BROKEN LOYALTY

JACKY LEON BOOK THREE

K.N. BANET

1

CHAPTER ONE
JANUARY 18TH, 2020

I wasn't expecting much from the day as I woke up, got ready for work, and headed out the door of my beautiful home in the woods. Another Saturday. Another opening. Another closing. Drinks to pour and finances to keep an eye on. Patrons to chat with.

More Heath Everson.

Just another day in the life.

Walking the trail between my bar and my home, I pushed my hands into my hoodie pockets to fight off the cold. I ran a little warmer than I had as a human, but that didn't mean thirty-three degrees Fahrenheit wasn't a bit chilly. If I were covered in fur, it wouldn't bother me at all, but I was in human form. I already knew my nose was going to be pink by the time I made it to the bar, but that was a normal occurrence for me in the dead of winter. Some nights, I didn't bother with the cold and just stayed in the upstairs apartment, but for some reason I hadn't this time.

I walked to the backdoor of my bar, passing my little old hatchback, which didn't look so good anymore. It was eight years old, and I knew I had to replace it soon, but buying a new car was more hassle than I wanted to deal with.

Locking the backdoor behind me once I was inside, I rubbed my hands together. For some reason, I wasn't really looking forward to work. The idea of just another normal day annoyed me as I went into the small work room behind the bar where the dishwasher was. I unloaded the clean glasses, feeling sluggish and tired, but I knew I had gotten enough sleep. Once that chore was done, I filled up two large trays with clean glasses and took them out to the bar, arranging them to use over the evening. I checked my liquor amounts, eyeballing what I would need to order on Sunday when I was closed. I considered the dirty floors, annoyed I would need to mop the next day as well.

"I love my job," I said to myself, frowning at my bar. Bad days happened. I loved Kick Shot, I loved my place, I loved the little thing I had carved out in Jacksonville, Texas.

But today, I just wasn't feeling it. What kept me going as I slogged through my chores was that it was Saturday. It was the last night of the week for me, and it was Heath Night. The werewolf Alpha would come to unwind, and I could do the same, kind of. I still had to run the bar, but it was nice to have an ear that listened when I needed to vent.

It was an hour before opening when there was a soft

knock at the front door. I frowned, unable to see through the window's closed blinds.

"I'm closed!"

The knock repeated, and I grumbled, realizing I probably hadn't yelled loudly enough. Instead of raising my voice, I walked to the door, unlocked it, and pulled it open. Without missing a beat, I glared at the two young men at the door.

"Kick Shot opens in one hour. Come back later." I'd moved to close the door again when one of them reached out and stopped it. They were human, but that didn't mean I tolerated anyone trying to force their way into my bar. I reached out and grabbed the young man's wrist, squeezing. "What do you think you're doing?" I demanded, a growl in my voice. I was in no mood for this.

"We're your new employees," he said quickly in a crisp English accent, not reacting in any way to my grip on him. He wore a perfect navy-blue suit, his auburn hair styled like he was about to walk into a board room. His face seemed too young and too calm.

"I didn't hire any new employees," I snapped.

"We were sent by your family from other establishments. It was said you needed help here, and we were chosen to come and get real world experience in the business by working for you."

I took him in, eyeing his face and sniffing the air. He was telling the truth. His expressive green eyes were wide and innocent, and his body language was relaxed, even though I was holding his wrist with enough strength that I could easily break it.

That means...I'm not sure what's more worrisome. If he had been lying, I could knock him around and definitely win, and I'd have to deal with whoever tried to send them. But he isn't. That means my fucking family has finally decided to stick their nose into my business. Great.

"I can't get rid of you, can I?" I asked blandly, letting the anger drop off my face.

"No, probably not. We were told to quickly explain to you what was happening, and if you still rejected us, to camp outside your door until you let us stay."

I sighed and let go of the young man.

"Come inside, you two. Tell me your names, exactly what you're supposed to be doing for me, and who in my family decided to send you. I need to know what region of the world to send you back to if I don't like the idea of you being here." I opened the door wider, and the first one, the talker, walked in like a professional, looking around the bar as if he already owned it. The other slunk in, his shoulders slouched, his eyes away from me. As I closed the door and relocked it, the talker walked to the pool tables and examined them. "Names. And don't touch anything."

"Ah. I'm Oliver Price. I'll be your new manager. I've been training to run restaurants and other similar establishments for five years since I was seventeen. Both of my parents are in the business. My father works for Mister Davor at his London location as the manager, and my mother is the head chef of Madam Zuri's restaurant, also in London. My family has worked for yours for four hundred years." The young man beamed. I did the mental math and wanted to kill my family for sending me a twenty-two-year-old *boy* to manage a bar in Texas. I already had two werewolves and a twelve-year-old human girl to keep an eye on. Oliver was going to be eaten alive by the locals.

"And you?" I demanded, turning to the slouching one.

"Dirk Jaeger," he mumbled. "Twenty-four. Bartender."

"For whom and from where?"

"Berlin. Niko's club," he said, not looking me in the eye. Other than his refusal of eye contact, there was no scent of a lie on his person. He just wasn't comfortable with the answer. It worked with his leather jacket and dark jeans look. His dark hair threatened to fall over his eyes if he let it go any longer. Avoidance—he wanted everyone to avoid him, including me.

"So, if I call Zuri, Davor, and Niko, they can all back up what you just said?" I asked, looking between them.

"Yes, Miss Leon," Oliver said confidently.

I pulled my phone out of my pocket and started texting, putting it into the family chat for everyone to see. I was ready to go for the throat, knowing I couldn't toss out either of the young men, but I felt violated; my siblings had sent two invaders into my personal space without warning. They knew better. They knew I didn't want employees or staff in any way. I wanted to do this on my own, and it was my choice.

Jacky: Which of you assholes decided the best way for me to have staff was to hire them for me?

It only took thirty seconds for an answer to pop up.

Hasan: I did. I told them to pick two people who would do well with some time in your territory and at a small location without too much pressure or stress.

That deflated my bravado immediately.

Of course, it was Hasan. I'm going to have to insult him by sending them back when he was the one who wanted me to have them. Fantastic. He's going to love this.

Hasan: It's a new year, and with your new role as my representative in the Americas, I thought it best you had some help with Kick Shot, so werecat affairs don't interrupt or hurt your business.

Jacky: We announced that seven months ago. Why so long? You know I'm just going to send them back to where they came from.

Hasan: You would, but I've sent them as a holiday gift, and you would never return a gift from your father.

Mischa: HAHAHAHAHA

I put my phone down on the bar slowly, knowing if I wasn't careful, I would break it. It kept going off as I looked at the two young men hovering around my space.

There's really no getting rid of them, then. I'll just have to make do.

"Dirk Jaeger and Oliver Price, bartender and manager," I said with barely restrained annoyance. "Well, it's Saturday night, and we're closed Sunday and Monday, so why don't the both of you head to wherever you're staying and come back on Tuesday? Say around—"

"We can start immediately," Oliver said, cutting in

with enthusiasm. "I've already read over a report of your business given to me by Madam Zuri. I'm certain Dirk will be more than capable of handling the bar without any special training."

"I'll be fine," the other young man said gruffly. "It's the American South. Everyone drinks cheap beer."

"Let's not stereotype my clientele." He was right. Everyone who came to Kick Shot drank cheap beer. By the look he gave me, he thought this was going to be a boring job.

"Okay..." I rubbed my hands on my jeans nervously. "I know what a bartender does, but what exactly are you going to do, Oliver?"

"Make your business grow and run it efficiently, so you can focus on the important things in your life," he declared, smiling. "Don't worry, I won't make any changes without your permission. I can also handle your accounting. Both of our salaries are covered for the next year since we're technically in training. At the end of the year, we'll probably go back home and work in other establishments."

"And I'll be alone again," I whispered blissfully.

"Maybe," Oliver said with that smile.

"Look. I like running and working in my bar. There's no way you two are going to be here five nights a week. I like working here alone."

"But, Miss Leon—"

"Go somewhere and enjoy the area for a few days," I ordered.

"Um. We don't have a place to stay yet. No one

arranged living quarters for us. We also don't have vehicles yet. We paid for a very expensive taxi," Oliver said softly, deflating a little as if he knew this was somehow going to upset me.

He was right.

"My fucking family," I muttered, shaking my head. "I have an apartment upstairs. You two can use it. I have a house back in the woods, and I'll stay there. How much was the taxi?"

He said a number that made me growl a little, and I went to find the cash for them. Oliver tried to say no, but I shoved the money at his chest.

"Next time my family sends you somewhere, tell them to arrange all of this ahead of time. I can't believe them. They know better..." I sighed. They did know better. They just wanted me to fret and start taking care of my new employees. *Sneaky motherfuckers.*

"Are we going to get started tonight? If we're going to be staying at the bar for a short while, we might as well get started." Oliver was chatty. I was quickly beginning to realize I was never going to get a moment's peace with him around. He was going to talk to all my customers, me, Dirk, and probably Heath, whenever he got the chance.

"Yeah, we can get started tonight," I answered, defeated. "Once we open, I'm going to run upstairs and get all of my things out, so that you two can move in. There's only one bedroom, so only one of you can stay there long-term, but for now, you two can flip for the bed or couch." I rubbed my forehead, wondering how I ever thought this would be just another day. This was completely out of nowhere and totally out of bounds on the part of my werecat father. "You said you got here by taxi...did you just fly in?"

"We both slept on the plane!" Oliver explained brightly. "We're ready to go!"

I wondered if the new manager had even asked the new bartender, but when I looked at Dirk, he was already getting behind the bar and looking through everything, familiarizing himself with my layout.

"Okay. Well, at open, go unlock the door, then...wait. I'll start clearing out my clothing upstairs, so whoever is going to stay up there can use the dresser and closet..." I walked away, stomping up the back stairwell to the upstairs apartment. I looked at the door to the office and knew Oliver was going to need access as well if he wanted to do his job right.

That annoyed me further, so I decided to put it off until another day.

Storming into the apartment, I went into the bedroom, wondering if I had washed the sheets in the last week. I didn't keep much clothing in the apartment, so throwing it all into a suitcase was easy.

I was even more annoyed with this new reality as I walked out the back of the building and started jogging home, encumbered by the suitcase I promptly tossed through my front door, baring my teeth.

I can't fucking believe this. Hasan has backed me into a corner, and I know it'll just piss everyone off if I send them back. Fucking hell. I can't even yell at Oliver and

Dirk. *They don't deserve that. My family pointed them to their new home, and they came.*

One year. I only need to keep them here for one year.

My stomach sank as I realized what that meant.

In one year, they're just going to replace Dirk and Oliver with two other new people.

I walked slowly back to the bar, needing to think. How was I going to get rid of them? I couldn't keep them. Maybe I could let them stick around for a few months, then send them back, saying it just wasn't working for me to have employees. I really liked working alone.

Without a solid plan, I walked back into the bar and checked the time. Two minutes before five. Without thinking, I walked out to the bar and went toward the door, passing one of my new employees. The moment it hit five, I unlocked it, flipped on the Open sign, and went back to the bar. Only to stop because Dirk, with his short brown hair and dark, narrow eyes was there, wiping down a glass.

"I looked in the back. You should get more glasses," he said softly, looking up at me.

"I've never run out. Run the dishwasher after closing every night. Takes ten minutes."

"Ah..." He sighed and put the glass down.

"I can put a stool back there for you."

"No, thank you."

Realizing I was going to get nowhere with him, I looked at Oliver and grumbled as I noticed something was different. Some of the tables had been moved.

"Oliver. Why did you rearrange?"

"Because there are specific patterns of tables and chairs used in bars like your own to optimize the customer's or a waitress' walk to and from the bar," he answered, smiling.

I bit my tongue; moving the tables and chairs wasn't the worst thing. How I never heard him doing it was beyond me. I should have stopped stewing in my annoyance and paid attention. I'd left two new people down here, unattended.

"Well, okay. Come upstairs, and I'll show you where I keep the books. Can you manage inventory and budgets?"

"Well, I would work with Dirk on the alcohol inventory, but if you would like that to be only my duty, then yes." He fell in step behind me as I walked to the back and up the stairs again.

"That's the apartment. There's some food in there and everything you need for cleaning. I left my towels for you two if you need them, and there's a washer and dryer for your clothes." I pointed to the second door. "That's my office, but since you'll be the manager for the next year, I guess it's going to be your office..."

"You don't seem very happy about this," Oliver said carefully. "I was told you might be resistant and to work through it, but..."

"My family knew better than to do this," I replied, taking a deep breath. "But don't worry, I'm not going to make your life difficult."

"Thank you. I was told you would at least know we were on our way, but..."

"Nope. They gave me no warning," I said, staring at the office door. "Look, Oliver? This is just going to take some time for me to get used to. I've been running and working at Kick Shot alone for over seven years. Just go easy on me and don't change things too fast or too often, and we should get along just fine."

"I can do that."

"Who the fuck are you?" someone exclaimed downstairs, making both Oliver and me jump. I knew the voice, so I raised a hand to stop my new manager.

"Let me handle this," I said quickly. "Why don't you go get acquainted with my office. Finances are sorted by month and year in the black filing cabinets. They should all have labels."

"Yes, ma'am." Oliver nodded, and I sighed.

"Just call me Jacky." I started walking away before he could call me Miss Jacky or Madam Jacky or something like he called Zuri.

CHAPTER TWO

I trotted down the stairs, ready to face my most consistent, if frustrating, patron.

"Joey, I know you aren't yelling at my new bartender," I snapped, walking into the bar and putting my hands on my hips. "His name is Dirk, and he's starting today. You'll be good for him. Before you ask, he's human."

Joey turned to me, then back at Dirk, his eyes narrowing with distrust.

"You could have asked me to help out around here. I would have taken the job," he said simply.

"My business decisions are none of yours," I said patiently then looked at Dirk. "He drinks Bud Light normally, but you might be able to get him to try a craft beer on occasion. He's a regular and a bit of a drunk. Cut him off if you think he's going too far, but other than that, he's harmless."

"Yes, ma'am," Dirk said quietly, grabbing a glass.

"Call me Jacky," I told him just like I had told Oliver. I turned back to Joey and raised my hands. "They're here. Be nice to them. I know Dirk has loads of experience as a bartender."

"Is there some other reason for this?" Joey asked, crossing his arms. "I like this bar because you're the bartender. Are you into something—?"

"Don't finish that. I wanted some help around the bar because I can't keep doing it full time and not having a life," I snapped. "Take your beer and go wait for your buddies, Joey."

He did as I asked, grabbing the drink Dirk put in front of him. When he was out of ear shot, I looked at my new bartender.

"They might all do something similar. I've been behind that bar for over seven years."

"They'll get over it," he said patiently. I wondered what was going through his mind. He wasn't very hospitable, and I was trying. "You lied to him."

"I did," I confirmed. "There's no reason for any of my customers to know you just showed up because my family decided you needed to work for me. So, you worked for Niko?"

"Yes."

"At a place in Berlin?" Now that I was thinking about it, he had an accent, though a very slight one. He was very good with English, but I figured it wasn't his first language.

"Yes."

"A restaurant? A club?"

"A night club. I'm used to more excitement than this," he explained. "Niko believes I would do well handling a calmer location for a short time."

"Any reason for that?"

"Ask him," Dirk said plainly.

I sighed and, deciding I needed to know more about these two sooner rather than later, grabbed my phone off the bar and checked the messages. Most were them teasing me, a regular occurrence but without the meanness that used to be there. Since Washington and everything that happened around the deaths of Gaia and Titan, they had accepted me into the fold. I was now the youngest sister and maybe not the best sibling, but they treated me as one of them. Even Davor offered to help with any situation in the Americas I felt I wasn't ready for.

I sat down on the wrong side of my bar, looking more like a customer than the owner as I sent out a few more texts, this time to different siblings specifically. Niko would have information on Dirk while I trusted either Davor or Zuri would give me the details on Oliver.

It didn't surprise me that my family would have two people they could send my way without a second thought. They owned businesses, both for money and pleasure. A couple of fancy restaurants in London for Zuri and Davor? Made sense. A night club in Berlin for Niko? I could see it. They probably weren't money making operations. I had a feeling Mischa owned places all over Russia, and I knew Hasan was neck deep in different businesses to maintain his extreme wealth.

Niko messaged me back first.

Niko: How's he settling in?

Jacky: I don't know. He barely talks to me.

Niko: There was a fight at my club recently. One of my waitresses had a problem with some of the patrons. He stepped in, and it became a brawl that poured out onto the streets. He didn't want to go down there, but I wanted him to take a deep breath and release some stress. An easy job he knows should help him settle. He's been edgy with all of my male customers since the fight and jumpy about stuff.

I frowned and looked at my bartender, deciding not to dig further. Niko didn't seem to point to the human bartender as being in any trouble, but there was a fight on his record, which meant I needed to be careful. I didn't want to give the young man a reason to get into another. It would defeat why Niko chose him to come down to Texas. He looked like the kind of guy who could really get into it. He had broad shoulders and definitely hit the gym to keep up a beefy figure to look intimidating. He screamed with an aura of 'fuck with me, and I'll fuck you up.' It didn't intimidate me because I knew I would win, but I could see him scaring half my clientele.

I texted back with a quick thank you, adding a promise to keep Dirk out of trouble.

As the night really kicked off, more of my customers gave Dirk a terrified expression or were generally surprised by his presence behind the bar. I quickly realized it was a smart move to stay at the bar and keep an eye on things as many of them tried to test Dirk into leaving from behind the bar and walking their drinks over to them.

"He's not a waiter," I called out. "Get off your asses and get your own drinks."

"You hired a new bartender but not a new waitress, the one thing we've all been begging for," John, one of Joey's friends, said as he walked up and grabbed his beer. "Why don't you run drinks around?"

"Because I'm the owner and not a waitress," I reminded him plainly, raising an eyebrow. "Are we really going to get into this?"

"No." He strolled away. It was a common complaint, had been for years, and I had no intention of fixing it now. I was already being forced to have the two new guys.

By eight, Oliver still hadn't come back down, and I began to worry he was lost in paperwork. Knowing I should have checked on him sooner, I stood up but didn't move as something caught my interest. A wolf was moving around in my territory. Tilting my head and staring at my phone with feigned interest, I paid attention to the movement of one of my two werewolves through my territory magic. I was beginning to notice subtle differences in them. Heath was easier to identify, for whatever reason. It was definitely Heath moving around, probably in his car and on his way to my bar.

It's Saturday night. Of course, he's on his way here. He hasn't missed a Saturday since Jabari was in town.

The normalcy of it made me excited, pushing away

some of the annoyance I felt at how the day had gone so far. As long as there were no new surprises, I would make it through another work week.

I jogged up the stairs, determined to check on one of the surprises before the wolf showed up. I opened the office door to find Oliver shuffling through papers with a pair of glasses on, making notes as he went.

"Are you doing okay up here? Want anything to drink?" I wasn't really sure what the protocol of having employees was, but he obviously wanted to do the job, so I wasn't going to stop him. At the same time, I didn't want to overwork him. It was his first damn day at Kick Shot, probably his first day in the country.

He looked up slowly, pushing his glasses up.

"No, ma'am, I'm fine. Thank you."

"Jacky," I reminded him.

"Yes...Jacky. Thank you, but no. I don't drink."

"I have soda or water."

"No, thank you."

"Okay." I closed the door again, leaving the young man inside the office. When I made it back downstairs, Heath was close. I slid behind the bar and prepared his drink, so I could give it to him when he walked in.

Dirk didn't appreciate it, looking down at me with a considerable amount of annoyance as I prepared a second drink for myself. Ignoring the apparent irritation in his dark brown eyes, I continued with what I was doing, knowing he should have an explanation.

"A...friend is on his way," I explained softly. "I always

have his drink ready for him when he walks in since I know when he's coming here."

"The werewolf?" he asked just as softly.

"So, you were briefed on that?" I raised an eyebrow at my new bartender.

"Yes. Oliver and I were both given the details of how you have two supernaturals living in your territory. A werewolf Alpha and his adult son. We were told to not get into any trouble with them, but that's a normal rule for supernatural customers."

"Heath is no longer an official pack Alpha since it's just him and Landon, but he is the official werewolf representative to our family." I kept my voice low, letting the music drown it out so my patrons wouldn't hear. On a dark winter evening, I was lucky to see a couple of dozen on any night, and tonight was no different. Only about twenty people were in the bar, and none seated nearby. "I'm also the official werecat representative to the werewolves since their largest Council is in the US now, and I'm friends with Heath. Playing nice with him and Landon will make everything about your next year here smoother."

"Of course." He seemed professional enough, and I hoped he would maintain it when the werewolf was in the building.

As Heath walked in, I left the bar and held out the drink to him. He immediately knew something was off, and curious confusion filled his grey-blue eyes.

"Meet one of my two new employees, Dirk," I said, smiling tightly, letting him know we needed to talk.

"Good to meet you, Dirk. Welcome to Kick Shot." Heath put the beer down on the bar and held out a hand. I breathed a little easier when Dirk took it. "I'm in every Saturday unless any of Jacky's family is. You'll probably be seeing both my kids run through here at some point or another as well."

"Both?" Dirk frowned at me.

"He has a human daughter, Carey. She's twelve, nearly thirteen, very sweet, and you'll put your life on the line for her," I said with the same tight smile I gave Heath.

"Sure." Dirk nodded slowly.

I motioned for Heath to follow me, heading toward the back of the building. There was no way I was going to sit in the bar and try to talk to him with a new bartender hovering. Slipping out the back door, we stood quietly for a moment, staring at the woods.

"You shouldn't talk about Landon like he's a young boy causing trouble," I said after a moment. "He's older than me."

Heath chuckled. I still both loved and hated the noise. I finally figured out why I hated it. It was a lethal weapon Heath wasn't careful enough with. In the year and few months I had known the wolf, it was becoming apparent that my attraction was growing, not dimming.

I just really enjoy spending Saturday nights with him at Kick Shot.

"I know, but he's not here to glower at me."

"That's a good way of putting it. Glowering. He

glowers at everything. You know, I think he's said all of fifteen words to me since I met him."

"That's not true. You two had a hot debate over the holidays about what was appropriate for a twelve-year-old girl to do about boys in school," he reminded me. "And you both somehow forgot that she's my daughter. You're just her pet kitty, and he's just her older brother."

"Pet kitty?" I crossed my arms, leaning against the wall as I stared him down.

"Mmm. Yup. She has you wrapped around her little finger."

"She has you and Landon, too," I retorted.

"Very true." He sagged in defeat, leaning on the wall next to him. "Want to explain what's going on in there? You didn't really hire two new employees without telling me, right?"

"Why would I tell you?"

"I don't know. You tell me everything?"

That's true.

"I didn't know until a little earlier today that I was getting two new employees," I finally explained, looking away from him to stare into the woods behind the bar. "You have three guesses who sent them."

"Your family."

"Be more specific."

"Hasan."

I nodded, sighing heavily. "Yup. With a couple of dumb reasons why. He thinks I need to be less hands-on with the bar now that I'm the face of the family for the region and all of that. Apparently, they're a gift from him for the holidays."

"They're humans, not chattel." Heath laughed then coughed in shock and exasperation with my werecat father.

"Damn. I should have used that line," I muttered, a little upset.

"Yeah, you should have," he said, the exasperation still there. He sipped his beer and looked out at the forest. "So, two new employees and we're relegated to talk out back? Should we get some patio furniture or something?"

I groaned. "I just...I didn't want Dirk listening in. I don't know these guys. The manager is a twenty-two-year-old boy named Oliver Price. His parents work for Zuri and Davor in London. Like...I don't know if I can trust them to..."

"To keep this secret?" he asked softly.

"There's nothing to keep secret," I said quickly, trying not to think about the way his voice, when soft, always turned a little husky. "We have no secrets, Heath."

"Sure. Then finish that thought about why you don't want your new employees listening to our conversation." He was being sly and pointing out the obvious. "We don't talk about anything that could come back on us. We vent, but nothing either of our kinds would consider a betrayal."

"I know," I mumbled. "I don't know them; therefore, I don't trust them. Dirk already knew you were a werewolf, by the way. Apparently, it was explained to both of them that you live in my territory. And there's another thing.

They know other people in my family, and they know about us. Our kinds, supernaturals. I never really put myself in charge of humans who were integrated into our world. Hasan has his staff, and I lived around them, and they...changed my sheets, but..."

"I understand. It's always an uncomfortable line, a boundary. By even working at your establishment, their safety is dependent on you."

"Yup. I've already got Carey, Landon, and you—"

"You don't need to defend Landon and me. We're not human, and we'll fight as any good werewolves fight to defend ourselves. Don't put my safety as a burden on your shoulders," he reminded me. "While there's only two of us, Landon and I have been fighting together for a long time. I'm certain we could defend ourselves well enough to get away from any fight we couldn't win."

It wasn't the first time he had to say something along those lines. The instinctive thing to say to him was, 'suck it.' He lived in my territory, and I was always aware of where he was when he was within my boundaries. I was the best person to keep everyone safe.

But he was an Alpha wolf, and he would die before he let someone die for him. He was a man who would fight in a charge, but he would always lead it. He would ask no danger of others he wasn't willing to take himself. I had a lot of respect for that.

"I know," I said, lifting my hands in mock defeat. "I just...they know better than to pull stunts like this. The new guys are going to be staying up in the apartment until one or both of them can find their own place to live.

That means I have to stay at your place or take Carey out when I want to see her."

"Or you can take her back to that house I know you're hiding."

"That's my private place," I whispered. "No one goes back there except me."

"Not even Carey? That's surprising."

"I haven't let anyone into that house except Jabari since I had it built. And Jabari didn't really give me a choice."

"Give it a shot. I happen to know she would love going to your house and sitting on your couch, not just to the apartment over the bar."

"Maybe. I'll have to consider it. I've got two days to figure out if I'm comfortable with it." It was frustrating. The longer I thought about my two new, forced-upon-me employees, the more I realized how much they would disrupt my life, and the more I wanted to put them in my car and drive them back to the airport. But I couldn't because it would be insulting, and now, there was the added thing with Dirk. If Niko needed him to have some time out of Berlin, I needed to help my brother with that.

"You seem really upset about this," he whispered, shifting his body to face me directly, his shoulder on the wall.

"Hasan asked my siblings to send two people to take over my job and force me to...I don't really know, actually. I have nothing to do outside of this. He said it was to free up my time and keep my business open while I was doing any official duties for the thing, but...it's been seven months. None of the werecats have contacted me with any problems they want to work out or even to introduce themselves. I was told it was normal, that I wouldn't hear anything until it was absolutely necessary, but there's still an information network among werecats. The family includes me in it now, but not the werecats of my region. I'm their go-to if they need anything from Hasan, our Tribunal member. You would think..."

"Hey..." He reached out and touched my shoulder. "You have a right to be pissed at your family for invading your space like this. Fuck offending them and send the humans back. I don't really like this either. It makes it feel like the friendship we've fostered is dirty, and we need to be watched. You're right, we don't have any secrets, but..."

"But..." I agreed. It was already unheard of for a werewolf to live in a werecat's territory, even more unheard of for us to be allies. It would be scandalous if anyone really knew we were close friends. While we hadn't yet done or said anything to be considered betrayers by our own people, I knew we were toeing a line that couldn't be crossed.

But when I looked into his grey-blue eyes, I wanted to cross the line and jump off a cliff. It was a problematic feeling. The steady wave of scent that came off him, increasing with each week, was challenging in its own way, evidence he was feeling the same. It had started as a joke when we came back from Washington, but like all crushes I'd had in my life, once I recognized it, it seemed to multiply. It looked like Heath was having a similar problem—close proximity was making the attraction grow.

I moved a couple feet away from him, and his hand fell off my shoulder.

"We have no secrets," I repeated, wondering if I could ever believe it. "We're just allies."

"Of course," he murmured, still staring at me. "We should probably go back inside before questions are asked."

I looked at the back door, sighing as I nodded in agreement.

"Yeah. This sucks."

"You can send them back," he reminded me.

"No, I can't. The entire family came together to send those two, and Niko needed Dirk out of Berlin for a little while. There was a fight that sounded rough. The guy obviously needs some time at a more...relaxed location. I can offer that. I haven't heard back about this Oliver kid, but he doesn't seem bad."

"What's your impression of him?"

"Young. Enthusiastic. Probably feels like this is his chance to establish the beginning of his reputation in the business, especially among my family. If he can chill out a little and his work is good, I bet he'll be working for one of my siblings until he retires." I opened the back door and tried to wave Heath in, but he reached over me, grabbed the door, and waited on me to go inside. It left his chest a little too close to my back, so I stepped forward before my mind spiraled out of control again. I tried to keep two feet between the werewolf and myself at all times, but I nearly always failed. He had this habit of taking up space, and while my personal bubble was pretty big most of the time, his was nonexistent.

I went upstairs to the office first, opening the door without knocking. Oliver jumped, papers flying, but not a single strand of his auburn hair was out of place. I watched as he tried to grab the papers and collect himself at the same time. His glasses were a little crooked, and his dark green eyes were bright, not showing a single sign of the exhaustion paperwork normally gave me.

"Is there anything you need...Jacky?" He practically choked, saying my first name.

"Want to meet Heath Everson?" I asked, trying not to seem intimidated or bothered by whatever was happening in my office. Or maybe it was his office now. Maybe I needed to start using the office in my house.

"Oh, I would love to!" The young man beamed and walked around the desk, leaning to look around me, his eyes going wide at the sight of the werewolf behind me. I stepped to the side to give them an open view of each other.

"Heath, this is Kick Shot's new manager, Oliver Price. A few members of his family also work for my siblings. Oliver, this is Heath Everson, previous Alpha of the Dallas werewolf pack, and currently, the werewolf representative to the werecats."

"It's an honor to meet you," Oliver said quickly, shoving out his hand. Heath took it with a bemused smile. Oliver, in all of his enthusiasm, shook fast and for a little too long, making Heath have to be the one to stop it.

I tried not to laugh. Oliver had to deal with cranky me when he arrived, but he was obviously not thrown off his game by Heath. "When it was explained to me that you lived in the territory, I did a lot of research on you. You've owned several restaurants and clubs over the years all over Texas. I was wondering why you never opened a location in Houston."

"It's not proper for an Alpha to build financial establishments in another pack's territory," Heath explained. I stepped back a little further as Oliver led Heath into the office. "We allow other species to work within our borders, though."

"Oh, I know that. The London locations where my parents work are both technically within the London Pack's territory. We allowed the wolves to visit as long as our..." I watched Oliver search for the right word, having to cover my mouth. This was entirely too funny.

"As long as the location owners weren't in the building?" Heath rephrased and finished for the flustered human.

"Yes. We also didn't make it public knowledge who owned—"

"I promise you, the London Pack knows who owns what in their city. They just know better than to cause anyone any problems. Wolf territories are important to wolves, but we can't and don't impose them on others unless someone of another species is a known enemy of the pack—say, a vampire who is known to hunt werewolves or a fae who conned a werewolf business. But an Alpha always knows who lives in their city."

"Oh...I wonder if my parents know that?" Oliver pondered, tapping his chin as he walked around the desk. "Do you help out here at Kick Shot?"

"I pay my tab once a month," Heath answered, smiling. "But no, this is Jacky's establishment. I'm just a customer."

"Ah, okay, then. I was hoping to draw on some of your expertise about the area and the local Texans." Oliver said Texans like they were aliens he didn't understand.

"It's a billiards bar or a dive bar, depending on how you look at it. It's not here to make me lots of money, Oliver." I wanted to put my foot down before I saw the wild ideas in the young man's eyes begin to take hold.

"Well, I was looking over—"

"Oliver. Slow changes. Small changes," I said, reminding him of our earlier conversation. "Now, with you two introduced, Heath and I are going downstairs to have a couple of drinks." I grabbed the wolf's shoulder and pulled him along. I heard the door click closed behind me and looked at Heath with an eyebrow raised.

"He's something," Heath said with a chuckle. "Well, at least things won't be boring for anyone in your territory any time soon."

I shook my head as he continued chuckling all the way down the stairs.

CHAPTER THREE

C ome Monday, I was already warming up to the new arrivals. I walked into the bar around noon just like I had on Sunday and looked around, noticing how clean it was. Dirk was efficient, and he didn't give me any shit the day before about doing a couple of hours of cleaning. Oliver was even willing to jump in, helping push around the furniture for the deep cleaning Kick Shot needed.

"Ah, Miss Jacky! Good afternoon!"

I stopped at the bottom of the stairs and looked up to see Oliver, trotting down like he was lighter than a feather. He was just the one I wanted to see today. Sunday had been my chance to really see how Dirk was going to be once I had him settled in. Standoffish, a bit angry—all things I had figured with him from Saturday night.

Now, I needed to really get into Oliver's head.

"How's your day been?" I asked casually. "Both of you settling in up there?"

"It's wonderful. Thank you so much for extending the offer to let us stay there while we look for our own residences." He stopped beside me, grinning.

"So, I asked Zuri and Davor to send me a little information about you, but neither of them has gotten back to me." *Not unusual. It could take them weeks to acknowledge I even messaged them. Davor dislikes me, and Zuri lives in her own world.* I pointed to the bar. "So, we're going to sit down and have a long discussion about who you are, why you want to do this, and why they picked you to come to Texas."

The blush that crept up Oliver's neck and face was almost cute in a boyish kind of way. He walked past me and sat at the bar like a kid put in a timeout, and I felt a little guilty. I didn't want him to think I was mad at him.

"Calm down," I ordered. "I just need to know the people who are supposed to work for me. You showed up right before I opened Saturday night, and yesterday, we had more work to do, and I had prior engagements." It had been bowling Sunday, where Carey and I once again defeated the werewolves of her family. "So, you and I are going to have a chat about who you are, what your goals are for the future, and the like."

"Oh, like you had with Dirk yesterday," Oliver said, nodding quickly.

"Yeah." *Which went nowhere.* He was going to bartend, and that was that.

"Well, I grew up seeing Madam Zuri and Mister Davor and wanted to do what my parents did. I wanted to work for them. I can't cook like my mother, so my father took me under his wing when I was done with sixth-form. I just graduated from university, but they wanted me to get more work experience, and finding a place for me took a few months. Then they said if I could tolerate America for a year, I could work for someone else in the Family at a smaller location. I didn't know it would be this small, but it's a good place to start." Oliver grinned, but something about it seemed fake. He was sent to another country to work at an establishment that was probably nothing compared to what my siblings had, nor carried any of the prestige.

"Do you think you could be happy here for a year?"

"Definitely. I know you want small, slow changes, but I really think you could expand Kick Shot into something amazing." He seemed too eager to please all of a sudden, as if he was trying to prove himself, and I recognized it. Deep in my fucking soul, I recognized it.

Someone out there had crushed his self-confidence at one point, maybe repeatedly. Someone made him feel like he couldn't do this job, couldn't succeed.

With the realization I had two rescue cases, not just one, I knew every piece of my argument about trying to send them back before the year was up would fail. Not just to my siblings, but to myself. I would hate myself, kicking out two people who needed help in their own ways.

"What kind of changes would you make to Kick

Shot?" I asked, hoping to start building the young man's confidence.

"I think you need to build a patio area. No pool tables, but a second bartender who would work outside when the weather is warm enough. A fire pit, maybe, for colder evenings and when people just want to sit outside. Even if you never open a restaurant or offer more food, that can at least grow your business and give people more options. Right now, it seems your business nights might see fifty people pass through the doors, and that's close to a full house for you, which isn't enough to sustain the business. You've been in the red for a long time. A year, at least."

"And since it was just me working here, with a lot of wealth behind me, that was okay." I hadn't been in the red the entire time Kick Shot was open, but the major repairs I did after defending Carey had slid my investment versus income into a bad place for the bar. On top of that, I'd lost some clients when the werewolves moved into my territory, and Heath started to frequent Kick Shot, another hit that I couldn't do anything about. Some people didn't want to drink with werewolves, and I couldn't fight that.

"But now, you have two employees," he pointed out.

"Who my siblings hired for me and have paid through the year, probably double what I make at this bar," I countered. "I know my books, Oliver."

"Still, a patio. You can at least invest a little to put the business back in the black and earn a little profit."

"Okay. What would phase two be?"

"Marketing. Bringing in more business with advertised special nights. Since you don't offer food..."

"You think if I offer more food, hire a couple of cooks and waitresses, this place will bring in more money and be able to support itself, including the staff I would need to hire?"

"Yeah..." Oliver was obviously trying not to smile.

"And this marketing?"

"Start with human clients, building up a more local image. Then we use the local image to build more of a legacy. You've been here for several years, a truly self-run business. We can get people passing through who have heard of this place and seen the good reviews. Tyler has a college, I believe? The small city north of here?"

"That's right."

"We're a bit out of the way, but I think we could swing some college students as well. Some like this type of atmosphere."

"And you want to do all of this in a year?" I nearly laughed in his face but bit my tongue. That wouldn't help anything.

"No, but I could leave a plan for whatever manager you bring in when I leave." His smile was innocent as if he had figured out all of my business problems in two days and could save me from financial ruin with just a simple plan.

"And we would start with some easy renovations. The patio."

"That's right! It can go out in the back. We could install another door that isn't near the staircase, and it could wrap around the far side of the building, away from the bar. And you definitely need to hire a waitress out of pocket. Dirk said there were complaints on Saturday."

"There are always complaints," I mumbled, shaking my head as the waitress problem was once again brought up. "I'll consider it, but don't expect much any time soon."

"Of course." Oliver's grin was beaming now as he realized I was listening to him. Really listening to him, as if his input mattered, and I would definitely consider it.

There was actually one thing I was willing to give him right now.

"If we started building the patio now, we could have it open in under a month, couldn't we?" I looked away from him, thinking about how Heath had joked about having a table and some chairs out back so he and I could talk in peace. Having outdoor seating was just a good idea. It would keep the pool players inside and free up some space for them when things got crowded, while others could wander outside. It would also give me a smokers' area, instead of them leaving their butts in the little ashtray right outside the front door.

"If you found a good contractor," Oliver said, nodding as he chewed on his bottom lip. I figured it was his thinking face. "Do you know anyone?"

"I do, actually. Now, I'm going to let you enjoy the rest of your day off. Thank you for talking to me, Oliver."

"Of course, Miss Jacky!" He jumped up and ran up the stairs in the back of the building.

Miss Jacky. I was just going to have to get used to that.

Checking the time, I realized I had a few hours before picking up Carey, but now, I had a reason to leave early for Heath's.

I left out the back and jumped into my hatchback. I knew he still had his feet in the real estate business, not that I found out much past that. He sat on the boards of a couple of companies in Dallas, and I had an acute knowledge that he had long hours some days, sometimes leaving my territory for a couple of days. Certainly, he knew a contractor or even had some control over a construction company I could use.

I stopped in the driveway, getting out as Landon walked out the front door, frowning at me.

"She's still at school," he said, eyeing me as if I was there to break into their house. Landon and I, even after more than a year, still hadn't found any reason to speak to each other on a regular basis, and he was as standoffish and defensive as he ever was. His dark eyes gave nothing away—no excitement nor distrust. He was just Landon.

"Actually, I was hoping to talk about some potential business with Heath. I know he's home."

Landon glowered for a moment before turning to walk inside. I followed in a rush, grateful to see he was holding the door open for me, an open invitation to go inside. I only went into their house for a handful of reasons. The last time I'd joined them was for Thanksgiving and Christmas Eve dinner. Before that, I couldn't really recall.

It was a clean, modern home. Heath preferred warm, neutral colors while I preferred cool neutrals, but I wasn't going to judge him for it- well, not to his face.

Everything is brown. I don't understand the fascination with having only brown furniture and things filling up every space visible. He gets fancy modern furniture in the oldest feeling color—brown.

While hating on his color choice, I listened as Landon went to get the werewolf Alpha. I could hear the muffled words they exchanged, Landon's more tense than Heath's, then footsteps coming back toward me.

"What can I do for you, Jacky?" Heath asked as he met me in his living room.

"I'm considering building an outdoor patio area for Kick Shot. Know anyone who can do that for me? Well, at least start the plans for it, take measurements, that kind of thing. That way, I have some idea about what I might be getting into."

"Why?" He gave me a confused look as he walked past me and fell onto his leather couch. "Don't tell me Saturday night brought this on."

"It did. Oliver's idea. I like it. I'm going to look into it."

"Jacky..."

"I have the money, and it doesn't hurt anyone," I said, ignoring his concerned and exasperated tone. "He thinks it's a good idea. I think it's a good idea. It's not a big step or anything crazy. I just want to see what the project might look like. And cost me. Think you know anyone who can do the job?"

"I own a construction company. I can do the job," he said, looking down at his hands for a minute. I wondered if he ever did any construction. I could vividly remember what those warm, calloused hands, hands that had done work before, felt like. "If that's okay. I live nearby, and we're allies. I don't see how it would be crossing any lines."

"I don't either. How do we start?"

"I can't believe you right now," he said, shaking his head in exasperation. "Jacky, really. Kick Shot is a little dive bar. I know you've loved what it is for as long as you've been running it. You wouldn't even hire one or two servers to take drinks around. Now, you're building a patio because some twenty-two-year-old human thinks it's a good idea."

"It *is* a good idea. Admit it."

"It is," he relented, still getting over the shock that I suddenly wanted to look into a construction project that would change Kick Shot so much. "If you're sure, I'll get it started tonight while you have Carey. There's going to be inspections, measurements, paperwork to fill out. You have a lawyer, and I recommend letting him know this is about to happen, so I can get my company lawyer in contact with him sooner rather than later."

"I know how this works. I've done major renovations on Kick Shot a few times now. Normally, I hire someone to oversee them," I said, grinning. "Thank you, Heath."

"Fine. One patio for a small dive bar in East Texas, coming right up." His amusement ended after only a moment. "Really, though, why can't you send them back?

Three days ago, you weren't thinking about building a patio, so I know this is about one of them. Big thing to look at, thanks to advice from a young man who's barely old enough to drink at the bar where he works."

"Do you really want them gone that bad?" I knew I did, but I felt a sense of obligation now that they were around.

I need to learn how to be less responsible.

"I don't like the idea that your family put people here. Have you asked them yet if they're going to report back to your siblings? Are you okay with being spied on?"

"No, but I'm not planning on asking them. I would expect them to keep in touch with anyone they know, like their family or friends, and if those people report to my siblings, I can't stop it. Do I want them reporting on my life? No. But that's a fight I need to have with my siblings, not two young humans."

Heath shrugged. "I can agree with that. I'll drop it."

By the look on his face, he wasn't happy. I knew Heath happy, and the man before me was smiling, but it wasn't anywhere close to real or pleasant. It was chagrined, annoyed. He was absolutely perturbed by this recent life change.

I didn't call him out. This was probably more about what we'd talked about the other night. Two new people around to potentially spy on us. It made me uncomfortable, but I couldn't send them back. I could only imagine how uncomfortable it made Heath. I tried to change the subject, to show I was willing to make this work for everyone.

"You've worked with humans before as a supernatural. How do you keep it...?" I couldn't find a way to phrase my question.

"Normal? Professional? Respectful? Pick something," he teased lightly, smirking.

"Respectful is easy. They both come from backgrounds that took them near my family," I said, shaking my head. "Normal is a good word, but...I need them to be loyal. They're in my space, and I need to develop that level of trust with them. How do I do that?"

"Learn their secrets and keep them," he answered softly, leaning onto the arm of the couch. He looked good, slouched on his couch, his legs outstretched. Even at rest, werewolves and werecats could seem intimidating. Wolves were just like cats that way.

"That..." I pointed at him, realizing what he just said versus how he met me. "Doesn't always work."

"You're here, aren't you?" he said with a sly smile that made me feel like I was being hunted.

"You're not a wolf; you're a fox," I accused.

"Not fair. But that's only one way. A very good way. You learn about them, learn what makes them tick, what they want, then you slowly reveal that you have the knowledge. You give them little pieces, build them up, and show they mean something to you. You, who seem very far above them, a thing they can't relate to. It gets worse as you get older. When the generations pass you by. I was always better at adjusting than Landon, but having kids helps. Especially Carey. She makes me relatable."

"Ah, yes, the good 'I also have a young child' shtick. Let me get right on that...Wait." I rolled my eyes. "You don't parade her around."

"No, but sometimes I show a picture to other dads who have daughters. The ones who have sons who know mine. The understanding and relatability were always there." He sighed, and I knew he was thinking about Richard. It didn't happen often, especially not around me, the werecat who ended up having to kill his oldest son. It only lasted a second before Heath was back in the real world and the conversation. "Learn who they are and learn how to make them feel like they matter. That's all you can do. Try to force loyalty with anything else, and they'll notice. Just be a good boss, and they'll give you the world."

"Hmm, see, that's where you went wrong with me. You tried to force my loyalty by protecting your kid, and I ended up loyal to her and not you," I teased, leaning back in the stupidly uncomfortable chair.

"I'm okay with that," he countered, the smile returning. "I'm sure they're great young men. I look forward to getting to know them better on Saturdays."

"We still lose our time to talk," I reminded him.

"That might be for the best," he reminded me. "We have no secrets, so we shouldn't look like we do."

"I'm going to wait on Carey," Landon announced, looking down at us from the large opening to enter the living room.

"Drive safe," Heath called as his son marched off.

When the door slammed, the wolf sighed. "He's warming up to you."

"Don't lie to me," I said, laughing loudly. "Please don't lie to me."

"Okay. He still doesn't know what to do about this situation. He hates change, which is funny since he was born a werewolf. He's been raised thinking werewolves and werecats don't get along, and part of that is my fault. He doesn't roll well with the punches like I do. I will say he respects you. He'll never say it, but he's glad Carey has one more person she trusts.

"She's such a precocious thing. Flings herself into the world like it's always going to catch her. Too smart for her own good and brave enough to give me a heart attack. If you think I'm alone in suffering through that, Landon is worse. He would smother her if I let him. Having you eases the urge to keep his little sister safe and allows him to step back the way I learned to do with him and their brother."

Wow. We're not even going to say Richard's name today. All right then.

"Well, that's good to hear. I'm not offended by him, Heath. It's just been over a year, and I thought maybe he would have warmed up just a little by now, but that's okay."

"Yeah. I wish he was as easy with the world as I try to be, but it's never going to be like that. A lot of it stems from the time period he was born."

"Half black, born during the Civil War, and growing up in the aftermath?" I asked softly.

"There were racist werewolves, too," Heath whispered, checking his watch. "Don't worry, I killed them as I came across them, but for Landon, life as a werewolf when he was a young boy wasn't easy. I couldn't always protect him, and neither could his older brother. One of my greatest regrets in life was not being able to protect him from it."

I didn't know what to say. Lost in thought, Heath played with his watch, checking the time, probably waiting for the minute Carey would be released from school.

"You're a great father, Heath," I whispered. "Don't ever think otherwise."

"It means a lot to hear that, thank you," he said, looking up. "I'll get back to you in a few days about sending people out to start the preliminary planning for a patio at Kick Shot. It's going to take some time to arrange."

The smile he gave me made me want to melt into my chair. His eyebrows went up slowly, and I bared my teeth as my face heated. After a moment of silence, the smile once again turned predatory.

"You don't make this easy, Jacky," he murmured.

4

CHAPTER FOUR

"Jacky!" Carey ran through the door, surprised and ecstatic about my presence on their uncomfortable chair. I grinned as she jumped on me, nearly thirteen now and getting bigger every day. The weight wasn't a big deal, but she had boney knees, and those could cause some damage. Kid was tough. I quickly blocked the knees with one hand and threw my other around her in a hug.

"Hey, Carey. How'd school go today?"

"It was okay. You're here early. Are you okay? You're never early." The questions continued before I could get a moment to answer any of them. "Is this about the new people? Are they good? Are they really bad? Are you going to send them back? Dad didn't tell me their names. What are their names?"

"Carey—" I tried.

"I mean, I hope they're cool. It would really suck if they aren't even cool."

"Carey—" Heath tried this time. I looked over her head at him, giving him a look of annoyance; he'd told her all about my new employees.

Before her rambling could continue, I gently put a hand over her mouth.

"Are you going to let me answer any of those questions or just keep rattling them off?" I asked gently, raising an eyebrow. I removed the hand once I knew I had her attention.

"You can answer," she said with a little shit-eating grin, knowing she didn't need to wear me down any more to get information. That grin was coming out in full force more often as Carey's skills at running circles around us only became more honed.

"I was here to talk to your dad about a possible project at Kick Shot. I'm considering adding a patio for customers. The new employees are fine. They're young. When you meet them, I'll introduce you. You'll probably be seeing them a lot over the next year. I don't know if they're cool or not. One is from London, and the other was working in Berlin before coming to help me at Kick Shot."

Carey's eyes went wide—people from foreign places. It wasn't like she had never met anyone from outside the country—I wasn't foolish enough to think she hadn't. Her father was a werewolf Alpha who probably had business and political connections all over the world. She had to have met some of them at some point.

"So...England and Germany," she said.

"Very good. How do you know the capitals of

European countries?" I smiled, glad to see she was still a sponge for knowledge.

She shrugged innocently.

"She has an atlas and keeps searching for information about places and trying to plan vacations for us. She wants to travel the world," Heath explained. "Popped up over the holidays when I told her we were going to take a vacation this summer but didn't tell her where." He stood up and came to grab his preteen off me. I snickered as she fought, but he tucked her under his arm and started walking away with her. "You can run off with Jacky after your homework is done. Homework first. It's the same every Monday. Don't fight me."

"Put me down! I'll go do my homework." That second line was full of defeat, and I could see her upset pout from across the room. Heath obliged her, though, putting her on her feet and letting her run into the dining room where Landon waited with an annoyed expression.

"Homework first," the big brother whispered to her. "Come on. We can do it together."

I smiled as Heath came back. He caught a glimpse of my expression before he sat down and looked back at his children. Landon had an arm around the back of Carey's chair, helping her pull out the right books from her bag. When she started her homework, he watched with keen eyes to see if she needed any help and instructed her.

"He's a good brother," I pointed out after watching this small scene unfold. It was precious.

"He loves school," Heath said softly. "Loves higher education. He's trying to get back in for his...fourth Ph.D.

When werewolves went public, he went back to the previous colleges he had attended and had them redo his diplomas in his real name."

"Ah, the old fake name to attend college trick," I said, nodding. "I've considered it. Would still have to since I'm not a werewolf."

"I bet everyone would just think you're a werewolf and not care," he pointed out.

"Like the humans do now? It's getting more frequent. I'm certain if I expand Kick Shot, especially since you live here now, everyone is going to be finally convinced of it."

"I don't think that's a bad thing."

"I'm a werecat, not a werewolf."

"I don't need a reminder."

We both laughed, and I stood up, gesturing to the walkway I knew led out the back.

"How's the horse?"

"Hating the winter, but I've owned horses before, and she'll be fine. We make sure not to spook her on full moons. Another six months and Carey will be able to ride her, with us in wolf form nearby, without a reaction."

"That's good."

"Don't think I miss your scent when you come near," he said, giving me a curious look.

"She's easy prey. Sometimes, I have to convince my cat that she's off limits. Does my scent spook her?"

"More than ours does."

I winced. "Sorry. I'll try to steer clear a bit better and stick to deer."

"A full moon hunt is important, but thank you for trying not to eat my daughter's new pony."

"You are very welcome." I was pretty sure I wouldn't even like horse if I did, but since I had never eaten one, I wasn't completely sure. I did know if I killed little Moonlight Dancer, Carey would never speak to me again, so I had to keep doing my best not to.

"I'm done!" Carey yelled. "Let's go, Jacky!"

I turned fast to see her standing up from her chair in the dining room. Landon coughed quietly, making Carey turn to him and wait. He flipped through the papers on the table, then nodded, giving her a thumbs up. I could see the big brother's exhaustion as his sister ran toward me. Homework was done, and he seemed like he wanted a nap.

"Looks like it's time for me and the preteen to go," I said to her father.

He took a long, deep breath.

"Preteen," he said softly. "Don't use that word."

"Why not?" Carey skidded to a stop next to me. "I am a preteen."

"Because it makes you too close to being a teenager," he mumbled, then waved a hand for us to leave. "Out of my hair, women. I have to get back to the work Jacky distracted me from."

I laughed and grabbed Carey's shoulder, leading her out of the house. As we got into my car, she was already asking questions again.

"So, the new people are nice?"

"They are. They were a surprise, no doubt, but I have

a good feeling about them. We just need to get used to each other."

"That's good. You have good feelings about people." She beamed at me, and my heart stuttered a little. In her world, I was a hero. I didn't much feel like one most days, but when she talked to me about me, I could almost see it.

It was the best confidence boost the world could ever give me.

"Let's hope so. My siblings have had people working for them for a long time. I hope they picked two who are going to work well with me." I really hoped for that because these two humans were about to meet the little girl who launched me on my current path of werewolves and responsibility. If anything went wrong, they would be the ones packing up and leaving, not her.

"Did Jabari pick them?"

I shouldn't have brought up my siblings. If there was one thing Carey was utterly fascinated by, it was them, and since she had met Jabari, she considered him the coolest and most interesting.

"I don't think so. They worked for Davor, Zuri, and Niko."

"Oh." The disappointment was clear as Carey's shoulders slumped, and her smile disappeared.

"What? The English genius, the African queen, and the German mystery aren't as cool as the ancient warlord?" I nearly laughed as I rattled off their new nicknames. I had come up with them months before to help Carey understand who all of my siblings were. She had wanted to know about them, and I needed to come up with short and easy ways of explaining each of them.

"I mean, they're cool, but..."

"But what?" I demanded, raising an eyebrow. I would have turned it on her, but I was keeping my eyes on the road.

"Jabari...wasn't he so...cute?"

"Never, ever, let your father hear those words come out of your mouth," I said quickly. "Carey, do you have a crush on my older brother?"

I could smell it. I could hear her pulse accelerate.

Heath's in for it if Jabari is the type of guy that gets Carey interested in boys. God save us all.

"He's super cool, and he started to teach me how to use a bow, and he loved Midnight Dancer, and...and..." She trailed off.

"He's way too old for you."

"He won't always be too old for me."

"Oh, yes, he will be." I shook my head slowly as she continued her argument, finally deciding to turn on the radio, which she protested. She was still trying to make her argument when I parked behind Kick Shot and got out.

"Jacky, please! Just..."

"I'm fine with you having a crush on Jabari, but if you think I'm going to let you act on it before you're forty, you've got another thing coming," I said with a laugh. Hopefully, by then, she would be over it, and this would be a thing of the past.

She did the dignified thing and stuck her tongue out

at me, then walked into the bar. I jogged to catch up, grabbing her before she could go up the stairs.

"They're staying in the apartment until they find their own places. One of them might move in up there permanently, so we're going to my house," I explained fast.

The squeal of excitement made me wince.

"We're going to your house?" she asked, her eyes wide with mischief and joy.

"Yes."

"Who's there?" Dirk called. I saw him move to the top of the stairs, looking down at us. "Oh, Jacky. That must be Carey? Heath Everson's daughter?"

"That's right. Carey, this is Dirk."

"Hi, Dirk!"

"Hello. Nice to meet you." He didn't come downstairs, disappearing from view and calling for Oliver to come out. The next thing Carey and I saw was the young manager showing up at the top of the staircase.

"You must be Miss Everson!" Oliver grinned, bounding down the stairs and extending his hand to the twelve-year-old like she was somehow going to be his boss too. "It's a pleasure to meet you."

"Call me Carey!" She shook like a kid shook hands, with too many movements. Oliver didn't seem to mind, though, and I remembered how he had shaken Heath's hand.

These two are going to be friends, and I'm not sure whether that should make me happy or scared.

"Okay. Carey and I have a short walk to get to my house. If there's anything you two need, send me a text."

"Of course, Miss Jacky." Oliver waved as I dragged Carey out, who was waving back with her signature grin.

"He's cute," she said as the door closed.

"Also too old for you," I said sternly. *At least he's human. That should count for something.* "What do you want to do today?"

"Can we play video games?"

"Yes, always." Throwing my arm over her shoulder, she wrapped one around my waist as we walked into the woods together. This was the first time I'd shown her the path to my house, and as we drew closer, I grew nervous.

Will she like it? It's not warm like her home or comfy like the apartment. It's really clean and sharp. It probably won't appeal to her at all, and she'll want to go back to the bar.

When it came into view, I heard her small gasp.

"Those are big windows," she pointed out as we entered the clearing around my home.

"I like being able to see my woods," I said softly. "Makes me feel connected."

"It's really...clean. White."

"I know." I loved it, the juxtaposition of the woods and dirt to the clean house with strong lines and hard angles. The large windows I cleaned once a week to make sure there were no smudges, so I could always see my woods without anything in the way. My front patio only had one chair and a small table, for those mornings I wanted to sit outside and enjoy the quiet.

I led her inside, letting her touch everything, my heart racing. Since the house was built, only one person had ever visited it, and that was Jabari. He hadn't stayed there for the entire visit after Washington while he healed, but he'd been over. I'd been just as nervous then as I was now. He'd inspected too, and I was left wondering what he'd thought when he was done.

Carey's exploration seemed less judging and more curious, though. She looked at things I used to clutter the shelves, read the titles of books I kept, and even inspected the rugs under her feet.

"What do you think?"

"I like it," she answered. "So, where do we play games?"

I chuckled and led her into the living room again, opening a cabinet and showing her the gaming consoles I owned, some of them older than her.

"Cool!" She jumped onto my couch, kicked her shoes off into the middle of the floor, then held her hand out, expecting me to hand her a controller.

It was perfect.

I should have brought her here sooner.

I gave her the desired controller, grabbed one for myself, and we got started. Time flew by, and I had to stop playing to make us dinner. I even made two hot cocoas with it, and she was delighted at how I put whipped cream on top instead of marshmallows.

"Can we put a movie on while we eat? Can we eat out here?"

"We can," I said, giving in to her every demand.

When I put her dinner on the coffee table, she dug in as I flipped through the DVDs to put on an animated movie I knew she liked and could watch a hundred times over.

"So, really, how's school?" I asked now that we were out of the hearing of anyone who could report back to her father. I never told him what Carey told me, never violated that trust. They both knew if I felt Carey was in danger, that changed. But how she was feeling, her secrets, things she needed to get off her chest- I was the friend who could hear those things and keep them secret.

"It's okay. I'm ahead because of my tutors. My teachers all love me, but other kids won't play sports with me. They think it would be unfair because I'm from a werewolf family, so I must be special too." Carey shrugged. "Same thing it's always like in school."

"And no boys."

She made a gross face. "None of them are cool like Jabari. They don't care about being strong. They think they're cool, but they're really boring and dumb. Jabari isn't boring or dumb."

"If you judge everyone against Jabari, you are doomed to end up with a supernatural, not a nice human—"

"So?" Carey frowned at me. "What's wrong with that?"

"Do you want to be one of us?" I asked softly. "Have you given it any thought?" I didn't know if Heath ever asked, and I knew his feelings on the matter. If there was one person he was totally okay staying human through her entire life, it was Carey. He didn't want their dangerous world for her.

"Not really, but I have a lot of time to make that decision," she answered, not giving me a real answer, which was for the best. If she said yes right now, I would have to tell Heath. He had the right to know if his daughter was strongly considering it, and she would need a certain education before she tried to jump in with both feet, asking for the Change. If she had said no, I was certain my heart would have broken.

I was more conflicted than Heath.

"Well, if you fall in love with a supernatural, they might not...want you to remain human, Carey." I couldn't believe I was having this talk with her. She was only a few months away from thirteen. Only one more grade, then she was going to be a high schooler.

She gave me a big shrug.

I'd opened my mouth to say something when cold flooded my veins, and a beacon of energy popped up in my mind. Without thinking, I was on my feet, a snarl contorting my face and making my chest rumble. My territory was mine, and within it, I defended things I was willing to kill for.

And the werecat who just stepped into my boundaries was going to feel every ounce of my rage at their presence. Like Gaia's land had felt angry and violent, I pushed similar feelings into the land, sending my warning.

Leave or die, cat.

I was just about to start stripping down to meet the

challenge in werecat form when it was gone. I stared through the windows, pinpointed on the direction I had felt the werecat.

Coward.

"Jacky?" Carey's voice was small and scared.

It nearly knocked me on my ass. I looked down at her, eyes going wide. She was pale and curled up on the couch, staring at me.

"I'm sorry," I whispered, realizing what she must have just seen.

"Are we okay?" she asked in that same tiny voice.

"I'm so sorry. Oh, Carey, I'm sorry." I went down to my knees in front of her.

"What happened?"

"A werecat entered my territory. Gone now. I..."

"So, we're safe?"

"Yes. We're safe," I promised. "Whoever it was left when they got my warning." I remembered that all of the Everson family now knew about my territory magic, the deep connection I had to the land. Carey had even seen it before when we first met, and the werewolves came for us. "Did I scare you?" I asked softly.

"No. I was scared someone was coming to get us," she said weakly.

Relief flooded me. Not me—she wasn't scared of the monster on its knees in front of her. She was scared of whatever monster I would defend us from.

"How did you know?" I asked, leaning to put my head down, my focus divided between her and monitoring my territory. I tracked Heath and Landon's steps. I waited for the intruder to come back.

"You were looking...away. Like you could see something I couldn't. It made me think of when the wolves came for us at Kick Shot. How you stood before you told me who was coming."

I'm lucky she's so smart. Or screwed.

"I'm going to take you home," I said gently but firmly. "I need to go check out the scent of the werecat who just entered and figure out if he or she might come back or was just looking around."

"So, it might not be a bad thing?"

"It's most likely not," I said, trying to lower my heart rate, which was still pounding, racing as if I had just run for miles. "I'm sorry you were scared."

"Not your fault," she said. "What about dinner?"

"We'll pack it up, and you can take it home."

I didn't feel safe leaving her in my home, the center of my territory, when a werecat could be waiting just outside the edge of my territory.

A fight was still very possible.

CHAPTER FIVE

"You're back early," Heath said as he opened the door and met us outside. Carey walked past him and held out the food for Landon to reheat. I stared at the Alpha wolf, wondering what he needed to hear and what I should withhold or fudge, so he didn't panic. A panicked father could turn a simple meeting between two werecats into a bloodbath.

"A werecat stepped in, then back out of my territory. I brought her back here because I need to check out where he or she was. Most likely, it was a rogue sticking their head in, testing the waters, and will have probably continued on their way by now. Another possibility is a werecat traveled down here and wanted to get my attention to talk since Hasan has asked me to represent him. That's bound to happen."

"There's more, isn't there?" he asked.

"There's a chance I get to the edge of my territory and find myself in a territory fight," I said softly, nodding.

"Not the most likely since a werecat willing to fight me would have come straight for me, no need for tricks. If someone took over my territory, they would find this area overrun with my family."

"Of course. Does Carey know?" He didn't seem scared or concerned, only serious. He knew I was trying to treat this as safely as possible, even if the chance it was a threat wasn't high.

"She figured it out when I reacted. She's seen it before and put it together on her own. She was a little shaken, though."

His eyes narrowed, but he didn't ask. He expected me to explain.

"The first day she was with me," I told him but didn't elaborate. He knew about the wolves who came to the bar. He knew how his daughter, eleven at the time, had to pull a silver bullet out of me, then we had to go on the run.

"Stay safe," he said finally. "Please." There was worry in the lines of his face, and he seemed a little older at that moment.

"I'll try," I promised.

As I drove, the anger came back.

How dare they? This is my home.

I was usually angry when rogues passed through, testing my borders. I'd had a number of territory fights already in my life, a regular occurrence for any werecat who held land. Rogues were always looking for a home or just loved to roam. Sometimes, their intrusion was purposeful, looking to claim something for themselves.

Sometimes, it was more accidental. One of the rogues I had met had been in human form, driving. They were on the road, and their path accidentally took them through my territory.

It had been nearly two years since I'd dealt with rogues coming into my territory. Things had changed. With Carey, especially with her as close to me as she had been, all my instincts had screamed to kill anything and anyone who approached. Territory fights weren't generally fatal, but I had people in my territory I would kill for.

I parked a mile from the edge of my territory and probably a ten-minute jog to the spot where the werecat had breached the line, which told everyone of my kind to stay back.

I debated on Changing into my werecat form before heading to the disturbance; with light fading fast, I knew it was the best choice. Keeping my eye out for passing cars, I quickly stripped, closed the car door, locked it up, and hid my keys in the dirt. Anyone with a nose could find them, which didn't mean much. I would know they were there long before they could take my car anywhere.

I hated having to be paranoid in my own territory, but I was living by the 'better safe than sorry' mantra, going out to check where the werecat had come into my borders.

I snuck into the closest trees and Changed, letting it roll through me and ignoring the pain. Over time, it hurt less, or maybe my tolerance for the pain grew.

I took off at a slow walk, keeping my nose in the air,

wondering if I could catch the scent of the other werecat. It was close to forty-five minutes since they breached my territory. They could be miles away, which was for the best.

When I reached the spot, I saw the footprints. They were big, definitely pointing to the werecat being a male. Sniffing around confirmed the assumption, but the scent was quickly fading. With no scent of the cat in the air, I could reasonably guess the werecat was gone, but I still followed the tracks to the very edge of my territory. He'd only come about ten feet in, and I could see how he wandered back on the same path he had used.

Something made me edgy, but I put the sensation down to this being the first rogue to come into my territory since I took the Oath to protect Carey and everything unfolded, leading to werewolves living within my borders.

It's been over a year. If someone was looking to get back at me for showing a little kindness to the wolves, they would have struck by now.

At least, that was what I wanted to believe. I wasn't generally paranoid, but the speed and unexpected nature of the werecat's step into my territory were trying to convince me that something was wrong.

Satisfied- if still edgy- the werecat was well and truly gone, I walked back to my car, staying away from my border since I could feel nothing outside of it. Beyond my borders, I was blind, and that worried me. The male werecat could be downwind and just outside my border, and I wouldn't know it.

And the fact that it's a male is a problem. He would be big enough to give me a real challenge, and there are no werecats younger than me, not that I know of. I would be going up against someone bigger and with more experience.

I was thankful he'd decided to leave. If there was anything good about the entire event, it was that he had decided to leave without a fight.

I made it back to my car and was back in it fully dressed within a couple of minutes, not wanting to stay out in the cold in human form any longer than I had to. I didn't go back to Heath's, instead sending him a text that the werecat was gone, and I would let him know if it came back. Then I focused on getting home, parking at my bar, and running through the woods back to my house.

Once I was secure in the center of my territory, the edginess subsided, but a small fraction of it remained, and I knew it would bother me for a few days.

I felt like I was missing something to do...

That's when it hit me. I had two new employees and had yet to tell them anything about what was happening.

"Fuck," I mumbled. "If I get kicked out of my territory, they'll be living and working in a building someone will probably burn to the ground." It was typical procedure for a werecat to erase evidence of the previous occupants. They would destroy my home and rebuild. I would be legally expected to hand over titles and deeds to anything I owned, and if I didn't, they would forge copies and signatures to take everything from me. If I was kicked from my territory and tried to fight legally, I would be expected to try for a rematch to take the land back.

Even considering it is a pain in the ass, I can't let some fucking werecat take my territory. This is why my siblings have many of their businesses outside of their territory. It keeps them safe from losing their sources of income. Hell, this is why most *werecats don't keep most of their business in their damn territory.*

I rubbed my temples as I sat down on my couch. With a sniff, I could still smell that Carey had been in my space. It was terrifying. A stark reminder that, under no circumstances, could I ever lose.

I checked my cell to see Heath had messaged me back, glad nothing was wrong. He even added that he let Carey know, something I was grateful for. I had given her such a fucking scare with my reaction to the intruder. It wasn't common to see any scars from what Carey had gone through, and like the men in her family, she didn't talk about it to me. But for just that moment, it had been there—the fear I would be shot at again, that she was going to be taken, and she wouldn't see her family anymore.

I had to stop thinking about it. I had to put Carey aside for a moment to consider my other problems. She was safe with her family. Those two wolves would fight to the death for her, and she would get away. She was smart like that. I bet Heath even had a plan already set for her if anything was wrong, and none of the supernaturals around her could or would protect her.

I dialed my eldest sister, Zuri, preferring to talk to her

over Davor about Oliver and what to do if I lost my territory. I didn't see it happening any time soon, but the intruder had been a wakeup call.

"Jacqueline, what can I help you with?" By the tone of her voice, I could imagine her regally lying on a long couch. I didn't know if she had an office and certainly couldn't picture her in one as I could with Hasan. I could see her poolside, eating cool fruits and having someone fan her. While it was probably a fantasy, it was the image I got nearly every time I spoke to her.

"I wanted to ask you about Oliver. Why him? Also, I had a werecat drift into my territory for a moment today, and there are some other questions I need answered about what to do with my employees if I lose my territory." Not wanting a lengthy conversation, I got to the point but realized my error and quickly corrected it. "Also, hi, Zuri. It's nice to speak to you this evening. Well, it would be closer to morning for you, wouldn't it?"

"It would, but I was awake, don't worry," she replied, a smile in her voice. "A late night, you see. I was about to retire."

"Of course. Now—"

"Oliver," she said with a sigh, cutting me off. "Yes. He's been a small problem for both Davor and me in the last year. Not that any of it was his fault but a problem, nonetheless."

"Care to elaborate?" I asked, leaning back and getting more comfortable.

"No. He wasn't at fault, but we felt it was best to

send him away for a little while, then Father gave us that chance."

"So, you're going to offer me even less information than Niko about the bartender he sent."

"Oh, we all know about Dirk," Zuri said with barely concealed annoyance.

"You don't like him?"

"His mother was a maid at Niko's home in Berlin, not that he ever used it, who had terrible taste in men. Niko didn't let it bother him that she was pregnant with a drunk's child, but after she had the boy, she fell ill. She passed away when he was about a year old, so the boy went to his father. Niko didn't want to step in unless he couldn't shape up and be a father." Zuri sighed again. "Of course, the father and the boy moved out of the country, and Niko lost track of them. A couple of years later, he went hunting and found Dirk in the care of the local government, so he took Dirk in, feeling responsible."

"Niko raised him?" I said softly, confused. "He's Niko's..." I almost said son. Typically, if a werecat raised a young human, they became parent and child.

"Yes. He's Niko's, in whatever context you want to think about it. Dirk isn't the first and won't be the last human one of the family has taken in. From my understanding, he's always been a good human and loyal to Niko, loyal to the only father he's ever known. A very good son, for the most part."

"But you called him a pain in the ass."

"To Niko, who had to deal with helping the boy grow up. All teenage boys are a pain."

"How would you know?" I asked, smirking. "You've never raised one, and stereotypes are rude."

"Don't make assumptions, and I do have a twin brother," she retorted. "I know young men. Pains, all of them."

"While I'm glad for more information about Dirk, I really want to talk about Oliver," I said, trying to get us back on track. "I know why Dirk is here. Niko already told me." And now I had even more of a reason to understand why he was seemed upset.

Niko didn't mention that he had raised Dirk, though. That was rude. The human is practically family. Hell, he's been family longer than I have.

"Oliver's enthusiastic and bright, but things happen," she said enigmatically. "And he's there to rebuild the confidence I know he has. Running a small bar with a stubborn owner is a good place for him. Not many employees to deal with and no overbearing father."

That gave me a clue.

"His father? He said he worked with his father."

"He did, but again, this is his story," Zuri repeated. "Take good care of him. He's a wonderful boy, and he'll do great things for your little bar if you let him. Now, you have a second problem you wanted to speak about? Something to do with losing your territory? Is there something wrong?"

"Like I said, a werecat drifted into my territory earlier today. What am I supposed to do if I lose a fight, and they're here?"

"You put in place a protocol, a group text, or a code

word. If an intruder comes into the territory, you send it to them before you deal with the intruder. It will initiate an escape plan. They'll pack up and drive out of the territory until you give them the all clear or find them at the meeting location. If you are chased out, I would expect you to have them both meet you close to Dallas, so you can put them back on planes to us, where we can protect them while you find a new home or just stay rogue, like Mischa. I would assume Dirk knows all about it. Oliver's family has never had a reason to learn since they're outside employees, away from our homes."

"That all sounds much less complicated than it probably is," I said, leaning over. "This is why I didn't want employees, Zuri."

"Talk to Father about that. He made the decision. I only used it as a chance to help a young man who has spent his entire life hoping to work for one of us. He's new, you're new. It seemed like a good fit."

"Are you worried about me losing my territory?"

"Does Carey still live there?"

I wondered for a moment how much Jabari had told Zuri about my little charge, my only real friend. If Heath and Landon weren't around, I wondered if I would be in a similar position as Niko. Maybe that was why Zuri made it a point to remember Carey's name.

"Yes."

"Then no, I'm not overly worried. A werecat with a charge will fight more viciously than a werecat without anything relying on it keeping the territory. It's actually not common for a young werecat to get overly attached to their home for the first century or so. Sometimes, older werecats will take the territory just to prove a point."

Haha. Great. A big male werecat might want to upset my life by forcing me out, just to annoy me. That would be some fucking bullshit.

"I think that's everything," I said, ready to get off the phone. "Thank you for talking to me."

"I would have gotten back to you sooner, but I was handling something with my territory in Cameroon. A rogue wandered through and thought she could freeload for a time. One of my staff saw the tracks, and I had to go in and chase her off."

"It's almost comforting to know you still deal with rogues like a normal werecat," I said, snorting.

"Yes. There's always one, maybe coming in from a different part of the world or too young to really understand we're in charge and why, so we have to put them back in their place." She sounded amused. "Now, I am going to sleep, little sister. Good night."

"Good night," I barely said before she hung up.

CHAPTER SIX

Jacky: You couldn't tell me he was your kid?

Niko: He asked me not to. Did he tell you?

Jacky: No, Zuri had to tell me. Why didn't I know you raised a kid?

Niko: You weren't speaking to us, and I'm very private about Dirk. Hasan let our siblings know, but I don't parade him around for the family. Don't call him nephew, he'd hate it.

Jacky: Has he ever met any of the family?

Niko: You're the first. I think it's best since you're a similar age.

I sighed and looked across the bar at my new bartender. Only someone in the supernatural world would think thirty-seven and twenty-four were similar ages. Humans would see two people from different generations with very little in common due to being at different stages in their lives.

And Dirk, even raised by Niko, was a human. Which struck me as odd as I watched him do inventory before we opened for the week. He was already twenty-four. The time to Change him in his prime was right now. Sometime between twenty and thirty was the choice of most to Change.

Dirk caught me staring, and his eyes narrowed.

"Yes?"

"Nothing," I said, looking back down at my phone, then remembered. "I don't have your number. Or Oliver's. We need to set in place some safety protocols. Should have done them Sunday, but I'm new to this."

"Niko said you were," he said patiently. "Let me get Oliver."

"Thank you." I played with my phone as I waited, and when they sat down in front of me, I slid the phone to them. "Were each of you given U.S. cell phones, or am I responsible for those?"

"We called the car ride company to take us out yesterday to pick some up," Oliver answered. "While you were with Miss Everson."

"That's good. I need your numbers. If there's an emergency, I want to be able to let you know."

"What's our meet up location?" Dirk asked.

"Dallas-Fort Worth International Airport," I answered, looking up at him. "If it's necessary, I want to be able to put you both on planes out of the country. If it's not, you can just drive the two or so hours home."

"What are we talking about?" Oliver looked between Dirk and me, obviously lost.

"We live in a werecat's territory. If she's challenged, she could lose the entire region, and we wouldn't be safe. So, she's going to let us know if someone shows up, and we'll leave, so we're not caught in the crossfire," Dirk explained before I could. "It'll be fine. She's one of the Family. I don't think any of them have ever lost."

"Don't have too much faith in me. I'm not that old," I said, trying to keep it light with a smile. "I'm closer to you two in age than I am to any of my siblings. It's good to have this in place because only yesterday, I had a werecat step in my territory. Nothing happened, and they left without incident, but it makes the point clear. We need a safety plan for the two of you."

"I'll make sure Oliver gets out with me," Dirk said, handing my phone to the young manager. "I plan on buying a car this coming weekend."

"Great. Oliver?"

"I don't know how to drive. If Dirk is fine coming to get me, I'll go whenever and wherever you need me to," he said, looking up from my screen. He looked back down and punched in his information, then held it out. "Here you are. I didn't know this was a concern. I feel a bit foolish."

"Zuri said you've never worked in werecat territory. Consider this a bigger learning experience than you thought it would be. It's one for me, too," I said, trying to ease the nerves at the table. What Dirk and I talked about was scaring Oliver. I could smell it in the air, even if he covered it up well. "We'll be fine. I don't keep prime territory with great resources."

"That's good," Oliver said, a wobbling smile forming. "Thank you for looking out for us."

"You're here. You're my responsibility. Now, let's get this bar open and get the week started." I thumped my hand on the booth table which I had claimed to work. Oliver took the finance books from me and ran up the back stairs, and Dirk went back behind the bar and continued his daily inventory. I unlocked the door and looked for a place to go.

"You can head out. Kick Shot doesn't need you hanging around," Dirk said, watching me wander. "We've got it covered."

"Yeah..." I hated that. I'd started working at Kick Shot to fight boredom and have my own meager income away from the millions Hasan had gifted me.

Now, it seemed I was back to twiddling my thumbs. I flipped my phone around in my hands, wondering if there was a good movie playing, or if I could go out to dinner. I almost considered calling Heath or texting Carey to see if they wanted to do something, but I felt like I was intruding even considering it. It wasn't my schedule to see them on a Tuesday.

I admitted defeat and walked out the back, heading for my house. I went to my home office and sat down at my gaming computer, booting it up to kill some time—a lot of time since I had nothing to do unless they called me. I didn't want to stay and hover when they were both capable, especially Dirk, who would be handling the customers all night.

Hopefully, there wouldn't be any fights.

I still thought it was interesting that Niko had raised the young man, but it wasn't my place to get involved. It was the same in reverse. Outside of what I told any one of them, they wouldn't get involved in my friendship with Carey.

I played around on my computer for thirty minutes before I gave up and sent a text to Heath, asking if I could come over or take everyone to the movies.

Heath: Let me guess. You're letting them manage Kick Shot and have nothing to do. I thought cats were good at being lazy?

Jacky: You're a very intelligent man, Heath Everson. Don't push your luck.

Heath: We're sitting down for dinner in thirty minutes. I'll have Carey put a plate out for you.

I sagged in relief and went to get ready. I ran down the trail, wondering where the hell my dirt bike was since I hadn't used it in three days.

Did I take it to the shop and forget about it? Maybe I do need an assistant.

I jumped into my car and flew out of the parking lot, ignoring the two lonely cars parked out front. A normal starting Tuesday for Kick Shot.

When I arrived at their home, Carey was already outside, waiting for me with the biggest smile.

"Hey!" I said, grinning at her as I got out of my car. "Hope you don't mind me dropping in."

"We're having pot roast, and you're going to sit next to me!" Carey ran forward and grabbed my hand, pulling me along to follow her. I couldn't get rid of the smile. Carey's welcome brightened my mood more, something I hadn't even considered I needed.

"That sounds amazing."

"Were you really that bored not being able to work?" she asked as she opened the front door, being a good, if short, host. I let her, knowing this was a special occasion to her. I didn't come to hang out unless I was already invited. I *never* asked.

"I was. I'm used to working. Like you got bored last summer without school."

"Yeah, but school sucks," she said, wrinkling her nose. "I don't know why I missed it. It's really boring too."

"Sometimes, work is like that, but it's still what we do every day," I reminded her. "So, when we suddenly don't have it..."

"We miss it, even though it's stupid?" She looked up at me, her eyes bright with knowledge and new ideas.

"Yes—"

"Carey, what did I say about calling things stupid?" Heath called loudly from the kitchen.

"Sorry!" she yelled back, then gave me a look. I could already see the teenager she was going to grow into, and that was a terrifying thing. She was smart, quick-witted, and a little defiant, ready to take on the world at the age of twelve.

She's going to kill us all when she turns sixteen and gets her first car. I already know it.

I didn't question anymore if they were still going to be living in my territory in a few years. With Heath's new position as a representative and mine, it was more likely than not, we would live near each other at least for another decade, and I was surprisingly okay with it.

She led me into the dining room, where I could see Heath in the kitchen, wearing the most ridiculous apron I had ever seen. It said Zookeeper and had a cartoon piece of meat on it. I could only imagine it was a teasing reference to the zoo his family might have been once, with two adult werewolf sons and a precocious human daughter.

Honestly, it reminded me of the boxers I had seen in Washington. My face heated as I remembered them and the rest of my view during that trip.

Terrible place for that memory to pop up. Cool down before he notices. Or worse, Landon notices.

Heath looked up and smiled, and I knew by the smile he could scent something from across the room.

"How're you this evening?" he asked, his voice betraying nothing.

"Bored. Thank you for having me."

"I understand. Go ahead and have a seat. Carey, go get your brother. He'll be outside."

"Okay!" Carey barreled through the back door into their massive backyard. The moment she was gone, Heath put down the very large knife he was holding and walked toward me. Once he was too close for comfort, I could hear him sniff the air around me, then he stepped back.

"Take a deep breath," he ordered softly. "Landon is going to notice, but I'm certain he's already gotten wind of it from me when I haven't been paying attention. He's not going to say anything, but you don't like being embarrassed, and I know you will be. Take a deep breath and bring your pulse down. Think of something else and try to let go of the emotion."

I followed his instructions, thinking of anything else, like what could possibly be going on in my bar at that moment.

"Thank you," I whispered. "Landon's not out back, is he?" I knew Heath could be a little devious when it came to his children and finding ways to get them to do what he wanted.

"No, he's upstairs, but she wasn't paying attention, and I wanted to distract her," he said patiently. "What were you thinking about?"

"Wouldn't that defeat the purpose of the breathing exercise?"

"Possibly, but I'm curious."

"Then I'm not telling you," I said with a bit of sass that wasn't like me at all. "Feeding your curiosity isn't why I'm here."

"It kind of is since I was curious to see what you would be like at dinner with my family, in my house, away from your comfortable place in the bar," he retorted. "But fine. I'll find out eventually."

"No, I don't think you will." I had no intention of telling him I was thinking about his boxers. I took several more deep breaths as those memories came back, and I had to divert my thoughts to anything else, like Carey.

She was stomping back in, looking annoyed. The back door slammed as she glared at her father.

"He's not outside! You did that on purpose!"

"I did. I wanted to talk to Jacky about adult things," he answered without a shred of guilt. Instead, he grinned mischievously and walked back into the kitchen. "Landon is upstairs in his office. He got a call from an old friend. Tell him dinner is about to go on the table."

I snickered as she threw her hands up and went to the stairs, a stomp accentuating every step, telling me when she was out of earshot again.

"I can help," I said as he started lifting dishes.

"No, you are going to sit down and wait like a proper guest. This is my house, and no guest ever sets my table," he said with a bit of that Alpha sharpness I hadn't heard from him in a while.

"Excuse me?" I raised an eyebrow and dared to grab a bowl off the counter, sniffing to identify it as a potato dish. There was a lot of cheese too. I put it on the table while he watched, his grey-blue eyes narrowing in on the bowl, then flicking up to my face.

"Why can't you just do things the way I want sometimes?"

"Because I don't recognize Alphas, and I'm not a subordinate," I answered, staring him down. "If you had asked nicely, I would have sat down."

I watched him work through that. This wasn't the first time we had the discussion, but asking him not to order me around was asking him to do something against his nature. As for me following orders? I could. I tried for

Hasan and the family if they needed me to or I was out of my depth with something.

But this? He had tried to be an Alpha with me, and I certainly wasn't going to ever let that happen.

"My apologies. You'd think I would have figured that out by now. It's because you're in my house. I'm used to being in charge of everything in my house. There aren't many people who willingly talk back to me in my own home." He gave me a small smile. "Kind of refreshing, actually."

"Sure." I snorted and found a seat, letting him finish setting the table, my job of reminding him that he wasn't completely in charge done.

CHAPTER SEVEN

Carey and Landon came down a few minutes later and took their seats. Heath sat at the head of his rectangular dining table, Carey and Landon on either side of him, and I was next to Carey. That left a couple of empty places for food to sit out of the way once everyone filled their plates.

Carey launched into a description of her day and how her tutoring went after school. Heath listened as if it was the most interesting thing in the world, and I thought it was touching.

"So, this is your first time not working?" Landon asked. It startled me enough to nearly drop my fork.

"Oh, um, yeah. I'm not used to this idea of running a business but not working every night. Dirk, the new bartender? He told me I didn't need to be there, that they could handle it. I didn't want to hover, so I left and..." I shrugged. I needed to keep myself from rambling to the wolf, who barely ever said ten words to me.

"You get used to it," he said. "Work comes and goes. Father and I have been on both sides, quietly controlling a business or being really hands on and helping out wherever we could. When you have to hide your immortality, it's important to know when either is necessary."

"Thank you. Kick Shot just feels like my home."

"It's the only business you own, and you've worked there alone for over seven years. Of course it does." Landon watched me carefully. "But in ten years, you would have had to step aside anyway and let others work there because werecats aren't out to the humans. They were already beginning to think you were a werewolf because of your interactions with our family."

"I know."

"You'll be okay. You could spend the time opening a second business. Throw yourself into a new project. That's what I do."

"My son doesn't know how to stop working," Heath said, cutting in. "Of course, I also can't convince him to move into his own place. He's an overachiever who refuses to leave the nest."

"I moved out for fifty years until Carey was born. Then you needed Richard and me home," Landon retorted. "Once she's old enough to need less help, I'll find my own residence again."

"You could find a mate and leave sooner, and we both know it," Heath pointed out. "Carey and I would be fine, especially since she's out of diapers now."

"DAD!"

I covered my mouth to keep from laughing.

"I'm not interested in a mate," Landon said evenly. "Or in being an Alpha of my own pack or anything else. We've had this discussion."

Heath sighed heavily.

"Dad! Why would you say that in front of Jacky?" Carey demanded, grabbing her dad's sleeve. Heath looked down at the hold and gave me a look.

"I'm certain everyone at this table understands that everyone else has been in diapers at some point in their life," he answered, finally looking at his daughter. "Including Jacky."

"Yeah, but..."

"I didn't mean anything by it, Carey," he said finally. "I would never embarrass you on purpose. I'm sorry I seem to have now. I promise not to bring up that sort of topic again with company around."

I was surprised by his even tone and the care he handled it with. Carey was the literal kid at the table, and I knew how fragile a kid's self-confidence could be. My own parents used to say all sorts of embarrassing things about my sister and me, more often about me. Unlike Heath, they didn't acknowledge it when it happened and an apology certainly never happened. Not that they had been bad parents, just normal ones for their time.

He's such a damn good father, and I must be getting old. I think that only makes him more attractive, and I hate it.

"Moving on," Landon declared, looking back at me. "The key is to find hobbies, something to fill your time.

Before Carey was born, Richard and I coached sports for young werewolves. It passed the time, and they couldn't play with the normal kids, so they would have missed out on the chance otherwise."

"That was very sweet of you," I said softly.

"It was Richard's idea," he said as if it was a curse.

"I don't want to talk about Richard," Carey said quietly.

My heart squeezed.

"Then we won't," I promised her. Looking back at Landon, he seemed distant, sighing heavily.

"My apologies, Carey. I wasn't thinking."

I looked up at Heath, who wore a dark expression as he looked between his children, then at me.

"You could volunteer for the community," Heath finally said, turning the conversation off Richard and back to me. It helped ease the bruised feelings at the table, ones I knew I was going to grill Heath about once dinner was done. "Help clean up a park, get your name on something, or not. You can coach sports or teach classes in something you have training or experience in. Most Alphas are passing their time by helping corporations learn how to work with werewolves with training courses about our kind and how to integrate us into their workplaces. Construction is big for werewolves right now, which is why you see a lot of us in real estate, so we know those industries. Since we see things as longer-term investments than humans, we offer unique perspectives and educate humans as we can about them."

"That all sounds like a whole lot of public speaking

I'm not really about," I pointed out, leaning back in my seat. "But that's it? When you have a little secret to keep, you do...nothing? Or you do it from the background?"

"Yeah. I'm certain your siblings understand it."

"I don't know. They have families who have run and worked in their businesses for generations. I think Hasan's butler is fifth generation or more," I mumbled. "I would need to start establishing those sorts of relationships now and hope I picked trustworthy people."

"And that's bad, why?" Landon asked, frowning.

"She hates people being in her space," Heath reminded his son. "Jacky is apparently even more of a shut-in than most werecats."

"Probably," I agreed, unable to deny it.

"Do you know the names of the Tribunal members?"

"Not off the top of my head, which is pretty sad since they wanted to execute me."

"Do you know how their government works?"

I waved a hand a little, answering with a 'kind of.' "I know they have a couple of groups that do their dirty work, and I know the werecat portion of the Law. Do I need anything else?"

"No, but you probably don't plan on doing business with other supernatural species," Heath said, shrugging. "I'm just trying to showcase to Landon how much of a shut-in you really are."

"Thanks," I muttered, staring at him. "No werecat does business with other supernaturals. We're not exactly well loved, and people tend to ask us to die for them when they find out we're around."

He winced at that. "I can't say you're wrong."

Heath and Landon had good points about my current situation. I needed hobbies, ones I could throw myself into to pass the time without feeling like I was doing nothing or getting bored, the way I did with video games. I easily got bored once I beat them and had to find a new one to pass the time. Constantly trying to find the next one could get tiring in its own right.

I needed something consistent I could do. Volunteering could be good, but I had no idea where to start. It was definitely something I needed to think more about later.

"Thank you for the advice," I finally said to Landon, who nodded but didn't otherwise respond.

As dinner ended, Carey was released to go play video games for a couple of hours before her bedtime. Heath made me a coffee, probably knowing I would be up for several more hours, and we went outside, letting Landon keep Carey company.

"What happened at the table?" I asked softly as we sat on his back porch.

"Landon is getting more comfortable talking about Richard, trying to get past it. Carey isn't ready to acknowledge it happened," Heath said, staring at the open field of his backyard. "My oldest son did a lot of good in his lifetime, and he had been a great brother to Landon. He protected Landon from a lot when he was young. What happened in Dallas was..."

"Unexpected?" I finished for him, hoping I got it right.

"Yes and no. Richard was always close to me until we took over the Dallas pack, and stronger wolves moved in. He found himself slipping out of power since a lot of my inner circle were wolves strong enough to be Alphas one day. Then Carey was born, and he found himself second fiddle again to a younger sibling, this one seemingly even more special than the last. He only turned bitter in the last decade or so. Looking back, it's easy to see. It wasn't at the time."

"And Carey will always remember the brother who hurt her, but Landon wants to remember the brother he was close to for so long, even if it's hard," I said, nodding as I understood. "That's a difficult place to be."

"I wish I could help them work through it, but I'm still trying to...I should have caught it. I should have been a better father to Richard. How am I supposed to help my remaining children when I'm trying to put my failure with Richard behind me?"

"So, the bluster about how he declared his side and you wrote him off, is you trying to convince yourself." I felt comfortable saying it. Heath and I had been through a lot. "Plus, you seem to look at Landon and Richard as if they were still children through all of this, Heath, and they weren't. Richard wasn't a child when he died; he was a grown man who made his own decisions. They weren't children. They don't...need their father to be with them every step of the way and their decisions aren't yours. You even pointed it out at dinner. Landon lives with you, and he's what? One hundred and sixty something years old? How long ago was the Civil War?"

"You're close enough," he said sadly. "He's only around for Carey. We all know it. Even if I joke that he can leave now, he knows I need his help, and he's never been one to do anything away from the family. Even when he lived on his own, he was ten minutes away, and Richard was his neighbor. We've always been close and that's even stronger thanks to being pack animals." He looked down at his whiskey and sighed. "You're right, by the way, about Richard. I keep trying to convince myself that it's all okay, and he made his choices. But it's never going to be okay, and I just need to live with that. He betrayed me, and I'm still trying to get past it. I don't speak to many of my friends in Dallas anymore. They all knew Richard and saw the clean up with his body there after you were taken away."

"You'll be fine in the end," I told him gently. "I know you will. Richard was not some sign that you failed as a father. I don't know how many times I've said that, and I don't care how many times I'll have to say it in the future, but it wasn't you. It was him."

"Yeah..." He threw back the rest of his whiskey and poured another. "So, back to you. We were talking at dinner about what you can do with your new free time."

"Eh, not me. Let's pick a different topic." I was done being the topic of discussion, but I wanted to say something about dinner. "Actually, let's talk about how Landon spoke to me tonight. That was new."

"I told him why you were coming over. He's generally good at these types of things. He's never been talkative, but he was my second-in-command, Jacky. He knows how to help someone find a new direction when they seem a little lost. He just extended that to you, which is a good sign. It means he is finally warming up to you."

"I don't know why it matters so much to me."

"He lives in your space," Heath pointed out.

"Thousands of people live in my space, and I don't give a flying fuck about them most of the time," I reminded him. "Half the time, I don't even care about my customers because they annoy me to the point of no return."

"He's a werewolf in your space. A threat?"

"Possibly."

Then the realization hit me, and it made my stomach sink.

He's your son, and I want him to like me.

I looked away from Heath, staring into the dark world beyond his back porch. When had this become such a problem?

"I should go," I said softly.

"Wait, have a real drink with me. Please." He looked up at me as I stood, and I stared down at him, swallowing as his eyes seemed to shine in the dark with the telltale signs of loneliness.

"You know, I'm sure anyone in Dallas you once considered a friend still is," I whispered.

"No, Jacky, they're not. They're my old pack, and I gave them away. Every time I go back, I become less of an old friend and more of the Alpha who left them. Tywin sees me more as a threat since time has passed. He wonders if I ever might want to take over again. If maybe I'll get bored with my life of fatherhood and normal problems. They were all relieved to hear the North American Werewolf Council gave me a job, which requires me to stay here. *Relieved.* More and more often, I call into meetings. I haven't driven into Dallas since before the holidays."

"I'm sorry. I thought..."

"I hoped it wouldn't be like this, but I knew better," he admitted. "I think we all hoped I would still be a good friend to the Pack, but it's too volatile. Tywin has the right to lead without feeling paranoid. The way I left was disastrous. The Pack suffered greatly for my mistakes with Richard, Emma, and Dean." He gave me a small smile. "Jacky, you're the only drinking buddy I have left."

I sat back down, understanding now why Saturdays were so important, and he kept coming back.

"You're the only drinking buddy I've had in over a decade," I said with a small smile in return. "We're a mess, Heath."

"We are. But that's why I said you could come over tonight. I wasn't going to leave you hanging out to dry when you needed someone or something to help pass the time."

"Thank you."

"No, thank you," he said, leaning back in his chair. "You know you're welcome here any time, right?"

"Don't try to make me part of your pack," I ordered, knowing what would happen if I suddenly dropped by several times a week. He would start to see me as someone he had to take care of.

"I would never." His tone was too innocent.

"Bullshit."

"Okay, yes, but still, the offer stands." His grin was wolfy, and if it wasn't so fucking attractive, I would have hated it.

"I'll think about it."

"Good."

An hour later, Carey ran out to give me a good night hug and one to her father. Once she was gone, I fiddled with my glass, staring at the liquid swirling around. Landon didn't come out and join us, but I noticed lights turning off inside, indicating he was preparing to head to bed as well.

Soon, it was just Heath and me in the dark. Even the porch light was off. We could see well enough in the dark, so that wasn't the problem. The problem would have been there even if the lights were on.

Heath watched my every move, and the moment both of his children were gone, there was no mistaking the heat in his gaze. Something had gotten him interested, and I knew it was time for me to leave if we wanted to keep up this act that we had no secrets, and the attraction between us wasn't threatening to boil over.

"I'm going to go," I said carefully.

"Have a good night," he said, not arguing this time.

8

CHAPTER EIGHT

S aturday came fast. I was clawing at the walls, wanting to work. All week, I tried to figure out what sort of hobby to do in my newly-acquired free time and failed to find anything that sparked my interest. Every day, I went to Kick Shot before opening, only for Oliver and Dirk to say I wasn't needed once I was done looking over the books from the night before.

Tonight, though, I was going to bartend, something normal. Dirk could take the night off, and he would fucking like it.

When I walked in, they were both there, ready for the pre-open talk we had every day.

"Okay," I said loudly as I strolled to them. "Tonight, I'm going to be behind the bar," I announced.

"What?" Dirk frowned at me, his expression as severe as normal.

"You heard me. I want my bar for a night. Tonight is the night Heath normally comes in for a drink, and I want my normal Saturday. You two dropped in on me a week ago today, and you've been amazing, but I want tonight."

"But Saturday is the best night for tips at most bars," Dirk said, sounding really annoyed. A quick sniff in the air and I realized he wasn't annoyed. He was getting pissed off.

"No one tips at Kick Shot," I said, confused. He pointed across the room, and I turned to see a new jar on my bar, 'TIPS' written on it, and I sighed. "How long has that been there?"

"Three days," he answered. "When I realized no one here tips. They should always tip their bartender, or he waters down their drinks. I made two hundred in tips just last night," he said with an evil smile. "You were too nice to them."

"Funny, because I'm pretty sure they all think I'm a bitch for not hiring a waitress," I mumbled, shaking my head. "Well...how important are tips?"

"Very."

"I would think Niko would make sure you're paid very well," I pointed out with care, hoping he understood my meaning.

He did. Oh, he really did. His face turned red, and his annoyed expression turned into a full glare.

"Niko doesn't treat me special because I don't want him to," he snapped. "Did he—"

"He didn't. Someone else did. Big family, not many secrets," I answered. "You should have."

"Whatever."

"Miss Jacky, you could always build that patio outside and have a bar placed out there to give a second bartender option," Oliver pointed out, clearly oblivious to the conversation or pointedly ignoring it, which was the smartest thing he could do. He seemed to be a very smart young man, so I went with the latter option. "Did you talk to your contact about it yet?"

"I have, and he'll send someone out soon to look over what he can and can't do with the building," I answered. "You can ask Heath about it when he gets in."

Both of them gave me a stunned expression.

"What?" I demanded.

"You would use a werewolf's company to do work on Kick Shot?" Dirk asked.

"Yes. Heath is an ally and a friend, and if you repeat those words to anyone, I'll send you back to my siblings without any sort of recommendation," I snapped. "He owns a construction company and has worked in a lot of real estate. He knows people, humans, not just werewolves. He also lives in the territory. Why would I go out and find someone else when I have someone I know right here?"

"It's just...a bit unusual," Oliver pointed out softly.

"If neither of you has noticed, everything about this is unusual." I looked between them, wondering how they had missed it. "Believe me when I say you're going to see things happening here no other werecat would put up with. Two werewolves live in my territory. If that didn't clue you in, we need to have a long discussion."

Neither of them said anything, looking at each other then getting up.

"We'll get to work," Oliver said. "And if Mister Everson is going to be doing the work, please send him up to the office. I've already sketched up a design he might want to see."

"Am I ever going to see it?" I had no idea he was playing around with design ideas already.

"Certainly, I just wanted to see if it was plausible first before handing it over to you."

"I'll come up and see it when Heath arrives, then." I was out of the loop about my own bar. Dirk had set up a tip jar, something I had never considered, and Oliver was probably making plans to knock down walls.

"You seem frazzled," Oliver said gently. "I'm sorry this has disrupted your life. We're just trying to do our jobs and make everything easier for you."

"It's fine. My family thinks they know best, and I'm not going to toss you out into the cold. Still adjusting, that's all." I took a deep breath. "I'm not mad. I'm just used to the world moving slowly. This has all been very fast."

"I might be stepping out of bounds, but have you considered a hobby?"

I nearly laughed as I walked out of the bar to my house. I would come back when Heath was due to come in.

Once I got home, I played on my phone and made something to eat. I had been so excited to go to work when I had woken up, that I had forgotten to get in breakfast and just ran out the door. Of course, it didn't help that I had woken up late.

I thought as I cooked and decided to call the sibling I was surprisingly closest to, thanks to nearly dying with him.

"Hello, Jacky," Jabari answered, seeming a little distracted.

"Hey, Jabari. How are you?"

"I've been well. Busy with a new project," he answered.

"What are you working on?"

"I'm helping with an investigation at a local wildlife park and training new patrolmen for the park. You know me."

"I do." It was the one thing I discovered he was passionate about while he was staying. He loved his local wildlife and had been helping them for hundreds of years as humanity expanded. It was a hard fight, but I knew he loved it. I also knew he wanted to help more, but it was hard being a secret species. "Are you still funding them?"

"I am. So, what do you need? You aren't the sibling I expect to call out of nowhere."

"Ah, well, funnily enough, I wanted to ask if you would help me find a new hobby."

"This has something to do with Father's meddling, doesn't it?"

"They've taken over my bar, and now I have nothing to do. It's terrible, Jabari. Yell at him for me. I've been avoiding it since I found out it was him. This is way over the line."

"I told him you would think so. He decided it was time. You know how he gets."

"Jabari."

"I can't help you with him, but I can help you brainstorm some ideas," he said, chuckling.

"You can't or you won't?"

"Both, but then, you know how I felt about your little bar while I was there. I thought it took up too much of your time. You need more than two days and a night to work on other things. Plus, you own it, and it's good to have employees. It helps the economy."

"Wow. I thought you told him I wouldn't like it, but it sounds like you agree with his decision."

"I never said I disagreed with him. Who else have you talked to about this?"

"Heath and Landon."

Jabari growled a little.

"Really, big brother? You nearly died with Heath, who helped me protect you while you choked on your own blood."

"I was even beginning to like him. Then I met his son," my brother snapped.

"Ah." Landon had been incredibly distrusting of Jabari. He followed his father around during the trip my brother had made through my territory, watching his father's back to make sure Jabari didn't attack. He also never let Jabari be with Carey alone. I had noticed it but never brought it up. Landon just thought he was protecting his family, and I had no problem with him doing it. It wasn't like he'd attacked anyone, but Jabari had been massively offended.

"Moving back to the topic. Have you considered doing anything with that nice piece of land up north?"

"No," I answered, not wanting to think about the place where a nest of vampires had tried to kill me. As far as I knew, there still wasn't a new nest in Washington after the previous nest was decimated. The entire thing had been messy, convoluted, and incredibly brutal. A lot of people had died because one nest master had decided to try to hide his crimes instead of cleaning up his mistakes. It shouldn't have even been a werecat problem, but two werecats ended up dead and became one. "I don't want to go back there yet. Not after what happened. Maybe I'll be more comfortable in another year or so."

"What about something local?"

"Heath brought up volunteering. I don't know what I would volunteer for, though."

"You don't need to really volunteer. Go to the city government and ask if you can fund a project for them, like a new park or something. Or you can go further up and work with the state," he said casually.

"Is there anything that doesn't require more people? I came out here and opened Kick Shot for a quiet life, Jabari."

"Expand Kick Shot. With those two working there, you can focus on different areas."

"That would make my new manager very happy," I

muttered. "It'll keep me here, and it would be nice to see my little dive bar get bigger."

"I know change is terrible," he said with compassion. "I have yet to meet a werecat who enjoys it. I know I don't. Father is better than most, but he's always ready for it, almost looking forward to it. The rest of us would be just fine if nothing changed ever again. As it is, it's getting harder and harder to hide from humanity. The wolves didn't make it any easier by going public. The fae being sloppy makes humans look over their shoulders for more and the witches are slowly getting outed. It's only a matter of time before we're revealed."

"I know, and you met Joey. He's..."

"Sensitive to supernaturals. He must have a drop of witch blood in him. That's what most people think about humans who are sensitive to us. He might even have enough strength to do a few spells if he ever wanted to try. I didn't like him much."

"I like him less every passing day. He's nosy and watchful. He used to be friendlier, but he's always suspected I'm something, werewolf being his best guess."

"Only because he doesn't know werecats are real."

"Exactly." I sighed. "Well, thanks for talking to me. My food is almost done, then I'm going to head back to the bar. I think I'm going to build this patio Oliver keeps mentioning."

"Oliver? Zuri sent Oliver?"

"Yes. Why?"

"No reason. He's a good kid. I know she's been wanting to use him but felt he needed more training away from home. It's good she sent him down there. Who else did they send you?"

"Dirk."

"Ah...I don't want to gossip about our brother, so I'll let you go."

"Good idea. Zuri gossiped a lot, and I'm still trying to figure out what to do with the information."

Jabari laughed and said goodbye, and I hung up once I said it in return. I grabbed my food from the microwave-Chinese takeout leftovers- and went to eat at my dining table.

I'm going to build a fucking patio. I can't believe this.

9

CHAPTER NINE

I was waiting at the bar when Heath arrived. He strolled in like it was a normal Saturday, this time unsurprised by the presence of my new employees, looked at me with a small smile, then stopped at the bar.

"Whiskey on the rocks, please."

"Yes, sir," Dirk answered. Heath, before even getting his drink, pulled out his wallet, took out a large bill, and dropped it in the jar. The wallet was put away right before the drink was placed in front of him. He gave Dirk a friendly nod and brought the drink toward me.

"Good evening."

"Hello, Heath. We're going to work tonight," I said, smiling at him.

"Are we?" He seemed only a little surprised.

"Yup. We're going to expand Kick Shot."

"And this is because...?"

"I need something to do," I reminded him, making

him laugh. "So, we're going to expand Kick Shot. I know Oliver already has some sketch ideas upstairs, and I told these two you're the man I want to hire. If you're willing, this is what we're going to do tonight."

"Let's get started. We can chat while we work."

"Is there anything to chat about?"

"I haven't failed to think of something yet," he said, leaning over to say it in my ear as he passed.

You know, ignoring what's going on between us would be a lot fucking easier if he didn't do that.

I followed him up the back staircase and let him open the office door to reveal Oliver flipping through papers. I stepped around Heath before Oliver even realized we were there. I tapped the desk and spooked the young man, who sent papers flying. Grabbing a few as they fluttered around, I tried not to chuckle.

"Miss Jacky, Mister Everson. Are you here to look over my sketch ideas?"

"We are," I said, smiling at him. "Tonight, we're going to really look at this and see if it's plausible. Expanding Kick Shot is going to happen one way or another."

"Oh, that's wonderful, ma'am. I have all sorts of ideas we can try. The building has such potential, and the location—"

"Let's stick to the patio for tonight," I said, holding up a hand. "And please, it's Jacky."

"Of course, Miss Jacky."

Heath looked at me and mouthed it, grinning wildly. *Miss Jacky.* It wasn't the worst thing to be called, but it still killed me a little inside.

"Let's see those sketches," Heath said, his grin matching the one his daughter often gave me.

Oliver pulled out a sketchbook and began flipping through it. I went around the back of the desk and sat in my chair, letting them claim the other half of the desk for their discussion. I kept my eyes on them, though, and listened in, ready to stop them from knocking down too many walls.

"We could wrap the patio around like so," Oliver pointed out.

"That is a strange ratio of patio to indoor bar. I would say expand the bar out by several hundred square feet, then do the patio," Heath said, grabbing a pen to make the revisions.

"We're not knocking down entire walls," I said before that went any further. I knew one of them would think about it.

"Hear me out," Heath said, shifting the sketch for me to see. "If you don't do it now, you'll have to demolish the patio we build to do it later. If you do it now, we can fold all the construction into one event. If it still needs to grow, you can build out from other directions after."

"We can build out the other sides without building out this side," I pointed out, grabbing the pen and making my own notes.

"But we could use that space later for a kitchen behind the main bar," Oliver said in a small voice, frowning. "We could also repurpose the upstairs—"

"Absolutely not. I don't want to deal with multiple levels. This isn't a club. It's a bar. There is a difference." I eyed him. "Plus, you would be homeless, and we would need to find a new place for this office."

"Good point. That would require even more major construction."

They continued to ramble on. In the end, I convinced them we didn't need to expand the bar right now, and all the patio needed was space for a wet bar and a few tables. It didn't need to be anything special.

"Are you okay with this?" Heath asked as we walked out of the office together.

"I need something to do. Jabari asked me if I wanted to do anything with that piece of land I have in Washington. I said no, not yet. I don't know what I would volunteer for, and I don't have much for hobbies except video games and the occasional book I always read too fast. Might as well expand Kick Shot."

"None of that answered the question," he pointed out as we went out the back door. I chuckled to see a table and two chairs placed behind the building. They hadn't been there when I came in to meet Heath, meaning Dirk had brought them out while we were upstairs. I sat down and waved a hand to let him know he could sit down. A moment later, Dirk came out with another whiskey for Heath and a water for me.

"You aren't manning the bar if you're running drinks, Dirk," I said softly. "But thank you for them."

"Hire more staff," he said before turning to go inside.

I sighed heavily as Heath started to laugh.

"Oh, these two are going to change everything, and you won't be able to bring yourself to say no," he teased.

"Why not? I'm very good at saying no."

"No, you really aren't. Carey—"

"I couldn't legally tell Carey no when she showed up," I reminded him. "And who is so heartless to turn away a child in need?" I pointed at the back door. "Right there. That's where I met your daughter for the first time."

"What about Washington?"

"I thought it was my fault," I pointed out.

"And this patio?"

"I'm bored."

"You had already brought it up and given it consideration."

"Oliver." I groaned. "He's smart and willing to do anything to please. I just wanted him to think I was going to take what he said as professional advice. To give him the feeling of being useful, in charge. You know how that is."

"I do. Wolf packs are like that. Now, you're making the patio because you have the expendable cash and nothing to do with it. It also makes Oliver think he's done something good for your business. He needs a confidence boost."

"You noticed?"

"He's too much of a people pleaser to not have a self-confidence issue. He's willing to do whatever is necessary to earn respect, including agreeing with bad ideas," Heath said with a smirk. "I wasn't going to knock down any of your walls."

"I thought you made a reasonable point..." Frowning,

I tried to figure out what he was thinking.

"I would rather build out, so the staircase is in the center of the building, not on the far end. It would also keep the building's center of mass toward the center."

"So, it doesn't seem lopsided...That's very smart, but you were testing my new manager by giving him an option you didn't even like. He's not your employee, Heath."

"They aren't just invading your space," he reminded me with a small smile. "I'm still uncomfortable with the idea that your siblings have sent their own people here to work for you or spy. Do you think anyone in your family would be okay with these long Saturday night talks?"

"I don't know," I admitted. "I don't ask for their opinions on my friendship with you."

He gave me a look, and I threw up my hands.

"I don't ask, but sometimes, they let me know they think it's foolish to let you live in my territory," I conceded. "We haven't really spoken about it in months. They're used to the idea. They even warned these two about you and your family before they came here."

"You understand my concerns, Jacky."

"I do and wish there was something I could do about them. I..."

"Can't say no," he said, smirking as we went back to that part of the conversation. "I know." He stood up, leaving his half-finished whiskey on the table. "I'm going to get home. You have a good evening, Jacky."

"Bowling tomorrow?" I asked before he could sneak away.

"No, next Sunday. First Sunday of February."

"The weekend before the full moon. Okay, I'll write that down."

"I'll remind you next week," he promised. He touched my shoulder for a moment as he passed, awkwardly patting it like friends would do.

I didn't watch him go, frustrated he was right. Frustrated I was bowing so easily to my family's forced intervention.

I didn't go back in, heading home, knowing Heath was headed for his own home.

I was halfway back to my house when I felt it. I spun to face the north. Just for a moment, there and gone before I could make another move.

Another werecat had crossed into my borders.

I ran home, pulling off my clothing as I went and dumped it all on my porch. I Changed, snapping my jaws as it completed and took off into the dark woods.

Maybe this time, I could get there fast enough to see if the werecat was still around. Maybe this one was a normal visit.

I skidded to a stop ten yards from the edge of my territory, sniffing the air. Another male, this one different from the last. That disturbed me. Werecats didn't do anything as a group, and rogues didn't go near each other. I had always been told rogues fought when they crossed paths. Two coming near and crossing into my borders within a week of each other?

It was a terrible coincidence.

The only reason I didn't raise the alarm was that he

had left even faster than the werecat before, not even giving me a chance to react.

I growled loudly as I approached my territory border, knowing everything outside it was the dangerous unknown. I had made it to the border fast enough, the scent was very fresh. Too fresh to know if the werecat was still around.

I saw nothing, and a small patrol revealed nothing. I couldn't see or smell him on the other side of the invisible line that kept me safe.

Heart racing, I headed home. I didn't return to my human form, opening my door with my paw and nosing my things inside. Since my fur could handle the cold, I stayed on the porch, wondering if the intruder would step in again.

I don't know how long I waited, but the dim glow of the sun breaking over the tops of the trees told me it was time for me to try to get some sleep.

I didn't tell anyone what happened. In my human form, I sat on the edge of my bed, trying to reason out what was going on.

The easiest explanation would be rogues passing by to get an idea of who I am. It's been several months since Hasan had word passed around that he would look to me to keep everyone in the Americas safe and represented. After everything else, they could have been wary to introduce their scents to me earlier, but why aren't they saying hello? Why are they leaving so fast? They could at least stop and talk to me.

Uneasy, I fell back onto my bed, my mind spinning until the very minute exhaustion demanded I rest.

10

CHAPTER TEN

I was exhausted as I parked in front of the bowling alley, feeling like I had barely slept in days. The reality was, I *had* barely slept in days. Every few nights, I felt a werecat step into my territory and leave.

I was being toyed with, and I didn't understand why or by whom. I had four different scents, three males and a female. There wasn't any schedule, and for all I knew, they were hovering on the outside of my territory, just to fuck with me. Werecats didn't toy with another of their own kind like this.

Part of me felt like I was just going crazy, like the lack of sleep after the first few visits turned into a recurring belief it was happening.

I have to put this aside and go bowling. Just this. Then I can call all the people I need to call and see if anyone can come up with some reason for this.

There were a few things I hadn't done yet, but I needed to. Calling my family was one of them.

Expanding Kick Shot was proving to be insanely time-consuming, and with the intruders, I devoted myself to being around Oliver and Dirk whenever the business was open and even hovered while they were off. It wasn't until Heath texted and asked if I was going to be late for bowling that I remembered I needed to keep up appearances for a while. Just one afternoon for Carey, so she didn't think she had to be afraid of anything. Heath knew part of what I was facing. I had told him someone seemed to be toying with me, hopping in and out of my borders. It was enough to put him on his guard without starting a panic.

I walked into the bowling alley like it was any other day, smiling at the werewolf family as they picked out their bowling balls for the day.

"Sorry for being a little late," I said as I walked over with my rental shoes.

"It's okay!" Carey replied brightly, falling onto the bench next to me. "We would have waited."

"Oh, you didn't have to do that."

"She wouldn't have let us start until you were here," Heath commented from his seat with Landon on the other side of the lane. "Because she's polite and you're part of bowling day. We don't leave people out of bowling day."

"Well, thank you for that." I tried to give him a smile, but I knew it fell flat by the way his eyes narrowed. His head tilted to the side as he asked me the silent question.

Again?

I nodded so quickly, I was certain Carey missed it,

but I knew Heath didn't. He sighed, but nothing was said as the first game started.

Three hours later, and I was finally feeling more relaxed. Too bad it was time for everything to wrap up.

"How's your science project coming?" I asked Carey as we walked out the front door.

"It's good. It's really easy. Plants, photosynthesis. You know. The easy stuff."

"That's good. It's an easy A for you." I squeezed her shoulder lightly, pulling her tight to my side. "You keep out of trouble until tomorrow, and we'll play a bunch of video games and go out to dinner. Wherever you want."

"Why?" She looked up at me with a frown. I only took her out to eat for special reasons.

"Because tomorrow is your presentation, isn't it?" I grinned as she nodded. "And you'll tell me you got the A you promised me, and I will take you out to dinner." I would take her out to dinner, no matter what. I always tried to reward her when she tried something uncomfortable or daring—not dangerous. Making that distinction was important with Carey.

"Don't worry, I'll get that A!" She grinned and jumped into Heath's nondescript black SUV. Landon checked her seat belt, then got in as well. Heath stepped up next to me and motioned toward the back. I followed him, knowing he wanted to talk.

"You're not sleeping," he pointed out.

"Would you, knowing someone is either staking you out or being an ass just to be an ass?" I asked, annoyed. I didn't want him to know the severity of the situation, so I altered the way I mentioned it. He didn't need to know how many there were. One rogue was bad enough. "Heath, it's been two weeks of this motherfucker jumping in and out of the territory, a shitty rogue looking to be an ass. If he wanted the territory, he would have picked the fight already, and I'm not stupid enough to hunt him outside my territory."

"Why not? He obviously needs to be taught a lesson."

"He's a rogue. The longer a werecat is a rogue, the better they get at fighting because it's really all they do. He also has to be older than me, and he's male, which sucks because he's going to be a lot bigger than me." I rubbed my eyes. "I'll figure it out, but I can't leave my territory to hunt him down. It would remove the one big advantage I have right now."

"Knowing where he is when he steps into your territory," Heath said, nodding. "I just don't like this."

"I don't either, but I'm going to make some calls today. Oliver and Dirk are off buying Dirk a car. They've promised not to leave my territory and should be back before nightfall, which gives me some time to get ahold of people."

"Do you think your family might have dealt with something like this before?"

"I don't know, but it's worth a shot." I hated lying to him, but really it was more of an omission. I phrased everything as if I was talking about one of the four werecats toying with my borders and keeping me awake at night, which didn't give him a hint of a lie in my scent. And I knew he was waiting for it. There was only so much more paranoid I could get until he knew without a doubt I was hiding something. We were beyond that point.

"It is. I know you could defeat anyone who comes in here. I trust in you for that. I just don't like to see you be toyed with like this. It doesn't seem right."

"I don't think it is," I whispered. "You go. I'm going to get home and make these calls. I'll let you know if there's anything you need to do if you're willing to help."

"Always," he said softly.

I walked to my car and drove home fast. When I parked in the back, I saw the new pickup truck and tried to smile. Of course, some car salesman convinced my two Europeans they needed a Ford F150. It fit Dirk, which was even more puzzling, but I couldn't go up and give them shit about it. One, I promised them I would leave them be today, and two, I really needed to talk to my family. I had asked for a family meeting about my current situation, and they would be waiting for me in only a few minutes.

I barely had time to kick off my shoes and let my hair out of the annoying bun when I walked inside. Dropping in front of my computer, I looked at the new communication system—a top-of-the-line camera that should please Zuri and Davor and not annoy the others.

I was the last one to sign in to the group video conference.

"Jacqueline, you asked for a family meeting," Hasan started. "Is there something going on?"

"Yes. I've had four werecats come into my territory

and leave before I could get to them, at least twice each, over the last two weeks," I said, laying it out quickly. "Three males, one female. I'm assuming they're all rogues."

"That's unusual..." my werecat father said, frowning into his camera. It felt like his eyes were opening my soul and baring my secrets to him.

"You've never heard of this happening before?" I asked, wanting to shake my monitor like it was him, and it would rattle some knowledge out of his mouth.

"Sister, are you okay?" Jabari asked softly.

"No. I'm losing sleep," I said, annoyed. "They...they keep stepping in just long enough for me to know what and where they are. I've even been able to process long enough to give a warning through my connection with the land only once, that very first time. I think the only reason I reacted so fast that time was because Carey was with me in my house at the center of my territory. That was the first time. The next time, I was headed home from work on Saturday. Then there's been..." I took a deep breath. "There's no pattern. It just keeps happening, and it's keeping me awake at night. I never know the next time they're coming."

"Is it ever more than one at once?" Hisao asked.

"No, never more than one at a time, but it's still four werecats, congregating around my territory. That's so many."

"It is," Mischa agreed, growling. "You are a toy in a game to them, sister."

"I figured that out." I eyed Mischa on my screen, then

looked back at Hasan's face. He seemed to be concentrating, thinking as he drummed his fingers on his desk. "Hasan?"

"I've never heard of werecats doing something like this," he said softly. "Be very careful, Jacqueline. Mischa, you know rogues better than all of us."

"I am one, of course I do," my Russian-born sister said with a mean look. "When I need to shake up a werecat who's pissed me off, I'll deploy a similar tactic. It reminds them I'm the real power. There are other werecats who do it just for a laugh. They'll toy with you for a few days to a few months until they get bored. There's not much you can do unless you catch one in the act and teach him or her a lesson."

"Is that really what you think? She's got a bunch of assholes?" Niko growled. "Dirk is in her territory right now. He's at risk."

"So is Oliver," Zuri snapped. "While I didn't raise him, the boy is a good human, and I don't want him hurt either. That being said, Mischa knows rogues better than any one of us. The same as you know werewolves." She turned on me. "Have you made a plan?"

"They have an escape plan now, and Dirk bought a truck today. They have a way out, and the meet up location is the airport. If anything turns serious, I'll put them on planes."

"If you make it there," Niko said softly. "What if you can't?"

"I can give them to Heath and his family, or I can have Heath meet them at the airport and make sure they fly out. It's not the same level of protection, I know, but it would at least give them strength in numbers and get them out of the country."

"You trust the wolf?" Davor asked, finally speaking up.

"I do," I said, nodding. "That hasn't changed and probably won't. He's just as at risk right now as your humans."

"I don't," Davor snapped. "Oliver isn't just Zuri's. He's also mine. If anything happens to him, we're going to have words, little sister."

"I was wondering when the asshole would come out to play," I snarled at him. "I didn't fucking ask for Oliver or Dirk. I'll do my absolute best to protect them, but don't shovel the blame on my shoulders."

"Stop it," Hasan ordered. "Let's review. Jacqueline has four werecats breaching her borders, toying with her. What's the worst-case scenario?"

"One of them attacks," Mischa said.

"All of them attack," Jabari countered. "It's not natural for werecats to congregate like this, which means they know what they're doing. If they came into her territory in full force..." I saw the flash of worry go through his eyes and over his face.

If they all attacked me at once, I would be a very dead werecat.

"Why would they do that?" Zuri asked. "Anything Jacky may have done, by now, has been proven to have no resounding effects on the werecats. Things settled down in the last six months, especially thanks to that incident last spring and our announcement about her position. On top of that, the repercussions from our family if werecats killed one of our own? Who gains anything?"

"I think I'm right," Mischa said with a shrug. "I think they're having a laugh. Rogues aren't all enemies. There's a chance some of them might not be rogues, but werecats in Jacky's region who want to toy with her. I have a feeling they'll call a meeting soon and talk it out with you or just disappear and not bother you anymore."

"Do we send someone to back up Jacky?" Hisao asked. "I'm willing to go. They'll back off a lot sooner when they learn I've landed in Texas."

Those words made shivers run down my spine. Hisao was a terrifying male. He had a lethality to him that couldn't be denied. I probably couldn't win a fight against any of my siblings, but I could at least give them a couple of good reasons to stop fighting me. Hisao carried himself as if he could kill me, or anyone for that matter, without a thought.

"Want to make her look weak?" Mischa snapped. "That's how you do it. Then, the moment you leave, they'll be right back at it. Jacky will continue to foster a reputation that her family has to save her from problems of her own making. First, the Tribunal thing with the werewolves, and now this? Which are probably harmless games? They'll be laughing at her for centuries, and she'll never have any respect among the werecats."

"Mischa is right," Hasan said sadly. "Jacqueline, you'll have to get through this on your own. If they attack you, we'll send the full family to you, but we can't overreact without reason."

"I know," I said. I was fine with that. "Should we discuss a possible battle plan?"

"If multiple werecats enter your territory looking for a fight, little sister, you better turn and walk away. Is that clear? None of us would ever take on a group of our kind. One of the reasons we have so much power is because we're such a big family, willing to throw our lives on the line for each other. While we don't ever use that tactic on other werecats, it doesn't mean the threat of it isn't real." Zuri huffed. "I couldn't win by myself against four others. Neither could Jabari, though he and Father would have the best chance. Father?"

"I've never had to, so I don't know," he answered honestly. "I'm certain if all of you decided to turn on me, I would be in for a difficult fight. I might take a few of you out, but I don't see myself winning. The problem is, fighting as a group is inherently uncomfortable for werecats. We can't communicate in our werecat forms, which is only one problem."

"We would also see ourselves as in charge," Jabari added. "That's how the werewolves were able to make ground on us during the War. We're stronger, faster, bigger, but we're not good at tactical, group fights, and most werecats didn't want to be a part of them. Then there's Jacky."

"Yeah, I still have that ability," I said with a sigh. "Let's not get into that right now."

"Let's. You're an oddity, not the norm," Hasan said. "Play this carefully, Jacqueline. Just be careful."

"And run if they attack," I finished. "But most likely, they won't."

"Most likely," he agreed. "Mischa?"

"I've said it already, but they're probably just fucking with you. Picked a bad time to fuck with you with new humans in your territory, but they wouldn't know that. You know, if they're playing around in a group, they could be a family unit as well. Let me dig around and see if there are any family units out there I might not recall off the top of my head."

"Are there rogue families?" I frowned, not wanting to consider that.

"Sometimes a rogue will turn someone, teach them the ropes, then drop them off somewhere. It's not common, and we try to step in when we hear about it," Niko informed me, his tone a little snappy. "We're not like werewolves in that way. We have very strict rules, and we don't tolerate accidents."

"Yeah, I knew that much," I snapped, not liking how he was in a bad mood. This wasn't my fault. I was just trying to best prepare myself for every possibility. "Plus, we naturally bond when we Change someone, right?"

"We do, but long-term rogues already have a hard time bonding to land," Mischa said with a rueful smile. "There aren't many out there like me, looking for no connection. It leads to rogues having way fewer children than other werecats. Maybe one every thousand years, if that. I've only ever Changed one person in my entire life, and it wasn't an accident."

That was interesting. I had no idea any of my siblings had ever Changed anyone, where those other werecats were, or who they might be.

"That was before you went rogue, though," Zuri said softly.

"A story for another time," Mischa said with a soft growl. "Either way, let me look into anything that might sound like your four cats and get back to you, little sister." Mischa turned off her camera and signed off.

"Well, we've lost the expert," Davor pointed out. "I'm leaving as well. Good luck, Jacky." Then he was gone as well.

Slowly, they all signed off and left me alone, Hasan grilling me before he finally left. He wanted to make sure I'd heard everything that was just explained to me.

I stared at my screen for a long time and snarled as I felt one of the werecats jump in and back out of my territory. I stumbled as I got up and went to my door, the snarl never ending.

Fucking assholes. I need this to stop. This isn't a fucking game. There are people here who rely on me. Don't they fucking realize that?

I decided not to run out to the spot and sniff who it was. I could do it later in the evening. There was one more phone call I wanted to make.

I hadn't spoken to Lani in nearly a year since before I went to Washington. She didn't see me as a friend anymore, and that was fine. I had other friends of a sort. I had my family around me, even if they were across the planet. I didn't need the friendship of the other Texas-based werecat.

But with this much rogue activity, I knew I needed to call her and check in. The phone rang and rang, but there wasn't an answer. I tried a second time before giving up and leaving to get the scent of my intruder. It was the female, twice in a row now. This was her third time breaching my borders. Her visits were definitely the shortest, always so fast I could barely react.

By the time I was back, Lani had texted me.

Lani: What do you need?

Jacky: I just wanted to check in with you. I've seen an increase in rogue activities around my territory. Are you having the same problem?

Lani: No. Sounds like a mess. Good luck with it. Don't get yourself kicked out of your territory. Would hate to see what a rogue would do to those werewolves you love so much.

Jacky: Do you need to be so bitchy?

I shouldn't have called her out, but her comment was uncalled for. I was trying to be polite. She didn't need to meet me with hostility.

Lani: No, but then again, you didn't need to lie to me for over six years. Forget my number, Jacky. I've tried to get over it, but I don't think I can, and I'm done trying.

Jacky: I'm not asking you to get over it. You're right. I lied to you. I'm sorry. But I am Hasan's daughter, and he asked me to do certain things. I'm checking in with a werecat who lives near me because there's increased rogue activity. Excuse me for worrying about you and your territory.

Lani: You don't need to worry about me. Good night.

I resisted the urge to throw my phone. Lani's attitude was the last thing I needed that day.

But she was right. I was the one who killed our friendship. Even if she could have forgiven me for the Dallas drama, lying about who I was for over six years was a betrayal I couldn't take back. I kept the most important thing about myself a secret from her, and there was no fixing that.

"I can't do this right now," I whispered to myself, sitting at the edge of my bed. "I shouldn't have contacted her."

I didn't sleep that night.

CHAPTER ELEVEN

Saturday, I felt like I was going to fall asleep on my feet or just fall to the ground to get some rest. Whatever those werecats were doing on the edge of my borders, I didn't know, but they were breaching my territory and keeping me on edge nearly every night now.

Almost as if they were ramping up to the full moon, which would be in just over twenty-four hours.

It wasn't even noon, but I was up and moving around, even though I was fighting the need for sleep. Just before dawn, one of them had breached and toyed with me, dancing along my border, and when I answered, they left. I didn't even bother to go see which one it was. I didn't care anymore. In the end, it didn't matter much. If Mischa was right, they would stop eventually and go off to have their laughs someplace else.

Hazing. That's what this amounted to if my sister is right. I'm being hazed for a laugh.

It was like college all over again, the werecat

equivalent of someone knocking on the door, then running when it was answered. It was rude and induced a level of paranoia that was beginning to drive me a little insane.

Cleaning my kitchen, I tried to focus on something while waiting for my new employees to be up and ready to work. Kick Shot opened at five, and we were falling into the habit of having a three o'clock meeting before opening to go over any possible changes. It never lasted long, but it was good to touch base before the day started.

I still didn't have a new hobby to help kill time, but I had replayed six different video games over the course of the three weeks since Oliver and Dirk arrived. A couple of days earlier, Heath and I talked to one of his company's architects about the new patio and would see official plans for it in only another week.

With all of that and the rogues, I was glad to be keeping busy, even if it was driving me further down the dark hole of insanity.

"Rude fucking cats," I mumbled, scrubbing a pan in my hand, gripping the side hard enough to leave dented fingerprints. Noticing, I cursed again and dropped the pot, stepping back from my sink. Frustration and annoyance, combined with the paranoia of when it might happen again, were starting to make me unfit for company. I took a few moments to breathe, then went back to the dishes, handling them with care. I would have to replace the pot, but it wasn't a big problem.

At one, I was ready to leave, my house spotless, and headed for my bar, tucking my hands into my pockets to avoid the chill. I chuckled to see that the table for Heath and me to have drinks at was already out, meaning Dirk was awake and moving around early today. His truck was parked next to my Nissan, telling me he wasn't running before-work-errands either, probably holding off until tomorrow. I knew he and Oliver were actively looking at rentals around my territory in hopes of leaving the apartment upstairs. Neither of them wanted to stay upstairs for their entire year in Texas.

"Good afternoon, Dirk," I called as I walked in the back door.

"Hey, Jacky," he called back. "Tomorrow is the full moon. Anything you want from me before that?"

"I don't know yet. Let me think about it, and if anything is unusual, I'll say something when we're closing," I answered, seeing him behind the bar. "Is there anything you need?"

"No, I'll be fine. I'll keep Oliver from doing anything dumb tomorrow night since this will be his first full moon in werecat territory. You're going to run the borders, right?"

"Yeah, probably," I agreed, sitting down across from him. "If I have time, I might go for a hunt, but there's been some strange activity, and I want to make sure my territory borders are clear of any intruders. It'll send them a sign that I have no intention of making my territory smaller and easier to defend." I found it was easy to talk to Dirk about werecat aspects of my life. While Heath understood the immortality aspect, Dirk was raised by a werecat, and Niko had obviously educated him in preparation for a potential Change. It was the one thing I could count on to get Dirk talking to me.

"Showing them you aren't scared is a good thing," he agreed. "Niko says it's more complicated than you've been letting on to me and Oliver."

"It is, but that's my business, not yours, and Niko should know better," I answered with a smile. "And if you want to live by the pretense that you aren't related to me in any way, you won't use Niko to get information I only tell my family."

Dirk's face flushed. "Yeah. Sorry. He called earlier this morning, wondering if you had made plans for the full moon."

"When I have, I'll let you and him know, but let's not go around me." My smile turned sharp as annoyance ran through me. Heath had been right. Who the fuck knew what Dirk and Oliver were telling my siblings if they felt they could call and ask about me at any time? My human employees most likely wouldn't know any better, and Niko was probably just worried about Dirk's safety, but it was still frustrating to think my family could be using these two to breathe down my neck.

Dirk turned away and started checking bottles on the back wall. It was funny, doing inventory every day at Kick Shot. It was mostly to kill time. The only stock we ever came close to running out of was beer, as sad as that was. Half the time, I replaced bottles on the back display because they were beginning to look too old, not because I was running out.

"How do you like it here so far?" I dared to ask,

changing the subject to him and not my current problems.

"It's quiet, but your customers are good-natured. Joey decided I was human last week, which I'm guessing is a good thing?"

"Very good. He knows, of course, what Heath is, and he's certain I'm a werewolf. I know some of them have always felt I might not be one hundred percent human, but it's become more...troubling in the last year," I explained with a sigh. "It's frustrating, and some of them avoid me completely, only coming here to have a drink and play some pool."

"You've gotten more customers in the last week than you did the first week Oliver and I were here," he said with a shrug. "Maybe they're glad the obvious supernatural creature is no longer behind the bar. Maybe they like you being the quiet, out-of-sight owner, not the potentially very dangerous bartender."

"Probably. Oliver showed me the numbers after closing last night and hopes they continue through the month. It's a kick to my teeth, but I'll survive. I guess I won't bartend anymore." Which I hated, but if that was what needed to happen to make Oliver happy with my books, that was what I was going to do—at least until they left. Then I fully intended to go back to my regular job, and my customers could all go somewhere else if they had a problem with it.

"For what it's worth, some of them miss you behind the bar," Dirk said with a small smile. "You know what they drink. You know their names. You're the constant at

Kick Shot, and they know you. I'm still getting to know them, and well, you know how it is being a bartender. The regulars come for the consistency, the relationship built with a favorite bartender."

"That does make me feel a little better, thank you." I truly appreciated the sentiment. It meant the seven and a half years I'd stood behind that bar weren't for nothing. "Maybe werecats should go public."

"Niko isn't against it," he said, shrugging again. "Werewolves could do it, why can't werecats?"

"Because we're solitary. Or that's the argument I hear a lot. We're easier targets than wolves, who would band together and fight anyone who threatens one wolf. A lone werecat could get killed, and no one might figure it out for weeks, if not longer. All it takes is a single silver bullet, and while werewolves are trying their best to regulate that, I promise you, human governments are stockpiling them for if it's ever necessary."

"Ah, yeah. The American government, without a doubt. I wouldn't say the same for Germany."

"There's not enough space in Germany for every werecat who needs to hide," I reminded him.

"There would be plenty of places where werecats would be welcomed." Dirk ignored my point about Germany and made me a drink, putting it in front of me. "I wasn't living with him when Hasan threatened to out werecats to...save you, right? That was the whole debacle, wasn't it?"

"Yeah, that was me," I muttered, staring at the glass in front of me.

"I knew I had heard your name before coming here, I just couldn't place where. Can't believe it took me three weeks to figure it out," he said, shaking his head.

"Why did you hide that you were Niko's adopted son?"

"Because he was never much of a father," Dirk answered. "He was always Niko, more of an uncle than a father, and while he was around, he wasn't...he didn't teach me to ride a bicycle or anything like that. He sent me to good schools, talked to me, and helped me get ahead in life."

"And?"

"And what? The only reason I was getting ahead in life was because he was handing it to me. So, I picked a job that would make me work. I dropped out of university a year before I was done. I don't want life to be easy. I want to be normal."

"Not normal," I said softly. "You want to be human."

"I am human. What would you understand about it, anyway?"

"More than you know, but that's a discussion for another time," I declared, standing.

Taking my drink with me, I walked to a booth to wait for Oliver. I played on my cell phone and sipped the water Dirk had given me until I saw my manager sit down across from me.

"Good afternoon," I greeted, looking up from my screen. Every time I saw Oliver, his reddish hair was perfectly styled for a business meeting, and his work suit was crisp as if he ironed it every day. I knew he wanted to look older, so he dressed well, but sometimes I saw a boy in a suit, and it just didn't fit. Today was one of those days.

"Good afternoon, Miss Jacky. I finished January's report this morning. I'm sorry it was late. Since all of February is in my format, it should be much faster in the future."

"Of course." I had done my books only for tax purposes and messily. My accountant hated them. I was certain that was going to change with Oliver micromanaging my business, doing more than I figured a manager should. "Don't worry too much about it, Oliver. I'm not going to go over your work. I gave you my accountant's email. Just send it all to him."

"I already have. I just wanted to let you know." He gave me a boyish smile. "Is Mister Everson coming to Kick Shot this evening?"

"He does every Saturday," I reminded him. "Is there something you wanted to talk to him about?"

"No, but he's one of our biggest spenders, and I thought maybe we could do something, up our game to show him we appreciate his business."

"Absolutely not," I said with a smile. "We're not going to shower Heath Everson in undeserved recognition just because he can tolerate more alcohol than the humans and knows how to pay his tab on time."

"Miss Jacky—"

"Oliver, he's a friend, and he doesn't get a trophy for that. His ego doesn't need inflating." And I didn't need to give him anything he could possibly use against me at a later date. If these two tried to pull out all the stops for him, I would get teased relentlessly.

"Okay." Oliver seemed defeated.

"You can do that for our human customers. Have a customer appreciation day once a month. How about that?"

"Where we offer a deal? Say, one-dollar pitchers? That's popular in pubs, right?"

"Yeah, depending on the crowd. I'll let you toy with the idea. Write up a proposal, including what sort of beers we would offer that we can waste for that cheap, and we'll look into it." I was constantly finding Oliver things to do. From the patio to potential hires to this, I had learned already that Oliver was the type who needed to be kept busy, or he felt like he wasn't doing a good job. It proved frustrating on some days, but he had an amazing work ethic I couldn't talk shit about.

He jumped up and headed upstairs. I chuckled at Dirk, who shrugged as he went to the door and unlocked it. I checked the time, surprised to see it was five.

"Well, let's get another week over with," I said to myself.

"And the full moon," Dirk said from the other side of the room.

"That's tomorrow, but yeah." I sighed, vacating the booth so humans could use it. I still had no idea what I was going to do about the full moon. I took a seat at the bar and waited for Heath. As humans came in, I waved and said hello, but I was getting used to not being behind the bar. I didn't hover over Dirk, making sure he got their orders or knew who they were. He was picking up their names and what some liked to drink just fine.

When Heath walked in, Dirk began pouring him a whiskey without needing to be asked. While I had always given Heath a beer, Dirk was falling into the whiskey habit. He also slid me another water, taking my nearly empty glass. Without a word, Heath and I walked out back and sat down.

"I'm beginning to enjoy this," he commented. "Dirk is good."

"Why whiskey, not beer?" I asked, wondering about the change.

"He knows what good whiskey is, and you don't," Heath answered with a smirk.

"I do know what a good whiskey is," I snapped, offended.

"Fine, he classes the joint up a little." Now he was grinning. "He makes me want to spend more money than you did."

"So, my good looks didn't get you drinking more, but his do? We need to have a long talk, Heath Everson." I gave him a smug look.

"Your good looks make me want to do a lot of things. Drink more isn't one of them," he fired back, looking at my face. When his eyes dipped down, I hissed softly, a warning not to push his luck. When he looked back into my eyes, I could see the victorious little light dancing in his eyes, thinking he had won.

"You shouldn't flirt so much. It's only going to get us into trouble."

"I find it impossible to resist. Flirting with you is fun."

"You just like seeing me flustered," I retorted.

"I like seeing your emotions," he said softly. "You're an open book, and I like seeing what's going on in that head of yours."

"That's not fair since you barely ever give me a sign of anything. You lock it all away and leave me hanging."

"I'm trying, though. I really am." He didn't stop smiling. "I can't explain it, but I've had so much control for so long, it really is an active choice for me in some situations to let it go and expose my scents."

"I bet," I mumbled. "I just wish I could do it."

"It wouldn't help you. You have the tendency to show what you're thinking all over your face, and I think it's refreshing."

"You like to see me flustered," I said again, back to that point. "And it's mean."

"I am never mean to you," he murmured, leaning close.

My face heated as I leaned away. "Heath."

He shifted away, looking to the woods. "Sorry. Sometimes it's harder to..."

"Control yourself?" I raised an eyebrow at him.

"Yes. I want you, and I know we can never...I should have never teased you about it. I should have never brought up how I feel."

"I find myself thinking the same thing sometimes," I admitted. "It's like having it out in the open means we can act on it when we can't." I went to take a sip of my water, staring out into the woods too.

"I was at the store the other day and saw Valentine's Day chocolates and gifts and nearly bought you something."

I choked on my water, thumping my chest several times as I coughed.

"Jacky? Are you okay? Give me a thumbs up, please." He was hovering over me as I doubled over to cough. I gave him a thumbs up and nodded, trying to talk.

"You what?" I asked, coughing afterwards, my throat feeling raw.

"I nearly bought you something for Valentine's Day," he said again. "I had to remind myself it was a terrible idea."

"It is," I agreed, rubbing my chest that ached a little from accidentally inhaling water. "Let's just not talk about it. Heath, we can't keep indulging this flirtation, and you know it."

"I do, but do you really want me to stop showing up every Saturday?"

"No. No, I don't. Do you want to stop coming by?"

"Not at all," he said, sighing heavily. "We're in a tough place, Jacky."

"We should see other people, or you should, and I'll go back to being a shut-in with no friends."

"Well, now we're both shut-ins with no friends, remember?" His expression was sad.

"Do you miss them? Being with other wolves?"

"Yes and no." He didn't elaborate.

I didn't get the chance to ask him, stiffening as my magic picked up on another intruder.

Then a second. And a third. A fourth. I was certain there was at least one other, but there were so many now, all in different locations, my mind felt like it was being yanked in different directions.

All hovering at my borders before disappearing.

"You should go," I whispered, standing up slowly.

"What?" He stood up with me. "Jacky?"

"Go home. Pack a bag, and don't come back until after the full moon. Actually, don't come back until I tell you it's safe." My heart pounded with the implications of what I had just felt. I had no idea why they were doing this but knew what this had been.

I knew a warning when it was so obviously written on the wall.

12

CHAPTER TWELVE

"Excuse me? You want me to leave?" He seemed confused and hurt. "Jacky, what the hell is going on?"

"I've been lying to you," I explained softly, my eyes directed to some distant point at the edge of my territory.

"About?"

"The rogue werecats."

"Werecats?" he growled. "As in more than one?"

"As in at least five," I said, turning to him finally. "Constantly toying with the borders of my territory."

"That's why you've been losing sleep. You've been edgy and distracted when Carey's been with you. You need to explain, Jacky. Why do I have to leave?"

"Not just you," I corrected. "You, Landon, and Carey. Fuck, can you take Oliver and Dirk with you?" I asked, running my hand through my hair, trying to push the brown flyaway pieces from my face. "Please?"

"Yes, I can but—"

"Heath, I don't know how to explain what's going on, alright? I've asked my family. My sister, Mischa? The Rogue as everyone calls her? She thinks they're toying with me, but..."

"But what?"

"For weeks, they've been stepping in and out of my territory faster than I could reach them, always only one of them. Just now? Five of them came in, and I don't know who they are or what they want."

I watched as he lost some of the color from his face. Even a proud and powerful Alpha werewolf had a reason to fear five werecats.

"Are they gone?" he asked softly. "Or should I run inside, grab your humans, and get moving?"

"They're gone, but I don't think they're going to stay that way."

"Tomorrow is the full moon," he mumbled, nodding as he seemed to agree with me. "You're coming too, right?"

"No."

"Jacky—"

"I have to stay. They might just want everyone around here out of the way to talk to me, or they might attack me. I don't know. I'm betting on the latter at this point since they've had weeks to talk to me."

"Then you need to—"

"I can't go anywhere until I know what they want," I snapped. "I can't."

"And Hasan? What does he think?"

"He and I are of the same mind on this. If he or any

of my siblings come to help, it's a sign of weakness on my part."

"Are you not even a little worried something could happen to you?" Heath ran a hand through his dark, curly hair, exasperated and deathly afraid. "Jacky, five werecats could..."

"A little worried?" I laughed bitterly. "Heath, I'm terrified. Finish that statement. Five werecats could easily kill me, you, and Landon. Could easily take over my territory. Could easily do a lot of things. I'm not a fucking idiot. I wish Mischa could figure out who they could be, but she hasn't been able to figure out anything. Werecats don't do this. We don't group hunt. One rogue playing games with me would have been easy to solve, but I've caught four definite scents, and just now, there were five stumbling into this territory. What form they're in, I don't know. I don't know if it's safe for me to even leave my territory, Heath. I don't."

"Because they could be laying traps for you outside your borders," he said softly.

"Yeah..." I had that worry when I had felt the first one, but now, I wasn't sure what to think. The only thing I knew for certain was my territory wasn't going to be safe soon and possibly already wasn't. There was no way for me to defend my home against this many werecats.

"Did you talk to your family about the possibility of them attacking?"

"Yes, but I need them to attack before backup can be called. It's complicated, it's..."

"Politics," Heath finished for me. "I understand. A

wolf pack can't go after another wolf pack unless they have a definitive reason to. It looks bad to attack another pack without grounds, based on paranoia or a feeling the other might be planning to encroach. Since we've decided to congregate in cities, fighting like that doesn't happen as much anymore. It keeps us away from each other and cuts out our need to fight for land."

"Hasan told me if they all attack, I just need to run," I said, swallowing. "It would be an unfair fight, and no werecat, including him, could possibly win a fight against so many of our own kind. Once I let them know it is an attack, they'll come to me, then it's on, but not a moment earlier."

"So, you have to potentially risk your life for proof," he whispered. "Jacky, this is stupid."

"I know, but it's the right way to do it. Tell me you wouldn't require the same thing as werewolves? Evidence the other party is in the wrong."

I could practically hear his teeth grinding together.

"Let me stay—"

"No."

"Jacky—"

"No," I snarled. "They'll crush you. I can at least dodge and avoid them in my territory. Damn it, Heath, this is not the time for the good guy to play hero for the lady he likes. This is the time where I tell you to help me get everyone out, so I can be prepared for this. If I'm alone, I only have to worry about avoiding them and getting out of my territory. Once I know for sure they're a threat, I call in the family, and we clean this mess up without looking weak."

"Why would they be doing this?"

"I don't know. It's been over a year since everything in Dallas and the Tribunal, and other than some increased tensions with overeager werewolves, no one has been hurt. No one has suffered for my actions or the actions of anyone in my family. This might not be violent, but I really think we need to treat it like it will be."

Werecats don't have pack magic. If they're going to come during the full moon, it's not going to be to have a chat. If I keep saying it, maybe I'll believe it.

"You think it will be, and that's good enough for me," he said, reaching out to run a hand over my cheek. "Do you want me to leave now and take them with me?" He nodded toward the back door. I pulled away from his hand and looked back to the closest place a werecat had been, wondering if they would come back in tonight or if tonight was the final show of force to fuck with me before tomorrow. This could all end up a bad, mean-spirited prank. Maybe I was too paranoid after everything I had done for Heath and my need to protect Carey.

"Go now," I ordered. "I'll come in and explain to them that they'll be staying with you, then I need to contact my family and let them know about this escalation before the full moon begins to claim them around the world."

"Okay." He opened the back door, letting me step inside first. I walked out to the packed bar and sighed.

"Damn it, this is going to look bad," I whispered to him.

"We can wait until closing," he reminded me. "If you get a feeling they're back, I can text Landon and tell him to go with Carey and meet him with these two as soon as I can."

"Let's do that," I said, frowning. "I really hope this is a bad prank."

"What are the chances it is?"

"In Mischa's opinion, very high. I just don't have a good feeling about any of it. It's too unusual with there being a group of them. Fuck, the roads might not even be safe for you to leave my territory."

"Let me handle that," he said sharply. "You don't worry about anything but keeping yourself alive, Jacky. Okay? And if they do attack me, Landon, or Carey, they risk another open war with werewolves all over the world. I'm the chosen peaceful liaison, remember? I should be the one wolf in the world safe from werecats because I'm trying to keep the peace."

"Don't tell any of the werewolves about this. I don't want this to seem like I'm weak outside the werecats."

"I'll keep it to myself," he promised.

We waited and watched. I was tense as the minutes ticked by into hours, and people began to leave. When Dirk called closing, some tension left me but not enough. I wanted them packed up and gone by dawn.

"What are you two waiting on?" Dirk asked as he locked the front door. "You've been standing there, a little too still and quiet for a couple of hours now."

"You need to leave with Heath to a safehouse," I said quickly. "I want you and Oliver out tonight."

"Is our safety at risk?" he asked.

"Yes, but it could only be a situation tomorrow night, then you'll be able to come back. If things don't go well, Heath will make sure you get on planes and home safely," I explained. "Five werecats just breached my territory borders and sent a very clear message. I want all of you gone before the sun comes up."

"Let me...let me pack a bag."

"Hurry."

Dirk ran upstairs, and I heard him talk to Oliver, who must have left the office when he realized it was closing. The young manager didn't come down. I heard both sets of footsteps moving in the apartment above me, half jogging as they grabbed whatever they needed.

"Thank you," I finally said to Heath, who waited patiently with me.

"It's no problem, but I feel I should say, I absolutely hate this and want to stay here and help you."

"That sucks," I muttered. "I...I wish this wasn't happening, but it is, and I need to make sure everyone around me who can be, is safe. You included. You have Carey and Landon, and they need you."

"Landon is a grown-ass werewolf," he growled.

"And I'm a grown-ass werecat," I hissed back. "Carey is more important than all of us and *she's* twelve-year-old human girl. I am not. You'll protect your daughter."

"I will, but I want to protect you too."

"I wish you could, but you can't. If I don't get ahold

of you on Monday, assume something is wrong. I'll text you Hasan's number, so you can coordinate with him if needed."

He nodded slowly. We heard the footsteps coming back down. Dirk and Oliver were each holding a suitcase.

"Follow Heath's orders at all times. He'll make sure you're safe."

"Can I take my truck?" Dirk asked.

"Keep behind me," Heath said. "Let's go."

I watched them leave, listened to the trucks fire up, and through the window saw their lights disappear as they turned onto the road and drove away.

I wasted no time locking up Kick Shot and running for my house. I texted Heath the information, then jumped onto my computer, quickly calling an emergency family meeting with whoever could spare a moment. Davor was the first to respond.

"What's wrong?" he demanded as his video came up on my screen.

"Five werecats breached my borders earlier, then left. I've sent Heath with Dirk and Oliver to pick up the rest of Heath's family and leave my territory until Monday. Just in case. The message was fairly clear."

As I was talking, Niko and Hisao jumped on, then Hasan.

"You think they're going to attack on the full moon?" Hisao asked, frowning.

"There are no other possibilities, are there? Unless this is just them fucking with me to have a big laugh tomorrow. In which case, I'll try to kill them anyway because this isn't fucking funny," I snarled at the end. "They're playing games with me, and I'm tired of it. I'm terrified, and I don't know what to do."

"You've done what you can," Niko said. "You sent away the vulnerable people who live in your territory. Are Dirk and Oliver getting on planes?" I knew he would worry about Dirk, one of the reasons I decided to call the emergency meeting.

"They will Monday if Heath doesn't hear from me. He has a safehouse somewhere. I don't know where it is, which is probably a good thing. He's a planner like that."

"He's an Alpha wolf. They have plans for everything," Hasan commented. "Jacky, if they come into your territory tomorrow, I want you to run. I don't care why they're there. You'll abandon and make it clear you aren't willing to get into a fight with all of them."

"That's my plan, but I figured we should all be on the same page."

"When do we go in?" Hisao asked. As he was talking, the rest of the family got on. Jabari, Zuri, and Mischa all showed up at roughly the same time with the twins sitting next to each other.

"What happened?" Mischa cut in before anyone could answer Hisao's important question.

"Five werecats breached Jacky's territory and sent a clear warning," Davor answered before I could. "Still think they're joking around?"

"No, not if they're doing it as a group so close to the full moon," Mischa snapped. "Do we have any idea what their agenda might be? Jacky?"

"No, they haven't exactly been leaving notes for me," I growled.

"Then let's start by asking the important questions." Zuri cleared her throat as someone tried to talk over her before she could continue. "Why Jacky? What's important about her? Why her?"

"She's the youngest member of the family," Jabari pointed out.

"She's allied with werewolves," Niko mentioned.

"She's been in trouble before," Davor grumbled. When I sighed heavily, he shrugged. "Sorry, it's the truth."

"Yeah…" I rubbed my face. All of those things were true.

"She's vulnerable. If there's one person in the family who would be easy to defeat, it's her," Hasan whispered. "But that would imply this is an attack on the family. On all of us, with Jacky being the first, the vulnerable warning shot."

There was a long silence after that.

"They wouldn't. No. We've been the most powerful family of werecats for at least a thousand years, and only more so in the last eight hundred since the formation of the Tribunal. With you and Mother being our active sitting members by Law, they wouldn't." Zuri seemed as if she couldn't wrap her head around that. "Why would they attack the family? Everything we've done has been to protect our kind and keep us from utter annihilation by the werewolves. We've protected other werecats for as long as we've been a family."

Honestly, I couldn't wrap my head around it either. The concept of anyone attacking our family through me was insane. It was definitely a death wish.

"Maybe they just hate Jacky," Davor said. "Young, impetuous. We've all had a front row seat to how unpopular she is among the werecats. Maybe they're fine with our family, but don't want her in power."

"Especially since she has werewolves so close to her," Jabari said, looking away from the camera with a thoughtful expression.

"Then all of the European werecats would have tried to kill me ages ago," Niko growled. "I don't think it's just because Heath and his boy are in her territory."

"Why?" I asked, realizing I had a chance to learn a little more about Niko. Why would anything like my situation relate to him?

The call was silent again, and I watched how my siblings discreetly looked away from their cameras.

"What do you all know that I don't?" I demanded. "Come on. I might die tomorrow. I think it's time for at least some of the family secrets to end."

"My biological parents were werewolves," Niko explained with an abruptness that caught me off guard. "Well, my father was, and my mother went through the Change after I was born. They were killed by other werewolves during the War. Hasan found me running for my life, so I wouldn't be Changed and turned into fodder for the War like the other young males of my pack. He finished raising me, and I decided I would rather be a werecat. Everyone in the family loved me and took me in, even knowing who my biological family was. Everyone except Davor, but then, he doesn't like anyone."

"Oh shit," I said, leaning back. "Well...fuck." Then it dawned on me. "Niko, The Traitor."

"It's been said, though less frequently now, that I betrayed my own kind," he said with a sharp smile. "It's also led other werecats to be somewhat distrustful of me since I spent much of my childhood with my pack, my werewolf family. I can't blame them. Both of my biological older brothers were werewolves. I was the youngest of three. They...fought in the War on the other side by their own choices."

"I'm sorry for being nosy." I felt guilty for prying.

"It was time you knew. You do have a point. You might die tomorrow." He seemed sad. "Please don't do that, by the way."

"I'll try my best. Hasan, do you want to tell me anything?"

"If you live through tomorrow, I'll tell you one of my secrets. How about that?" He also gave me a sad smile.

"Ah, going to use it as an incentive. Cool." *I hate this. It suddenly feels like I'm at my own funeral.* "I'm going to hold you to it this time, Hasan."

"You'll be fine," Jabari said sternly. "I know how well you fight. You learned well with Hasan after you were Changed, and you have a good head on your shoulders. I believe in you."

"Thanks for the vote of confidence."

"If you don't make it out, just know, we'll come, and

we'll kill every single one of them in your name," he promised with a snarl.

"And burn down their homes and take their land?" I asked.

"If we have to. If these rogues even have anything to their names. This is why I hate rogues. Classless, unruly, and—"

"Excuse me," Mischa cut in. "But let's not treat all rogues like they're fucking shitheads. These are, sure, but I play by our established rules, and it helps me maintain my region for Father."

"Sorry," Jabari grumbled. "But you can't deny this is underhanded and mean. This is disrespectful. This is unacceptable."

"You're right, but let's not write off an entire portion of the werecat population because you don't agree with their life choices."

"Can you two have this conversation after I run for my life?" I asked impatiently. "We never answered Hisao's question. When do you all come here and help me?"

"With the full moon so close, we can't possibly fly out right now. We can leave the moment it's over and head to Dallas. From there, we'll converge on your territory." Zuri seemed confident in her answer.

"I think we wait even longer," Davor said softly. "And that's not because I don't like you, Jacky. It's practicality. If we fly out right after the full moon, we're possibly going in blind."

"I must agree with him, my sister," Jabari said to Zuri.

"It would be best to wait for word from Jacky...or the ones who are doing this. They won't kill a child of Hasan without making it public knowledge as quickly as they can, no matter their reasons."

That made my stomach flip.

"So, I'm on my own until I can get ahold of you, or they do because I'm dead."

"I don't find that acceptable," Hasan growled.

"Father—"

"No, Jabari—"

"Hasan," I said, trying to stop the argument. "He's right, and I don't want any of you getting killed for me. We don't know what's going on, and we need to. If I get away, we can meet up after I call you. If I don't, you'll need to worry about how to protect everyone else."

"Then we should let you go, so you can prepare," he said gently. "You could leave right now."

"Yeah, I know. Abandon my territory and seem weak. Give the werecats of the Americas and the world the impression a few jokesters could chase me and mine off my territory because I'm young and inexperienced. Because my family wasn't around to defend me. We all know how that would play out. It would destroy the small reputation I do have with the werewolves in Dallas and in Washington with the vampires. I would be a laughingstock. I can't leave until I know they're here to kill me. I can't do it."

He nodded slowly. "I know, but none of us would judge you for it."

"Sure." I played with my computer mouse. "I'm going

to go. I guess I have a lot to think about until tomorrow. I gave Heath your number in case he hears from me, and you don't. I'll text you his contact information in case the reverse happens. Good night, everyone."

"Good night," Hasan barely got in before I hung up.

I quickly texted Hasan Heath's number and added Landon's, just in case.

Then I went to my room and waited.

13

CHAPTER THIRTEEN

The full moon was only an hour away when I stepped out onto my front porch. I knew they were coming. I could feel it in my bones that come sundown and the moon rose high, I would be called by the curse, and they would come.

I had no idea why, and I probably wouldn't learn any time soon. I texted a few people, hoping they would appreciate knowing I was still okay, then put my phone away in the duffle I planned on carrying while escaping my territory. I could only hope I held onto control well enough that my feline didn't decide to do anything dangerous, like fight any of them.

I knew they were coming, and so did my cat. I figured it was my cat that understood the threat better than my human mind ever could. Maybe the animal mind was more knowledgeable and had been trying to send me this message for weeks.

My territory wasn't safe, and they were going to attack.

I just wished I knew why. What was going on, and why did they telegraph their intentions for nearly a month? What was the objective?

I stared into the woods and said words I needed to get off my chest one more time.

"Goddamn it, I didn't sign up for this. Why did Hasan have to choose me for a daughter?" Frustration, anger, and fear rolled around in my chest and gut, making me want to be sick. This was what they had been doing for weeks—throwing me off balance with an unknown purpose.

My phone buzzed in my bag, but I ignored it, watching how the sun fell slowly. I was already nude with a fresh pair of clothes in my bag for dawn. Everyone knew the plan was for me to run until I thought I was safe, then contact everyone to let them know I was alive. There was nothing to do now but wait.

When the full moon's power claimed me, I Changed but didn't move from my front porch. Picking up my bag with my teeth, I dropped it in front of me, making it easy to grab and run with when they arrived.

I flexed my paws, extending my claws and scratching the wood of my porch as the stars began to twinkle, and the moon rose high. A couple of hours after nightfall, I finally felt them come into my territory.

They covered the four cardinal directions, and to my horror, they covered the intermediate directions.

Four to five to eight werecats—more in their numbers

than I could have ever considered. I didn't know all of their scents, blind against four of them, not knowing if they were male or female, old or young. Nothing.

It was all I needed, though, to know without a doubt what they planned tonight.

They're here to kill me.

As I grabbed my bag and started to move, I quickly decided I should run northwest and try to get through there, which would put me on the road toward Dallas. While the Dallas pack might not consider Heath a friend anymore, they would let me pass through. There wasn't any reason for them to tell me I couldn't be there.

I ran, knowing where the other werecats were every step of the way. I skidded to a stop and sank into a creek when the one in my way of escape was close, only a hundred yards away. I used the noise of the running water to cover my sound as I went upstream, letting the water wash my scent away. It wasn't a perfect technique, and most predators were smart enough to scour the banks of any water source to find where the trail would continue, but it would give me a little bit of an edge.

I jumped out of the water close to my territory border and heard a roar from the south. The werecat I passed must have encountered my scent. They were moving more erratically now, and the others were converging faster.

I didn't take the time to see what would happen next, making a mad dash for my border and escaping my own territory. The immediate feeling of blindness, losing my idea of where my enemies were, was an uncomfortable one. I never liked leaving my territory, and tonight, that dislike was amplified into a general hatred and fear of the unknown.

It made me slow down, move more cautiously, keeping a watchful eye out, and my ears open for anything out of the ordinary. One thing I almost never did was leave my territory in cat form, with only a couple of notable times I'd had to. I didn't know the land well, and the area wasn't unpopulated, so avoiding human homes was a necessary part of my plan.

I heard them before I saw them, two werecats coming fast behind me, not nearly as cautious or careful as I was. With a snarl, I moved into a full sprint, trying to leave them behind.

I wasn't fast enough. Like any smart cat, one was able to get on my heels and swiped at my back legs, causing me to miss a step and stumble, losing my run. I let go of my bag and rolled to catch one of them as they tried to land on me. Claws out, we rolled in the dirt, snarling and biting.

"Let's go, bitch," I snarled into the other werecat's head, smelling it was a female. She was stunned for only a moment, and I sank my fangs into the soft place between her neck and shoulder, shaking hard, trying to tear a chunk out of her.

The other werecat grabbed my back-left leg and yanked, making me fall off balance, but I didn't loosen my grip on the female.

This is fight or die, and I have no fucking intention of dying tonight.

The werecat I was holding onto pawed my face hard enough to make me dizzy. I tugged harder, feeling and hearing the flesh rend from bone and tendon as the blood began to pour. The female screamed an unholy yowl I knew I would have nightmares about.

If I survived the night.

I knew the wound on the female was fatal, but I didn't have a chance to turn and go after the larger male holding my leg. He pulled me off my feet just as a third werecat barreled into the side of me, knocking the wind out of my chest. The impact twisted my leg uncomfortably, and I had to use my free leg to try to kick the male off as my fangs searched for the new combatant trying to pin me down. I hit something and heard a yowl as the male released my leg. I brought my back legs up and raked them against the werecat over me, but not before the new male was able to give me several scratches on my chest and sides.

A feline scream greeted me as I felt my back claws tear through flesh. I rolled, taking my attacker with me, and got him on his back. Instead of continuing my attack, I took my chance to hop off him and started running again.

I can't win this.

I darted into the woods, this time not caring where I was going or who I might run into. Even the cat that lived within me decided this was a losing fight, and consequences be damned, running was the best choice.

I heard them pursue, an innumerable footsteps racing behind me, trying to catch me. I dodged trees and logs as I ran, panting as the pain of my injuries began to settle in.

I wasn't fast enough. Two fresh werecats gained on me, and one leaped. I tried to get out of the way, but several hundred pounds of feline landed on my back, taking me down. We slid for a few feet as I rolled to try to knock off the female werecat.

Fangs grabbed my shoulder and sank in, taking hold. Another werecat caught up, grabbed one of my back legs, and yanked hard, forcing me out of my defensive position.

"*I'm not dying tonight,*" I roared in their heads, swiping a paw at the side of the head above me. Bone crunched, and the cat was knocked unconscious, slumping to the side. With a snarl, I clawed at the one on my shoulder, trying to knock it loose. It eventually let go, but I could see more ready to join the fight.

"*You'll pay for this,*" I growled.

I knew I could have asked why, but I wouldn't have gotten a response. There was only one werecat who could properly communicate in feline form—me.

The one holding my leg released his hold, and I scrambled to stand, turning wildly to see the seven living werecats around me. I was blocked in.

"*You'll never get anyone who lives in my territory. I sent the wolves away. I sent my humans away. They'll be under the protection of my family until the day your bones go to dust.*"

One of the larger males snarled. He was nearly as big

as Jabari or Hasan, a testament to his age. He had to be a few thousand years old to reach that size.

I faced off with him as he prowled into the circle. I had no intention of fighting him. I knew the others would only wait a moment to join in, especially if I was winning. There was only one way for me to live through the night—I needed to get out of the circle of death they had made just for me.

He left a gap, and once he was ten yards away from it and I was closer, I turned and went for it.

I'm not dying tonight.

I made it through the hole, but not very far as the two werecats closest to me gave chase. One knocked me with a painful slap to the bites I already had on my back leg. The other rammed his shoulder into me, sending me twisting and falling into the dirt. I didn't spare a moment to think, fighting to get to my feet and keep moving. One of the werecats jumped on my back and clawed me open in several places. When a loud snarl echoed through the trees, the cat jumped off, and I staggered from blood loss as I walked.

No. I'm not dying tonight.

I wanted to get back to Carey. And Heath. I wanted to see my family again.

I tried to keep moving, but with a lazy nudge, the biggest male knocked me off my feet and snarled in my face. I weakly snarled back.

Huffing in my face, the big male brought up a paw and hit me across the jaw. It didn't quite knock me unconscious, but it was close, making my head spin. He did it a second time, and I was driven closer to failing. I tried to get on my feet, and he slammed me back down, snarling viciously in my face. He put his weight on his front leg over my neck, and my air was nearly cut off.

"Don't do this," I said desperately.

He didn't stop, and soon, black spots filled my vision, and I passed out.

14

CHAPTER FOURTEEN

I woke up feeling as if every part of my body was in pain in some way or another. I was still in werecat form, and I could barely move, thanks to stiffness and pain. I was almost certain none of my bones were broken, but I didn't discount the possibility of small fractures in my bones where enemy fangs had hit them.

"She gave us a real fight last night," a man said, his words colored with a deep southern accent from somewhere like Georgia or Alabama.

"She did. Smart one, too. She knew she couldn't take us and based everything she did on the chance of getting away," a deeper male voice said. He didn't have an accent, and for some reason, that bothered me more. Most old cats learned how to speak languages fluently, cover up old accents, or even speak in new ones. All good skills to have when someone had to blend in for centuries on end as humans changed. It also destroyed any ability to place the person with any reliability unless you knew more about them.

"She has fucking pack magic," someone snapped, this one female. "Tell me I'm not the only one to notice that."

I opened one eye and realized they weren't in the room with me. I was in a basement, and the cage around me was well built and probably had silver in it because anything else wouldn't do. I didn't immediately Change, deciding to remain in my werecat form for a time. If I didn't move or try to return to my human form, they wouldn't know I was awake.

I spent the time taking in the room, knowing I needed to be able to describe it later when I got out. The ground was concrete, and the walls seemed to be barely finished unpainted plaster. The bars of my cage were built into the ceilings and floors. On one wall, there was a shelving system, holding the normal things that could be found in a basement or garage—cleaning supplies and construction hardware. Across the room was a door, probably the only exit.

"You aren't," the deep voiced male said. "It's why I didn't kill her. If their entire fucking family has that ability, we have to expose them. Wolf magic in the leading werecat family? Why haven't they shared that with the rest of us? We could take the wolves down and finally reclaim our place as the most powerful supernatural species."

"And get out from under the thumb of the Tribunal," the southern male growled in satisfaction. "Fucking entire thing was just created by Hasan to secure his own power."

"And to stop a war one of his friends started," a female added softly. "Either way, we have her, and now, we can move on to phase two."

My stomach rolled, and my chest tightened as that voice registered.

Lani is one of them. She's betrayed me and helped them. Why?

The hurt was nearly too much. I wanted to get up and see her, ask why she would do this to me, but I resisted. I needed every advantage I could get, which meant I needed them to keep talking. I needed to know what the fuck was going on and how to use it to my advantage.

"Lani, love, what do you recommend when Jacky wakes up?"

"Promise not to kill her little human girl or her werewolves," my friend answered. "She'll give you the fucking world for them, I bet."

"I want the wolves," the obvious leader replied. "We can promise the little human girl will be unharmed and take her in once all of this is all over. No reason to leave a kid an orphan."

"When was the last time you raised a child?" Lani asked.

"Four hundred years ago, not too long. I'll manage, or one of you can take her. Lani, you've met her, haven't you?"

"I've seen her. During the Trial over a year ago. I could point her out in a crowd."

"Maybe you can take her."

I heard the annoyed sigh and knew Lani didn't agree. The very idea that they were talking about who was going to take my Carey pissed me off. It was almost too good of them and also the cruelest thing they could do.

And the leader wanted my wolves. Another problem, but it made me grateful I'd sent Heath and Landon out of my territory to protect everyone.

"You know what I'm surprised by?" another female spoke up. "She didn't call any of her siblings. We were certain she would get backup from at least one or two of them if we ramped it up and made her scared. She was the only werecat in her territory."

"Do you think they abandoned her?" a third male asked quietly. I could barely hear him.

"Possibly, or she didn't tell them what was going on. Whatever the reason, she was there alone, and we have to make do. Hopefully, Hasan gives enough of a shit about her to bend."

Hasan. My werecat father was going to lose his fucking mind when he caught wind of this.

I looked around the room as the group talking above me fell silent. With the silence, I took a moment to consider my surroundings again, wondering if there was anything that could help me through this.

Looking up, I saw a very tiny window, too small for me to get out, even in human form.

The basement was an effective prison, and I didn't see myself getting out any time soon.

I huffed a werecat sigh and began to Change, my body screaming in pain as it slowly happened. The gashes and punctures all over me opened and bled as new scabs had to form through the Change.

I panted once I was in human form. I heard footsteps above me and the thudding of a group jogging down the stairs. The door opened, and I caught a blurry look at the stairs beyond—a way out. I just had to get through that door, up the stairs, and out of whatever building I was in.

"Look who's awake," a tall man said with a smile. He was white, most likely of European heritage. How long he'd been in the United States, I didn't know. "Jacky Leon, daughter of Hasan."

"Jacqueline, daughter of Hasan," I corrected, moving to sit at the back of my cage, not taking my eyes off him. "Jacky is the nickname I prefer, though, so if you could keep using it, I would be grateful."

"She wakes up with a fuckin' attitude," the southern male said, moving to stand on the older male's right. Lani stood behind both of them. I could see her between their shoulders, her eyes hard. "Thought we would have taught her a lesson last night."

I didn't pay him any mind nor the male leader, staring at Lani, making my intent very clear. I knew she was there, and I was pissed. If anyone paid for this, it would be her.

The leader stepped into my line of sight, blocking my view of Lani.

"We're going to talk," he said with a smile. "We have your phone. We need the passcode."

"Why?" I knew the chances of leaving alive were slim.

"Tell me, or we kill the girl."

"Her name is Carey Everson, and she's human. You also have no idea where she is, and you won't get that information out of me because I don't know where she is." I bared my teeth. "And if you think what you've already done is bad, I fucking dare you to drag the werewolves into this by killing an innocent twelve-year-old *human*."

"Don't test me," he growled softly, coming to the cage, the smile never leaving. "I've lived thousands of years and dealt with more powerful werecats than you, and have succeeded every time. I'll find little Carey, and I'll flay her alive if I have to."

"You'll never find my girl. Answer the damn question. Why do you want the passcode for my cellphone?" The fact that it still worked after my crawling around in a creek was amazing. I sure as fuck wasn't comfortable with them getting their hands on it.

They could use it to text everyone and bring them into my territory, a perfect trap. Heath and Landon were safe wherever they were, but I had to remain strong, or they would accidentally give themselves away.

They could also use it to convince my family everything was okay. It wouldn't last nearly as long. A family meeting would be called, and if I didn't show up, they would know something was off, but it could take days for any of them to get to Texas and figure out what was going on. I could be long dead by then.

I could be dead in the next ten minutes if I didn't figure out what to do.

"We need to contact some people," he answered, eyeing my face.

"Figured. You're not getting it from me," I said, keeping my teeth bared, a warning that if any of them came into the cage with me, it was going to be a fight.

"If you don't give us any information, you're worthless. If you're worthless, you die," he said patiently. "I'll give you some time to decide whether or not you want to be worthless." He turned away and walked out of the room, the other two werecats falling in around him. Three had visited me, one of them fucking Lani, and there were still four in the building or nearby who were a part of this.

There was an agenda here, and I couldn't put my finger on exactly what it was. Wanting the wolves and talking about defeating the werewolves for good was a sign they were pretty fucking pissed at me. At the same time, they were pissed none of my siblings were in my territory to help me, pointing to hating my family. The leader was old, really old, and that pointed to him knowing Hasan personally. There weren't many werecats, and the oldest of our kind tended to know each other from ancient times. There was no way that one didn't know my werecat father.

"You didn't even introduce yourself!" I yelled.

I heard one of them come back down the steps and watched him come through the door.

"You may call me Mikkel, son of Ishkur." He turned and left again. At least I had a name now. One thing Hasan never told me was anything about other specific werecats. Whatever secrets or histories he knew about other werecats, he'd kept to himself, and I had always respected that.

Now, I was in a cage, wondering who my enemies were. I had no way of knowing who else was helping with this, and why Mikkel was the leader. I had no idea what sort of reputation any of them had. In a sad way, I knew more about werewolves than I did about other werecats. At least when it came to knowing who was who.

I looked over my injuries to understand exactly how fucked I was. My left leg was more torn up than the right, taking the brunt of the damage and covered in bruises. My shoulders were stiff, and I could feel where one of them had bitten me.

Beyond the notable, deep bites, I had myriad scratches on my chest, abdomen, back, and sides. Most were shallow in my human form, but I knew they had probably looked severe in my feline form. Luckily, claws between werecats didn't amount to much damage unless one of the cats was gutted. There was no ignoring the black and blue patchy network of bruises. They would slow me down just as effectively as the bleeding injuries. Remembering how I was hit across the face a couple of times, I knew my face probably wasn't much better, but without a mirror, there was no way for me to see.

I gingerly touched my nose and was relieved to feel it hadn't been broken, and neither had my jaw. No teeth were missing, something that would carry over between forms if it was the correct tooth.

All in all, I could have come out worse. Like dead. I could be dead right now. That's a plus.

I needed to stretch my aching muscles, so I began to pace, letting my legs loosen up. I gently stretched my arms over my head, ignoring the pulsing ache of pain in my shoulders. I needed to be ready to run the moment I had the chance. It could be hours, days, or even weeks, but I couldn't allow myself to grow complacent. I had to stay strong. That's what Hasan would want. He would want me to stay strong, so I could help any potential rescuer.

I wasn't hopeful for a rescue, but I had to believe. I had to believe my family would try to find me because the likelihood I would get out on my own was slim.

I have to try. I have to at least try.

15

CHAPTER FIFTEEN

It felt like hours later when I heard footsteps coming back down. No one above had spoken loud enough for me to hear, which meant they knew the walls and floors were thin.

I was surprised to see Lani come through the door with a bowl.

"We're not going to starve you," she said politely, refusing to look me in the eye. She put the bowl down on the other side of the cage. "Come get it." Stepping back, she finally looked at me and winced.

"Yeah, I probably don't look very good," I said with an angry, mean smile. I didn't think I was a hateful person, but at that moment, I fucking hated her. "Probably look better than that werecat I killed, though."

"Her name was—"

"I don't fucking care," I growled, walking forward slowly. I didn't reach for the food as I sniffed the air and caught the distinct smell of drugs in it. "She invaded my territory with the explicit wish to hurt or kill me. You captured me, so I'm going to assume that was the objective." I reached out and flipped the bowl, spilling the rice and meat everywhere. "I don't care about her fucking name, and I won't eat a god damn thing you give me. Try harder."

Lani looked at the bowl of food I spilled and sighed, kneeling to clean it up and put it back within my reach.

"You'll eat, or we'll dart you. One will fill your belly, the other will just knock you out. Your pick."

"Why are you doing this?" I demanded. "I thought you were loyal to Hasan. I thought..." *I thought you were my friend, or at least not my enemy.*

"I'm tired," she answered. "For six years, I knew you with no idea where you came from or how you became a werecat. For over six years, you lied to me."

"Then kill me for it. Why all of this?"

"You...you showed a wild disrespect for the way things are done." Lani gave me a pained, angry look. "You neglected to have any connection or responsibilities to other werecats. You took in werewolves. You laughed in the face of everything we are and our history. I tried so hard to forget about it and forget about you. Forget about how I thought I'd made a positive impact on your life, thinking no one taught you very well, and I had. And then you..."

"Yeah..."

"Yeah. Then Hasan, instead of punishing you, he gave you power," she growled. "Because you're one of his precious fucking children. You, the one werecat who has never paid any mind to what's going on outside your little territory."

"That's not true. I went to Washington..."

"You went because you felt guilty," she snarled. "You went because you were trying to clean up your mess for your own reasons, not because you cared at all for Gaia and Titan."

"They weren't my fault," I whispered. "The vampires killed them."

"Yes. Vampires. You, the Seattle pack, and fucking Heath Everson defeated the vampires while the mighty Jabari was laid down by a simple car accident," she sneered. "The great and powerful family of werecats who rule our kind, now resorting to the help of werewolves who would see us dead if they could." She pushed the bowl closer, and this time, I grabbed it.

Word travels in the supernatural world. I knew that. Everyone knew that. Werecats, for how isolated we are, gossiped like old humans with nothing better to do. Of course, she would know about all the little details of the events in Washington. It wasn't like it was ever a secret.

"There's nothing wrong with change. There's nothing wrong with becoming allies with someone who should be an enemy. So what if Heath Everson is a werewolf? He was once human, just like me and you. He's a good man, and he helped me keep Jabari alive. You would have been laid out by that car accident too."

"The werecats here with me? We would have gone into that nest to kill all of them from the start. A strong showing for the deaths of two old werecats who deserved more from their leaders." Lani shook her head at me. "It started with Liza. You know her name, right?"

"Yes."

"A weakling. A peaceful, quiet little female who was easily taken advantage of and killed by a pack of werewolves. And what does Hasan do? He doesn't even avenge his own daughter. He disappears and abandons us for a century while his children are left in charge, and that was fine. But when he finally came back, it was for you. You, the most irresponsible, arrogant, little werecat anyone has ever heard of. You're barely over a decade as a werecat, and you thought you could enforce werecat Law? Is Hasan so arrogant to think we would be okay with that? You love the enemy more than you love your own kind!"

"The pack killed those responsible to appease Hasan," I reminded her. The hatred I heard in her words rocked me to my core. "And I was just doing what was right."

"What was right was to let the werewolves clean up their own messes."

"By Law, I was on Duty—"

"And we plan on getting rid of that Law. Hasan allows other species to use us to protect their own. We get hurt and die because of them, and for what? So the Tribunal will think we're controlled? So we don't look like a threat to the other supernatural species?" Lani took a deep breath. "Mikkel came to me shortly after the Washington incident. I was so ready to congratulate you for stepping in and working with your family and taking your place, but then he and I talked. Mikkel has been my lover on and off for a couple of centuries now, and he made some good points."

"Lani..."

"Why do our people have to die for them?" she asked softly. "Because Hasan decided so to keep some other species happy? Is that what peace is worth? And in the end, when he finally stands up to the very Law he helped write, it's not for any of the werecats around the world who have been loyal to him for thousands of years. It's for the daughter who willfully knew she was breaking those Laws. His children killed werecats for centuries to defend them, then he proved himself to be the ultimate hypocrite."

"What are you saying?"

"You thought I was loyal to Hasan? You're right, I was, but that loyalty had been stretched thin. The declaration of you holding any kind of power you don't deserve finally snapped it. It's time for your family's nepotism to end."

"There's nothing I could do, is there?"

"Tell us where your werewolves are so we can kill them. That could possibly save you from death. You'll never be important the way Hasan wanted to make you, but you might live a long time. Maybe."

"When are you going to kill me?" I wasn't going to entertain giving up Heath and his family. Once again, I was grateful I had no idea where they had gone into hiding.

"I can't tell you that," she answered, stepping back from the cage now. "Just give us what we want, Jacky."

"You know, Hasan Changed me without my permission." I was angry, and a plan formulated. It wouldn't help me escape, but it might make me feel better. "I was dying from a car accident, bleeding out, barely conscious. My human fiancé was dying right next to me. His name was Shane. I woke up a werecat, and he never woke up at all. Hasan never wants to tell me why he let Shane die and not me." I dropped the bowl again and grabbed the bars, leaning forward on them. "I've had years of going back and forth on whether I loved or hated the man for that, but I never considered betraying him. I was never that *stupid*."

Lani's eyes went wide as I spoke, and I saw the hurt and anger on her own face at the last things I said to her.

"Then you're a coward," she hissed.

"Maybe I am," I whispered. "But I'm alive, and he gave me that when he didn't have to. Just like he gave it to all of you by fighting so hard to end the werewolf and werecat war. You're throwing it back in his face."

"He's a self-serving tyrant," she snapped at me, coming close to the cage.

I took my chance, grabbing the front of her shirt and yanking her into the bars. The force of her face meeting the metal would have broken a human. She screamed and pulled away, holding her face. Footsteps moved around upstairs, and I stepped back from the bars before they arrived, some of my anger subdued now.

The plan worked. Seeing Lani scream in pain made

me feel a little better, and a belly full of guilt quickly followed.

When did I become so fucking violent? I used to help people more than I hurt them.

I didn't dwell on the thought, glaring at Lani, who was clutching her face. I could smell the blood in the air, knowing I busted open at least one part of her face, probably her nose. I picked up the food, not really caring about the dirt and dust. She did have one point. The food would fill my belly. Even though it was dosed in tranquilizer or sleeping medications, it was food.

As I took the first quick bite, the other werecats made it downstairs. Mikkel went to Lani first and looked over her face, then glared at me. I bared my teeth.

"She came too close to the cage," I explained as if it was reasonable; it should have been expected the monster inside would lash out. I wasn't going to be the perfect prisoner for them. There was no way in hell I would give them anything they wanted.

"Carter, get Lani upstairs," he ordered, his eyes not leaving me. The southern werecat helped Lani up, cursing at the blood still pouring from her face. Once they were gone, Mikkel came close to the cage as well. "Come and try that on me."

"No, I don't think I will," I said softly, taking another bite of the meat and rice. "This is good. You should try seasoning to cover up the smell and flavor of the crushed sleeping pills, though."

"Will it keep you from assaulting anyone here?"

"No." I smiled tightly.

"You're going to make this hard, aren't you? All we need is the passcode to your phone, Jacky."

"I'll give you a number," I said, lifting my chin in defiance. I rattled off the phone number almost too fast for them. Someone scrambled with my phone and began punching it in, but Mikkel didn't pay attention, keeping his glare on me.

"It didn't work," the female said with a bored sigh. "She's playing us."

"It's not her passcode. It's a phone number," he said, his eyes narrowing on me further. "Whose?"

"Call it and find out," I dared.

I wasn't finished eating and knew if I ate slow enough, I could possibly get around the drugs in it. If I inhaled it like I was starving—and I was starving—I would be out like a light. I took another bite, looking down at how much I had left. There was a lot, and from the lack of a powdery texture, it meant the drugs were thoroughly mixed in. My prior EMT training and failed medical school classes were still helping me.

Mikkel pulled out his cellphone and punched in the number from memory. I was surprised he had been listening well enough to catch it.

"Who are you, and how did you get this number?" Hasan asked, not sounding scared or worried—angry. By now, my entire family would have figured out that something went terribly wrong during the full moon.

"Hasan," Mikkel said in greeting. "It's Mikkel, son of Ishkur."

"Did you kill my daughter?" Hasan went straight to

the point. It almost made me laugh when an offended look flashed across Mikkel's face. Everyone in the room could see how little Hasan cared about Mikkel and only wanted to avenge me.

"No. She's right in front of me, having the dinner I so kindly gave her."

"It's drugged," I called out. Mikkel snarled at me, and I heard Hasan snarl in return on the other end of the line.

"Quiet or I'll send someone in there to fuck up your face," Mikkel threatened. "I wasn't planning on talking to you so soon, Hasan."

"Don't threaten my daughter, tell me what you want," Hasan growled. "You were clearly intending on talking to me, eventually."

"Ishkur wouldn't have wanted us fighting," Mikkel said with a sigh. "I want you to step down from the Tribunal."

"And what would that get you?"

"I think werecats need to leave the Tribunal completely, and you stepping down will be a clear sign of our intentions. We should no longer be beholden to the other species and their inane rules to keep us in line. We should no longer have to listen to an old male who decides his family is more fit to rule than anyone else. Jacky here is the best example of that, isn't she? Young, inexperienced, and has gotten into trouble. She also allies herself with werewolves. Did you really think the werecats of the Americas would be okay with that?"

Hasan's answer to him was a long moment of silence. I swore I could hear every heartbeat in the room and Hasan's on the other end of the line. I could hear Lani whimpering upstairs as someone cleaned up her face and the trickle of running water in a steel sink. I heard the animals outside as night fell, coming alive for a night of foraging and hunting.

"Let her go," he finally said. "She never wanted power; she was just trying to do what was right, and I thought it would suit her to represent me in North and South America. I thought it would give her something to pass the time and teach her. She's not a ruler, I am."

"I really love how you don't try to excuse the werewolves," Mikkel pointed out with a chuckle. "We all thought Liza was weak, but maybe it was you. Maybe you've weakened and passed it on to the little, delicate flower of a daughter you lost."

My heart jumped into my throat. That was cold. If I knew anything about Hasan, it was that he didn't wear his anger on his sleeve, but he was probably fuming now.

"Tell me," Mikkel said gently. "Does Jacky have the same problem? Created by weakness, therefore, she's weak?"

"She's stronger than you know," Hasan answered. "Liza always had a tender, trusting heart."

"Yet you still aren't trying to excuse the werewolves."

"She's a woman in her own right, and her relationship with the werewolves could bring a resounding, permanent peace between our kinds. You weren't there, Mikkel—"

"I was there during the War," he growled. "They killed a human child of a werecat and laughed about it.

They killed my *brother*. We made them suffer for it. And now we talk about peace."

"It wasn't the first war," Hasan explained. "It was the third, though the first two were much smaller. Our kinds have been fighting since the dawn of time, since our creation, but you don't know this because you weren't there. Jacky has a chance of creating a symbol of peace with just one werewolf, and I decided I would let her try. And you're forgetting, her relationship with the wolf has nothing to do with him being a werewolf. She loves his human daughter; saved the girl's life. That kind of bond is permanent. We all know this. It's deeply ingrained in what we are."

"They—"

"If you are so foolish as to think werecats can survive without coming together with the other supernatural species, you are more of a fool than I ever thought. Ishkur would be disappointed."

"How dare you."

"He was my brother. I dare." Hasan's tone was cold. "I was there when he approached the wolf pack that killed his son, and they laughed in his face and refused to offer the wolf who did it to face justice. I was there when the War began as your father exacted his revenge and killed the entire pack in a single full moon. I was there when he died, *boy*. You weren't, but you hold on to all the anger many of us have fought to let go and move forward."

"You let them cut off your balls," Mikkel accused.

"You walked away when they killed Liza. I'm amazed your own children speak to you."

"Justice was done. The Alpha of that pack knew to kill the wolves who had done it, and he did so without a fight. He wanted to maintain the peace just as much as I did, even when I was angry. Continuing in that good faith, I walked away, yes. I think I deserved a chance to grieve the death of a child."

"You'll step down," Mikkel ordered. "Or Jacky dies by the next full moon."

"You won't live to the next full moon," my werecat father promised. "Let me speak to Jacqueline."

"She can hear you," Mikkel snapped.

"Daughter, do you know anything?"

"No. They beat the hell out of me and brought me somewhere, but I have no idea where. They thought I would call the family for help and have protection if they made me paranoid enough. I guess they were hoping to have more bargaining chips. Or the chance to kill a few other members of our family."

"Most likely," he agreed. "I'm sorry you're there."

"We knew it was risky. I nearly got past them. They didn't catch me until I was out of my territory."

"Good job. I love you, my daughter."

My heart pounded, and I closed my eyes. He was saying goodbye just in case.

"Yeah. Love you too, Father." Father felt formal, but it was good for Hasan.

I hoped it wasn't the last thing we would say to each

other, but Mikkel hung up the call and turned his phone off.

"Check that every twelve hours for voicemails," he ordered one of the other males, tossing the phone across the room. When he looked at me, he slowly took me in, judging me, weighing me against some scale in his mind. "You nearly did make it out. If you weren't so... disrespectful of everything being a werecat means, maybe you would have lived a long and powerful life."

"Go to hell," I growled.

He was laughing as he led the rest out of the room. Someone mocked me saying goodbye to Hasan, and I distinctly heard the comment 'weak child'.

I would show them a 'weak child'.

When I ripped their fucking throats out.

16

CHAPTER SIXTEEN

Monday turned into Tuesday. I barely ate, and I tried my best not to sleep.

The next full moon was still weeks away, but I knew better than to think it would take that long. For them to kill me, for me to get rescued, or for me to escape—one would happen long before the full moon came overhead again.

Tuesday turned into Wednesday, and I was beginning to notice a pattern. They woke up around noon and stayed up late into the night. They left one person downstairs with me while I was awake, and that person changed on a rotation with the others.

It was Wednesday evening when Mikkel came back down, holding dinner.

"We want the wolves," he said without any preamble. "You're going to deliver them to us."

"No, I don't think I will," I said with a smile. "You've lost your ability to trick anyone by making that phone call, and no one I care about is stupid enough to accept a trade."

"He's your ally."

"He has a daughter he wants to see grow up. If I were in his shoes, I would pick her too," I retorted. "There's nothing on this earth that will get him to choose me over his daughter." *And that's what I like about him. He's a good father, and nothing is going to change that.*

"Why don't we call him and find out?" He lifted my phone and waved it around. "Certainly, you want to go home."

"You're planning on killing me, and that's okay. This isn't the first time I've been held for potential execution. I was okay with it the last time, too." *So long as I'm not being tortured.*

"You're stubborn. You have a strong will. That's a good thing, but don't let it lead you to stupidity. The werewolves don't care about you enough to attempt a rescue, so why throw your life away for them?"

"I thought I was weak. You said I was weak to Hasan, just like Liza. Mikkel, do you possibly think you can win this?"

"Yes, because Hasan won't risk another child."

"You're right. He won't risk another child. He'll burn down this world for me or any one of my siblings, you fucking idiot. There's no winning here. There's only destruction. There's only a lot of dead bodies at the end of this."

Let's just hope that mine isn't one of them.

"You have a lot of confidence in him."

I only shrugged. Even if I was killed, my siblings would scour the land near my territory for months—even years if they had to—to get at him. Hasan would make sure no one in this building lived when he was done. Was I confident I was going to make it out alive? No, but I was very confident Mikkel wouldn't either.

"Why don't you tell me how you learned pack magic? Certainly, that won't betray anyone." He didn't bring the food closer, and I was starting to realize that starving me may become a new tactic. That was an unpleasant thought. Werecats needed a lot of calories, and they were already barely feeding me anything worth its weight.

"No, I don't think I'll tell you that, either," I answered, stepping back from the bars. I couldn't. If I told werecats I couldn't trust that a fae had gifted me the ability, the fae wouldn't be safe. I didn't even know if every fae could even do it. Brin hadn't been normal, that much I was certain of.

"Did you make a deal with one of them? Perform some sort of ritual with a werewolf? Was it Heath Everson?"

I sighed, giving Mikkel the best bored look I could muster.

"Would any werewolf ever give pack magic to a werecat? And before you ask, no, they don't know. If you think I told two werewolves, allies or not, I had the ability to use pack magic, then you have lost your mind. Which I should have realized sooner since you're here, holding me prisoner when you know who is going to take you on.

Picking a fight with my family is absolutely something that could get you committed."

He sighed and walked out of the room with the food, proving my private assumption correct. Wonderful.

"Well, this was a fun chat," I called out as he left. He didn't stop, continuing upstairs. I heard the bowl clang in a sink upstairs, the distinct metal and ceramic clattering.

"Lani, you didn't tell me that she thinks she's a comedian," he commented. "We're going to starve her out. I'm tired of the attitude. Maybe hungry, she'll be more willing to cooperate."

"It's a defense," my once friend replied. "She's freaking out. Keep her down there longer, and she might crack, but it's unlikely. She has a spine of steel, and she's not afraid to die."

"Odd for someone so young," he said thoughtfully. I heard something thump but couldn't identify it. "I was really hoping to get one of his older children. Zuri would have been a fine catch or Mischa, one of the older daughters. They both know me and would listen. They would recognize the problems I'm trying to fix."

"From the sound of her conversation with Hasan, they anticipated it being a trap to prey on Jacky and use it to get to more of them. They left her to rot, and she's still holding out for them. Maybe..."

"Maybe?" Mikkel seemed interested in whatever Lani might be thinking. To be honest, I was too.

"Maybe I can convince her. Give me a few days, maybe a week." A heavy sigh punctuated that. "I wish we were in my territory. I don't like flying blind like this. We need time with her, and we might not have it. If we were in my territory, we would at least have some defenses."

"The same could be said of Carter's territory or mine, but you know why I picked this location. Our territories would be the first places they checked, and they would go in force. We can't win an all-out fight against the entire family. That's why I was hoping to get one or two with Jacky, but in the end, they didn't give us that, so we make do." Someone walked around above me. The basement seemed to be directly under the kitchen, and they didn't much care if I heard whatever they were talking about. Who was I going to tell? "You can talk to her more, but stay away from the cage, love. Please."

I rolled my eyes. The only important thing I just learned was at least three of these weren't rogues. They were werecats with territories, used to relying on that magical bond with the land, just like I was. They were just as out of their element, being in a location without the distinct feeling of ownership and away from home.

"She won't pull that cheap stunt again, don't worry."

I snorted loudly, shaking my head. I knew any minute, another of the werecats would come down and sit with me, which meant silence would be expected.

"How did you deal with her for six years?" he asked, and I knew he'd heard me.

"For six years, all she did was exist. It wasn't so hard," she answered. "Everything changed after Dallas, though. She changed. Something about whatever happened with being called to Duty made her a bit harder, a bit more aggressive. Like she's come into...something."

"What was she saying? That Hasan Changed her without asking for her consent?"

"I'm not sure if she was lying about that. She got a rise out of me, then..." Lani snarled. "It was the stupid underhanded move of an angry child. She just wanted to inflict some pain."

I nodded to myself. She was right. I was pissed off when I did that.

The voices went unintelligible, meaning Mikkel and Lani were whispering now, keeping it from even my hearing. All that told me was they didn't want me listening in anymore.

It felt like hours later when Lani came down the stairs, a gun at her hip and without food in her hands. She sat in the chair one of them brought down and placed next to the door. The bruising on her face was already yellow, a sign of accelerated werecat healing. By the timeline, I figured most of my bruises were nearly gone, and many of the holes were closing up well, but it was going to slow down if they starved me.

"Good evening," she greeted, crossing her legs. It was a pose I was familiar with.

When we met, she had been the first werecat to ever come calling to my territory, curious to see who the new face was. She had sat on my couch, in the exact same position, explaining she had a territory between Houston and San Antonio. We had talked, and I had lied to her about nearly everything. I could still remember the lies, even if they were just lies of omission.

"Hi," I greeted in return.

"I wanted to ask you something."

"Sure, I'm not going anywhere." I threw my hands up, gesturing to the cell I was in. It must have taken months for them to set up.

"Did you ever really hate him?" Lani gave me a concerned look, the look of a friend who knew I had a rocky relationship with my werecat father.

"Yes. There was a time I hated him. I never lied to you about that or how complicated it was between us. I just never told you who he was."

"No, you made him sound like someone unimportant. For years, I looked into different werecats I knew, and it seemed like you had come out of nowhere. For all I knew, you were an accident a rogue made, not the daughter of Hasan."

"That was exactly the way I wanted it. I didn't ask to be...royalty, I guess. I didn't ask for anything. I needed time to myself. Then everything started happening."

"What changed for you? I'm sure you heard me talking to Mikkel about it. It's been stuck in my head since."

I didn't know how to answer. I looked at my hands and considered the things they had done, both in human and in feline form—crushed wolves, fired guns, eviscerated vampires.

"I was forced to acknowledge I'm a werecat," I finally said, looking up at her. "That the world we live in is violent, and if anything I love is going to be safe, I have to be willing to kill for it and...die for it if I have to."

"And kill you have," she said softly. "You killed a

good friend of mine while we were trying to capture you." She didn't seem to be very hurt, but I figured they all went into this insane plan with the belief they might die or wouldn't all make it out.

"I was once your friend," I reminded her. It still hurt. The betrayal of being in the cage with her on the other side. I would have survived the loss of a friend, I could have done that, but to see her in that chair burned my gut, making me sick, a deep ache in my chest.

"Sometimes," she said, looking away. "Most of the time, I just felt sorry for you. I thought you were so lonely. You didn't seem to have adjusted well to being a werecat, and I thought 'I can't leave her alone. She could accidentally hurt someone because she lacks training.'"

"Ah. So, I wasn't the only liar." It only made the hurt worse, burned a little more.

"I guess not." She seemed a little guilty.

I didn't know where to go from there. If she was there to try to turn me to their cause, she was failing. I wasn't going to turn and join their little cause, their rebellion, but at the same time, I understood their problems.

It wasn't fair that werecats were able to be called to Duty. We had a protective streak that was taken advantage of, and it put us at risk of dying for people we didn't know or care about. I knew the logistics, why Hasan had wanted it in the Laws; it was to give the werecats some purpose in the changing world. It made us functioning, useful members of the supernatural society, and that gave us a wall of protection.

"Are you on watch tonight?" I asked, going to the back of my cell.

"Yes."

"Want to give me any hint on how to get out of this?"

"I don't think there's anything you can do now, Jacky." Lani sighed, almost like she was disappointed. "You won't give us the location of the wolves—"

"I don't know where they are," I reminded her. She nodded in recognition of my words.

"Fine. You won't tell us where you got the magic you aren't supposed to have."

"And I won't."

"So, really, the only thing that will stop Mikkel from killing you now is Hasan conceding to our demands. We're tired of his decisions not being in the best interests for the werecats. We're tired of the nepotism and the strict rule he enforces at the cost of werecats' lives."

"How many werecats have died since I went to Dallas?" I asked, leaning on the back wall. "Truthfully. I know of three. Gaia and Titan, who were the victims of vampires. Jabari and I handled that for the rest of you. We made sure that due was paid for all of you. Then there was your friend, but when you invade the territory of another werecat, death is a possible outcome. If she didn't want to die, she wouldn't have done it. Are there any I'm missing?" When Lani didn't immediately respond, I continued.

"While werecats of this country don't talk to me, my family does, and I've heard nothing. The werewolves got the message and backed off, realizing no one was interested in pursuing closer ties. No werecats have been dying except the ones I've dealt with personally." I sighed. "You know what I think this is? I think Mikkel has been pissed off for over eight hundred years that Hasan brought peace, even if it meant losing a little freedom. He's probably always wanted to do things differently but couldn't. Now, he's found some reasonable excuses to push forward to claim his own power."

"You don't know fucking anything, Jacky," Lani snapped. "The whole lot of you have broken the backs of werecats for centuries. Mikkel told me how it was before the War. He told me how a werecat could do as he or she pleased. We could take territory where we wanted it, not having to dodge other species because we're not allowed to force them out."

"I know Hasan," I said evenly. "And I know he would never purposefully do anything to hurt the werecats, his own kind. If you had contacted him peacefully, he might have listened. He might have come to an agreement about this, but you let that motherfucker push you into the deep end."

"I let him?" Lani shook her head. "No, I could see the writing on the wall the moment word went out you would be Hasan's representative in the Americas. For a long time, I thought Hasan was doing the right thing, then there was you. Do you know how disgraceful everyone sees you? You are the smudge tarnishing the great Hasan. You are the evidence that, in the end, he only cares for his family. You are the piece we all needed to see that the isn't looking out for us. He's just propping up his own family."

"Why don't you let me step down, then? Why did none of you come to me and say no? I would have. I would have backed down and taken it to Hasan, telling him the werecats here didn't feel comfortable. I would have done that for you, damn it, but you never gave me the chance. You went straight to violence, Lani."

"He wouldn't have let you," she answered. "He would have sent Jabari and Hisao to put down the dissenters. Everyone here knows that. He doesn't even fight his own battles anymore. He sends his little army and hides."

"No..." I refused to believe he wouldn't have listened. I refused to consider him a tyrant.

"Yes. Not every werecat wanted to be a part of the new experiment with the Tribunal. What do you think happened to those who didn't?" Her bitter, cutting smile told me exactly what she wanted me to know.

Hasan...Did you really kill everyone who didn't agree with you?

I was rattled because I could see it. I could see him, Jabari, and Hisao hunting down the ones who wanted to continue the War. I could see Zuri, honey on her tongue, convincing others to stand down or die. I could see Mischa, roaming, grabbing rogues, and forcing their compliance.

"Mikkel is still here," I pointed out, looking to hold on to something.

"He's been very good at hiding for a long time. For

the longest time, I didn't understand why he was so private, much like you. He would visit me but asked me to never tell anyone about our relationship. He was hiding to stay alive, to keep the hope we wouldn't be ruled by Hasan. We're werecats. We deserve to live our own lives, away from the rules and stipulations of others. That's how we lived for so long before, and Mikkel has only been keeping that dream alive. There should never be a werecat forced to bow down to anyone, especially not an irresponsible child."

"You can't win this, Lani," I said, shaking my head in dismay.

"Yes, we can. If you haven't noticed, we already are." She reached into her pockets and pulled out ear buds. I heard the music come on and knew she could still hear me if I spoke, but the message was clear. The conversation was over.

I slid down and sat at the back of my cell. My stomach growled in protest, angry that a meal, no matter how meager, had been skipped.

17

CHAPTER SEVENTEEN

I was awake and starving four days later. I realized on the second day without food that they were serious, even if nothing was ever said. The message was clear—give them what they wanted or starve to death long before they planned on killing me.

My guard walked out, probably for a shift change, which wasn't out of the ordinary. As long as the cage stayed closed, the idea I needed constant supervision was overkill. They were lax, and they had reason to be. I wasn't going anywhere. I knew that because I had tested the bars already. Sure, if I shifted into my werecat form, I could knock them down, but that would take time I wouldn't have. They would be waiting on the other side by the time I was free, and I would be a very dead werecat for the effort.

I needed something else.

And now six days into my captivity, I was stumped. Even if I got out of the cell, I had to get out of the basement, out of the house. With seven werecats between me and freedom, that seemed unrealistic. The hunger wasn't helpful as my body burned through calories I desperately needed. I was certain I was already dropping weight, an unpleasant thought since four of the werecats holding me were bigger males.

"Are we going to feed her today?" Fiora asked upstairs. I knew all their names now, picking them up as they talked among themselves. "She'll fade and die before Hasan meets our demands if this keeps up."

"I want her to beg," Mikkel answered. "Where are Carter and Sam?"

"Outside on patrol," Lani answered. "Since this isn't any of our territories, I thought it might be best to send out people and keep an eye on our surroundings."

"Damn it, Lani! I told you we can't leave the house! Our scents could be picked up outside," Mikkel snarled, and something slammed onto a table or countertop.

I shook my head sadly as Mikkel's true colors peeked through the charismatic leader he seemed to be. He had a temper, something I had seen a glimpse of several times.

"We can't let anyone sneak up on us, either," Lani growled back. "They'll get in and kill us before we can even fight back. You know I'm right!"

There was a short silence above me as I knew everyone upstairs were weighing the points Lani and Mikkel made.

"You're right," Mikkel conceded. "They could think Carter and Sam are just rogues, checking out the area or passing through. There's no reason they would jump to it being us."

"There's plenty of reason," Fiora pointed out. "But I'm with Lani on this one. Better to have some idea we're about to be attacked than have no idea what's going on."

"I'll relent to the women in my life," Mikkel said with no small amount of sarcasm and annoyance. "You win, but I only want Carter and Sam doing the patrols. Do you understand? If it's just them, they could be seen as two rogues looking to settle down. If they smell more of us, they'll pick up on it much more quickly."

"Of course," Lani agreed. "Fiora and I were going to take their shifts downstairs."

"Ah. You can spread them out a little more than that. I don't want both of you exhausted all the time." He switched from annoyed to sympathetic and sweet. I perversely wondered if Lani was okay with Mikkel's other lover being in the house. It was clear by every conversation I heard, Mikkel was fucking both of them. He was unabashedly into both of them, and they were both into him.

Maybe they're all down for some fuck fest of a relationship, and it works for them. Live your best life, Lani, because it's going to be a short one once I get out of this fucking cage.

"You never answered my question. Are we going to feed her today? I know you want to break her, but it seems like she's going to starve herself. Her face has already thinned out, and we need her alive." Fiora pressed the issue, annoyed. With what, I couldn't really tell. It wasn't like I was asking to be starved. That was their decision. I was just going to live with it.

Or die with it. Whatever comes first, I guess.

"I should go down and talk to her again," Mikkel said thoughtfully. "Maybe she'll listen today."

"Good luck," Lani said with boredom.

I hadn't broken down in the six days they had me and had no intention of giving them anything anytime soon. Lani tried every day to talk to me about the Hasan problem, about how they were right about wanting to overthrow him and my entire family. She was hoping to sway me, and I continued to throw it in her face. If she couldn't do it, none of them would be able to.

I heard Mikkel coming down the stairs and narrowed my eyes on him as he came through the door. He grabbed the chair and pulled it closer, sitting close to the bars. I stayed in the back of the cell, staring at him but refusing to speak first.

"Good evening," he said lightly. "Here we are, yet again, Jacky. I grow tired of these talks."

"Me too," I snapped.

"I guess you still aren't ready to play nice. That's okay. I'll wait. I have all the time in the world."

"Good for you."

"We're asking very simple questions. All you need to do is answer them, and this all stops."

"I don't know where the wolves are, and I'm not telling you how I have pack magic," I growled. "We've gone over this."

"Then maybe you can tell me how to sweeten the

deal for Hasan. What else do I need to get him to step down?"

I stared blankly at him. I didn't really have an answer for him, but I wanted him to understand I wouldn't even tell him that. Mikkel sighed, shaking his head.

"Don't make me torture you."

That got me. A shiver ran down my spine as the rush of fear quickly raced through my system. Mikkel grinned, all teeth.

"There's a reaction. You don't want to be tortured. No one ever really does, so I can't say I blame you. You see, though, we've had you for nearly a week, and I grow tired of having you down here. Either answer me now, get something to eat, and don't get tortured, or I'll start tomorrow night, and it won't be pleasant."

"Torture is never pleasant. I look forward to seeing how you make it somehow worse than anyone else. Somehow, I think it's not going to be all that bad," I said, swallowing the fear. *Fuck.*

He growled, annoyed with my answer, and stood, stomping out of the room. I heard clanging upstairs and Lani's and Fiora's shocked gasps. When Mikkel stomped back into the room, he carried a toolbox and dropped it at the cell door. In his other hand, he had a large loaf of bread.

"You have twenty-four hours," he snarled. He tossed the bread into the cell. "You can eat that. It'll settle your stomach and get it to stop growling. Maybe it'll give you the energy you need to survive what I plan on doing to you if you keep up the attitude."

But offer nothing much else in the way of sustenance. Fucking asshole. I shouldn't have taunted him. I crossed a line.

I picked up the loaf, my eyes on the toolbox as I took a bite. Mikkel walked out, leaving me to ponder my next move. The loaf wasn't drugged, meaning he had probably taken it from the other werecats to feed me.

Fuck. I need to get out of here. Where the hell is my family? Have these motherfuckers hidden me so well, no one can find me? That's not good.

My eyes welled up for the first time since they had captured me.

I was well and truly alone, and that realization was sinking in.

A tear fell down my cheek.

THE MINUTES TICKED BY. They came down and asked questions, and I ignored all of them, refusing to budge. I knew what I was asking for. I knew what I was risking, but my secrets were mine.

When it must have been twenty-four hours, Mikkel walked back downstairs, looking me over.

"How was the bread?"

I didn't answer. My best idea for this entire event was to say nothing. The moment I started to speak, I didn't know if I would be able to stop. If they got me answering anything, they might be able to get me to answer difficult questions. I couldn't risk it.

The rest of the werecats walked down after him, flanking him, lining up alongside the cell.

"This is going to hurt," he promised me softly. "This is your last chance to tell us what you know, particularly about how you got your pack magic. You found a way to get the one advantage the werewolves have over us, and we deserve to know how. We're done letting them set the terms."

I said nothing, staring him down. I knew better than to taunt him now. With all seven of them in the room, I knew this was going to be a long, painful event.

"Fiora, guard," he ordered. I watched the werecat pull a gun from the back of her pants and hold it on me. Mikkel opened the cell, and I still didn't move. He strolled across the cell.

Without warning, he punched me in the gut, knocking the air out of me. I doubled over, but he wrapped a hand around my neck and forced me to turn my back to the rest of them. He lifted me up as I tried to breathe and let go of my neck before giving me a mean right hook and sending me back down.

"We're starting off easy, Jacky. We're going to make this slow. Let's say...we're going to test your limits. Why get out the pliers when a few punches could get you talking, right?"

He sounded as if it was an interesting discussion. I pushed up, only to regret it as the tip of his boot connected with my ribs. A second kick hit my gut.

"Rules, everyone. We're not breaking her bones. We'll save that for later. Always make sure Fiora has a clean shot on her. There's no reason for any of us to get hit back if she knows she's going to die for trying. Right, Jacky?"

Yeah, I wasn't stupid enough to try to grab one of them when they had me in a crowd like this. I was going to take the beating. A beating I could live through, even if it hurt like a son of a bitch.

He grabbed my hair and pulled me back to my feet. I clamped my mouth shut to keep from screaming. I wanted to scream more than anything in the world, but I didn't want to give him that, not this early. I would eventually, but not yet.

A hand reached through the bars and yanked one of my arms back. My other arm was yanked back next, and a chain was weaved around both of them and the bars, holding me in place. The last loop of it went around my neck, forcing me to keep my head up as best as I could.

Mikkel started in for real after that, and I could see the fury on his face as he started beating me.

Blows rained down on my abdomen and ribs, and he nailed my face a couple of times.

I started to whimper as blood poured from a cut lip and bleeding nose. I could only hope it wasn't broken. It didn't feel broken. He said not to break anything. I held on to that little silver lining.

After what felt like an eternity, he was done and I was left whimpering in pain. He left the cell, and another male walked in, but I didn't have the ability to string thoughts together, much less tell which one it was.

The hits continued. I started to scream in pain as

they started landing on other bruises. My legs tried to give out, but the chain held me in place. Someone pulled my hair from behind.

When the second guy was done, Mikkel came back in front of me.

"How did you get pack magic?"

I opened my eyes, trying to blink away the blood that made them sting. The second guy had given me a cut on my forehead.

Mikkel was staring at me intently, thinking he would get what he wanted.

I spat my blood at him, seeing it splatter over his nose, mouth, and cheeks. He wiped it off slowly, then backhanded me. He moved aside for someone else again, and it continued.

I held on because the alternative was worse. If I gave up Brin, the fae would become Mikkel's next victim, and I refused to be the cause of that. If I gave up anything I might know about Heath, it wouldn't just be him in danger. Carey and Landon didn't deserve my family's enemies. They didn't sign up for this. Carey deserved better than this from her werecat. I was supposed to be her knight in shining armor as Heath once called me. There was no way I could tell them anything that could endanger her.

And Hasan. I couldn't disappoint him. Not now. He was my father, the only one I had who mattered anymore. He was my family. Jabari, Zuri, all of them—they were my family, and I couldn't betray my family.

"If we go much longer, we'll break her doing this,"

someone said. My ears were ringing. "I say we let her pass out and heal a little. We can inflict more targeted pain for answers tomorrow."

"I was hoping she would fall to a little brute force," Mikkel muttered. He came in front of me again. "Jacky? Are you going to talk to us?"

I couldn't even lift my head up. I wanted to fall down and sleep, and I didn't much care who else was there. Keeping my eyes cracked open was hard enough.

He sighed.

"Let her down. We'll continue tomorrow. We'll step it up to the next level."

"Mikkel, you know I can get her to tell us her every secret in an hour," a male said with a little too much excitement. "Let me have her tomorrow."

"I don't want to go to that level yet. I know where and how you developed your skills. She's another werecat. We start slow. We don't want to resort to torture you've done on wolves yet."

My stomach flipped, but when the chains released, I sank down and managed to crawl to the back of the cell as a couple of them jeered. I curled into a tight ball and fell asleep. If the sleep was good enough, the bruises would heal a little faster. That was all I cared about.

18

CHAPTER EIGHTEEN

I was in a restless sleep when the loud footsteps overhead shook me awake. I sat up fast, looking up. My body screamed in protest after the beating I'd taken the day before, and I knew it was only the beginning of the torture I was going to have to endure. I was alone in the basement, something I was somewhat grateful for because I was pretty certain there were tears on my cheeks.

"What's wrong, Carter?" Mikkel asked, growling in annoyance that must have carried over from the conversation I had with him.

"We smelled wolves out on a couple of the trails," the southern male answered. "Fucking wolves, Mikkel. The two we scented in her territory."

Heath and Landon. How...What the fuck are they doing? They can't beat seven healthy werecats.

Fear gripped my heart, but at the same time, a little bit of relief came through.

My wolves are looking for me.

"Goddamn it," Mikkel snarled. "Wake up everyone. I want to get as many of us out there as we can. Maybe we can track them down and make an example of them like we planned."

"We're hunting to kill?" Sam asked, his slightly Boston accent helping me know it was him.

"Of course, we are. I wanted those wolves, so I could drop them at the feet of the fucking Tribunal werewolves. A lesson that they don't get to fucking meddle in our affairs." By the bloodthirsty way Mikkel said that, I had a feeling Heath and Landon were in for a hard fight I knew they would lose. He wanted to rip them to pieces.

There was a lot of moving around above me as Mikkel barked more orders. I heard people shuffle around, getting outside, and even some growls and the cracks of bones as a few of them Changed into their werecat forms. Fiora and Mikkel stomped down the stairs, Sam following them.

"Are you in any contact with them?" Mikkel asked, coming to the bars. I stayed on the far side, knowing not to go anywhere near him. I had given Lani a love tap compared to what he could do to me.

I also didn't answer, keeping my mouth firmly shut as I glared at the werecat.

"She's not going to answer," Sam said in a mutter. "Let me have her, boss. You know I can work out the information you need."

"I'm leaving Fiora with you. You won't maim her. You won't scar her. Not yet. If she tells you anything, lock her back in there to lick her wounds." He stormed out of the room, and I heard the signs of him Changing and heading outside.

"It's just us, then," Fiora said with a smile. She was wearing gloves, which disturbed me a little. Was she scared of blood getting under her nails? "Sam, you really know how to do this?"

"I tortured wolves for information during the War."

That put him at least eight hundred years old, which didn't fit anything I thought. His accent was suddenly very out of place.

"I thought you were from Boston," I mumbled, looking over his face. For some reason, casual conversation seemed like a good idea. He gave me a twisted smile.

"I came over when England decided to colonize the New World and get away from the troubles of the homeland. Picked up a little of the accent to blend in better, and it's stuck. I like it." He reached down for the toolbox and popped it open. I tried to keep my breathing steady. "Now, we're doing this because you've been surprisingly close-lipped this last week. With the fucking werewolves out there running around, it's a good time to get answers. You're going to tell me what we want to know now, or I start hurting you. Your choice, *Jacqueline*."

I bared my teeth at my name. "Only Hasan calls me that."

"I don't like you, but I don't want to see you get tortured," Fiora said gently. "Just tell us what we want to hear. Are you in contact with the wolves through pack magic?"

My mouth stayed shut. After a moment, Fiora sighed and pulled handcuffs out of her jacket pocket. I realized the need for the gloves as I could tell they had silver in the mix. Once those were on me, Changing into my werecat form would be impossible without cutting off my own front paws or breaking bones and disfiguring myself. She pulled a gun out next and pointed it at me as she flicked off the safety.

This can't be happening. They fully intend to torture me, and there's no way in hell I have a chance once they start doing that. I have to get out now. There's no other option.

With that thought, I started planning. There were only two of them. Silver handcuffs and a gun, probably loaded with silver bullets. Sam was pulling out things I didn't expect to see from a boring toolbox—torturer's tools.

"Get her out here and handcuff her with her arms behind her. I've got two other pairs for her ankles. That should secure her to the chair."

"Get the door," Fiora said, keeping her eyes on me.

I was only going to have moments to pull this off, and I was hurting.

Sam unlocked the cell door and opened it slowly, his eyes on me as intently as Fiora's. She slowly walked in, the handcuffs ready in one hand, the gun pointed directly at the center of my chest.

My heart was beating wildly as I assessed the

situation. I had to get that gun off me because she was probably going to be trigger happy and take a shot. Killing me was probably their plan if I tried to escape. Then there was Sam behind her, waiting in the door of the cell as she drew closer. I was going to have to fight both of them, but I knew this was the best chance I was going to get. Maybe they knew it too, or maybe they thought I was going to submit to being tortured.

And in the back of my mind, I knew Heath and Landon could possibly be outside, looking for me and this house. They were going to get killed now that Mikkel knew they were around.

I can't let that happen. I have to get out there and help them.

"Turn around and put your hands behind your back," she ordered me, stopping in the middle of the cell. I did as she asked, breathing hard, my fear stinking up the air.

"Still silent and strong. Impressive when we can all smell how much you don't want this to happen," Sam commented lightly as if he was mildly impressed and amused. "All you need to do is tell us what we want to know."

I waited as Fiora came up behind me, slowing my breathing as I concentrated on her heartbeat, her breathing, the light shuffle of her clothing.

I only had one chance.

When she was close enough to touch, close enough to feel her breath on the back of my head, making my dirty brown hair move, and I felt her fumble with the handcuffs to get them in position to cuff me, I knew it was time.

Spinning around, I lifted my hand and pushed the gun to the side with a snarl. It fired a moment later, and a flash of burning pain erupted as the bullet grazed my shoulder and hit the wall behind me.

Throwing my head forward, I slammed into her nose. I had no idea how to fight like this and was just going for it. She screamed and stumbled back. I took my chance to reach for the gun in her hand before she could pull it back up and take another shot.

Right as my hand wrapped around hers, Sam rammed into me and sent me into the back wall, bringing Fiora with us. The gun discharged again, and someone screamed, probably hit. I brought my knee up as hard as I could, hoping to hit either of them and felt an impact, but nothing came of it. One of them stumbled back, and I could smell the blood in the air. I shoved the other back with my free arm, keeping my hand on the gun. It was Fiora, and she tried to yank the gun from me.

"I'm going to fucking kill you!" she screeched.

I lifted a bare foot and kicked out, hitting her on the thigh. She brought her free hand up and sucker punched me. Neither of us let go of the gun. It fired again, hitting the concrete floor, and I knew with three gunshots, the other werecats would possibly be coming back. That was going to leave me pressed for time, and time was not a luxury I had.

I snarled and brought my free hand up as well, landing a full powered hit to her jaw. Before she could retaliate, I grabbed the front of her shirt and swung her back toward the wall, enjoying the crunch of her hitting it. Her grip loosened just enough that I could take control of the damn gun, then I kneed her again in the gut.

I turned around to run for the cell door, but Sam was already up, jumping into me, his shoulder hitting my gut hard enough to knock the wind out of me. I had the gun, though, and fired down at him.

He went limp, and I ran for the door, trying to breathe as Fiora screamed. I threw the door shut and kept running, not wanting to waste any more time. I didn't need to kill them all right now.

I just needed to not die.

Once I was running up the stairs, and she wasn't following me, I felt more comfortable. Not by much, but a glimmer of hope was there. I hit the kitchen floor and began my Change, letting it whip through me painfully and without a fight. I didn't care if the door was open or not, slamming into it and knocking it open with the sheer force of my body weight.

I was elated to see grass on the other side, but I didn't stop to enjoy it, running at full speed toward the trees. As I ran, I saw a werecat come out and stop in what was probably shock at my appearance. I didn't miss a beat, leaping and landing on the other werecat, rolling painfully as my teeth and claws sank in to cause some damage that might slow it down in the chase I knew was going to follow.

It wasn't until I let go and continued running that I

realized it was Lani's blood on my tongue. A roar filled the air, and I knew the hunt was on.

They're all going to be coming after me. I can't stop moving. The more distance I get, the better chance I have.

I had already played this particular game once and had made the mistake of hesitating because I was outside my territory. This time, I didn't slow down or look out for possible humans. I only ran. I wasn't as fast as normal, tired from lack of proper sleep, weak from lack of a proper diet, but I was smaller than most of the others, and hopefully, that translated into more speed.

Another roar filled the night, and I realized I needed to try for more than just running.

"HEATH!" I screamed desperately into the mental void of pack magic, knowing it was probably going to go into every head within a mile. Hopefully there were no humans around with roaring werecats and voices in their heads.

I heard the thudding of paws behind me and hoped it was only Lani trying to keep on my tail.

"Heath!" I yelled again.

"Jacky?"

It was so faint. I didn't stop moving, but there it was. He was somewhere out there.

"Where are you?" I yelled. Behind me, someone snarled viciously as they ran. I cut a tight turn and tried to leave the pursuer scrambling to make the turn.

"Where are you?" he asked back, still faint.

"I don't know!" I screamed desperately.

A howl filled the air, and I was certain every werecat

within twenty miles heard it. I turned for it, running at full speed.

"You fucking idiot!" I screamed, now more enraged than anything else.

"Don't worry about me. Keep running!" he ordered.

For once, I followed the Alpha tone without back talk or smack. I hauled ass, hoping to get to wherever he was. Now that I had a general idea which direction to go, finding him would be infinitely easier.

But it was also going to be so much easier for the other werecats, and I knew they would want him dead. By now, I was positive everyone realized I had escaped.

I was heading fast down a trail when another werecat hit the side of me, sending me into the bushes. The feline scream that left me was ear piercing as claws and fangs broke skin, and we kicked at each other, a bloody, brutal fight for survival. I kicked the other werecat off though, because I had a different objective. I didn't want to fight all of them, not right now. I needed to run, and I needed to keep my wolves alive. Heath and Landon were only there trying to find me. I couldn't let them die.

I left the other werecat and was able to get a running lead on him, continuing to move for the area the howl had come from. Finally, I caught the scent of wolf on the ground, knowing it had to be one of the trails they used. Refusing to slow down, I kicked up dirt and left my claws out, hoping the traction would be helpful.

Finally, I broke through the dense thicket and saw a road. I hit it and turned to see that fucking truck. Heath's fucking truck. I hated the obnoxious thing, but I wanted to cry as it came into sight.

Heath stood in the bed of it, a shotgun aimed and ready to fire.

"It's me!" I yelled. *"I'm coming—"*

A werecat hit me and sent me tumbling across the asphalt. I swatted at its head when it tried to bite me. We circled, and I snarled.

"Jacky!" Heath yelled. "Let's go!"

"Start driving. I'll catch up. Go before the other werecats get here." I couldn't run for him with another werecat on my heels. He would end up being the target.

I heard the truck moving, and the other werecat realized it as well. We both started running after it. I saw Heath keeping aim, waiting for anything to jump at him. The shotgun wouldn't be enough stopping power for an over five-hundred-pound werecat mid-leap, but close enough, he would kill it as he died underneath it.

The other werecat shouldered me, trying to knock me off my pursuit of the truck. I snarled and tried to pick up my speed. I wasn't paying attention, but Heath must have put the shotgun aside because the gun that fired next was a rifle. He'd come ready for a fight. The werecat beside me was hit with the second shot and tumbled to the ground. The truck slowed down, and I made a jump for it as Heath tried to get out of my way.

I landed in the bed of the truck hard enough that the entire damn thing bounced. The speed picked up again. Landon was in the driver's seat and must have stepped on the gas the moment I was in. I lifted my head, ignoring Heath for a moment as I watched werecats fly out of the woods and watch us drive away, knowing they couldn't keep up with the truck screaming down the road. Soon they became dots, and eventually they disappeared.

I wasted no more time, beginning a slow Change back into my human form. I was exhausted and injured, and it didn't come easy, but I was eventually panting in my human body, staring at the black bottom of the truck bed.

A hand reached out and gently touched my shoulder, carefully avoiding my bruises.

"Stay down," he ordered. "We're both naked as the day we were born, and we could get in serious trouble. Last thing we need is human law enforcement getting involved. With the way you look, Landon and I would go to jail for a very long time."

I turned my head slightly to see he was right. He wasn't wearing a shred of clothing. If I wasn't torn up and tired, still more than a little scared for my life, I would have tried to appreciate it. As it was, I was grateful I didn't immediately grow red in the face. The nakedness was practical, not sexual.

"Did you just shift back?" I asked softly. I hadn't been paying attention to how long I was running.

"I had about thirty seconds to get ready with human hands, then you showed up with that one on your ass," he answered. "You were running for us for a good long time."

"Five minutes isn't long," I whispered.

"It was an eternity, and we almost missed you, Jacky. We almost missed you."

"What do you mean?"

"Landon had already Changed back and was prepping the truck to go. I was about to Change after he was dressed in case a human came by so they didn't see two naked men on the side of the road. We had caught the scent of the werecats and knew they had caught our scents. Luckily, we had laid down a lot of trails in preparation, and they were lost in them, trying to track us. Then you called out."

"Fuck."

"Let me get a blanket. I'm sure I have one in the truck. You need to stay warm, and I...I can't keep looking at this. They..." He lifted up and tapped the back window. "Landon? Got a blanket in there?"

"They beat me," I finished. "I know."

I felt it land above my head as Landon shoved it through the small window. Heath arranged it over both of us but kept a proper distance between his warm body and my tired and beaten one.

"How did you find me?" I finally asked.

"With the help of your family. Landon and I did a lot of groundwork, finding scents and trails in your territory and where they drove off with you. We tried to track the specific car, but that's fucking hard. Not impossible, but really damn hard. We lost them, but by then, Hasan and Jabari could reasonably guess a few locations where Mikkel was likely to try to hide you. This was the fourth place we tried. When we caught the scent of the werecats, we headed back to the truck to report it and knew we needed to head out as we caught even more scents on the wind. We were hoping to mobilize your family to get you, then you called out."

"I escaped," I said heavily. "They were planning on torturing me. I had to try." My words were getting slower, thicker. "Got lucky."

"Jacky..." His fingers brushed my face. "You did good. Get some rest. You're safe now."

My eyes were suddenly heavy. He was right. I was safe now. With Landon flying down the road, probably going over seventy, and Heath right there—I was safe now.

19

CHAPTER NINETEEN

I woke up when the truck slowed down. I thought I was still in the cage, but it only took a moment to remember where I was, and I was moving, which meant Heath was right beside me. He and Landon had looked for me. They had waited on me to get to them.

Tears welled up in my eyes.

"Are you okay? We're nearly there. Another fifteen minutes. Hold on," Heath said suddenly. "Jacky?"

"Thank you," I choked out. "You didn't have to risk everything for me. If they had caught you, they would have killed you. You didn't have to help find me. Carey—"

"Yes, I did," he said back in a hard tone. "Damn it, Jacky, yes, I did. Don't tell me I could have left Carey without a father. Don't go there. Landon and I knew what we were risking. I made the call."

I turned my head to see him better. His eyes were the frosty ice blue of his wolf form, and his dark hair was falling over his face. The entire thing became too intimate in a single heartbeat.

"Heath—"

"If you think for one minute Carey would ever have loved me again after leaving you to the 'bad people,' just to keep her safe, you are sorely mistaken," he growled. "If you think I could have lived with myself, then you have lost your mind, and I'll talk to Hasan about seeing you committed. I couldn't not help, Jacky. I had to be there to find you. And now here you are, away from them."

Feelings choked me—the overwhelming, crushing sensation in my chest making it hard to breathe.

"I was so scared," I finally admitted. "I tried to be strong, and I kept silent. I didn't tell them anything, but I accidentally slipped with my pack magic when they attacked me. They were going to torture me to find out how I got it. They want to overthrow Hasan and restart the war against the werewolves. I was so scared. I didn't think I would ever have a chance to get out, and..."

An arm wrapped around my waist and pulled me close.

Fragile. I was feeling so fragile, the strength that had carried me for nearly a week failing as my forehead touched his chest, and tears fell. The intimacy was gone, only a strange comfortable feeling like I belonged there. That Heath comforting me was as natural as breathing. A funny feeling that should have scared me more than anything that had just happened.

"You did well," he murmured. "You got out. You're

going to our safehouse. Hasan is there, along with all of your siblings. I think. I don't know them all."

I nodded silently against his chest. Words failed me as I soaked in the comfort, the solid force he represented —unfailing loyalty, unfailing friendship.

He'd come when he never had to.

After another minute or so, I pulled away, knowing it was time to break this up.

"This is all so wrong," I said, running a hand over my face, trying to wipe away dirt and possibly dried blood. "This was never supposed to happen."

"Rulers must face challenges from all angles, including those from within. Hasan and I spoke long about it, about how the signs were there, but he felt confident his children would be able to fight and confident his werecats would always follow the rules of engagement, like one-on-one fights."

"But you know better," I said softly.

"I do, and I didn't need to impress on him that he fucked up by leaving you defenseless. A group of werecats was possibly planning an attack on you. You needed backup."

"We're not werewolves, Heath. We're werecats. We don't naturally do anything with the whole in mind. We're solitary and prefer to be alone and dictate our own lives. We don't group hunt. That's a wolf tactic. Ironic since Mikkel hates werewolves but used your tricks to capture me. Fucking hypocrite..." I groaned. "If we had met his force in kind before this happened, before I was taken, he would have painted it as my weakness. As

Hasan's. My friendship with you would have colored it as us using wolf tactics, not him."

"He explained all of those things to me," Heath growled. "Ask me if I care."

"You didn't have to get involved. You won't impress wolf ideology on us. It doesn't work that way," I snapped back. I wasn't sure why I was pissed about this.

"You worked just fine with Jabari," he reminded me.

"In special circumstances, and look at how he reacted to having help. It's not natural for us."

"It's natural for you. You work well with me. Maybe it's not true of other werecats, but it's true for you."

"Apparently I'm a freak," I grumbled. "Maybe it's the addition of pack magic. I don't know, Heath. I'm easygoing? But don't try to turn Hasan into a werewolf Alpha. The werecats will turn a very small revolt into a very big one. If he starts acting like you or trying to do things the way you do, this is going to get worse, not better."

The truck turned down a dirt road that got bumpy. Heath stood and jumped out of the truck bed, leaving me there alone. We must have been on his property if he felt comfortable enough to do that. I sat up, holding the blanket to my chest, and looked over the field, completely empty except for the five parked cars. There was a small house at the back with trees along the back of it. I scooted to the back window of the truck and opened it.

"Where are we?" I asked Landon, now that Heath had run off.

"Richard's farmhouse," he answered. "We've been thinking of selling it, but..."

"It was perfect for a safehouse," I concluded. "Who's here?" I had a feeling Landon paid more attention than his father.

"Hasan, Jabari, Zuri, Davor, and Niko."

We were missing Hisao and Mischa, which surprised me. Landon stopped by the other cars and got out. I sat in the truck bed for a little longer as I could already see what was going to happen.

Carey was somehow the first person out of the farmhouse, running for the truck. Zuri was right behind her, looking flustered, but I saw the moment she caught my scent on the wind and saw my head poking up from the truck bed. Hasan and Jabari were next.

I tried to stand as Carey screamed incoherent syllables. Keeping the blanket on was tough enough, but when Zuri reached me, I realized quickly, I needed to give up that hope. She pulled the truck bed down, jumped in, picked me up, and jumped out with me in her arms. It was an awkward sensation since she always seemed delicate. She was a werecat, so I knew she was strong, but this was strange.

"Let me walk," I demanded, struggling. "I can fucking walk, Zuri."

"Shut up, little sister," she snarled at me. "You're bleeding and bruised. If you think I'm letting your feet touch the *dirt*, you are sorely mistaken. I can't believe you."

My face heated as we passed Hasan and Jabari, who

had stopped halfway to the truck. Carey was still screaming in the background, and I looked over Zuri's shoulder to see Landon pick her up and hug her tightly. As I was carried inside, I saw a wolf run to his family. Why Heath had decided to Change was beyond me. His ice-blue eyes found me, only for a second, then Hasan's body blocked my view, and I was inside.

I was dropped on a couch, and Zuri grabbed my cheeks, holding my face to stare at her.

"Does anything need stitches? Was any silver used?"

"I was grazed. Right shoulder. Probably doesn't need stitches, only bandaged."

She snapped her fingers, and Jabari disappeared from the room, running off to get a first aid kit, I guessed. Hasan stood silently, staring down at me, but Zuri was still leading this charge.

"How many?" she demanded.

"Um..." I did a rough count. I knew the answer to this, but for some reason, it was suddenly hard to put it all together. "Eight attacked me. Killed one...When I escaped, I think I killed another, but I don't know. He was shot with silver twice, but another one could have stopped him from bleeding out. I don't know."

"We'll plan for seven, then," Zuri said with a growl. "Father?"

"Mischa and Hisao will be here tonight," he said evenly. "Did they beat you, Jacqueline?"

"Yes," I whispered hoarsely. "Yesterday."

He snarled in barely disguised rage.

I caught new scents and heard footsteps. Turning my

head, I saw Niko, Davor, and my two employees come in through a back hallway.

"Shit, Jacky," Davor muttered, shaking his head. "Did you have a fight?"

"A few."

"How did the wolves rescue you with seven werecats around?" Zuri asked, pulling my attention back on her.

"They...didn't, really. Well, they waited for me, so they were a big help." I explained the chain of events, from the werecats scenting the wolves to my desperation, knowing I needed to get out because I was going to be tortured for information about my pack magic. The fact that Heath and Landon had been around had pressed the issue but also gave me the chance to escape. I wouldn't call them my rescuers, though.

"How did they find out?" Hasan asked.

"I was sloppy," I admitted. "During their initial attack, I...called out, trying to tell them it was stupid to try to kill me. Or something. I think I might have even begged for my life. Sorry." I was ashamed of it now. I had begged Mikkel that first night to not do what he was doing. I had said *please*.

"Don't be sorry," he said in return, going down on one knee next to me. My heart squeezed as he leaned over and put his head on my shoulder. "Don't be sorry. I should be the one apologizing."

"I don't..." Frowning, I looked over him at my oldest sister, the one who knew our father the best. Jabari walked back in at that moment, his eyes dark with feelings I didn't understand.

"It was always a risk," Zuri said. "We knew when the Tribunal was being formed, many werecats wouldn't appreciate the idea of a centralized ruler, not even one like Father. Younger werecats fell in easier, not knowing any different and respecting us for our age and power, but older cats..."

"Hated the idea, even if they liked Hasan," I finished.

"Exactly. Before the formation of the Tribunal, werecats weren't centralized. We answered to no one except each other in a more communal fashion. If a werecat pissed off enough other werecats, we banded together to kill the troublemaker. But there were no Laws, no leader, and no one was forced to bow," Zuri explained as if it was out of a history book, but her eyes gave me a sense of the weight my family had been burdened with in those early days.

"Why do we do it now?"

"It was a condition of peace," Hasan answered. "To make peace, to form the Tribunal, I agreed to control the werecats. If I was to keep them safe from outside threats, I had to keep them from being a threat to others."

"Mikkel says you killed dissenters," I said softly, trying not to make it seem like I believed the accusation. I needed the truth, then I would make a judgment.

"I killed a few," he told me honestly. "And that's why I'm the one who should be sorry. None of you were ever supposed to be at risk like this. I always thought if anyone had a problem with one of you, they could and would come to me. Then I hid for a century. I lost touch, lost my relationships with everyone. They don't know me anymore; therefore, they can't trust me. We announced you, and I thought if anyone didn't like the idea, they would just come talk to me, or Jabari, or Zuri. Any one of us."

"It was the final straw that broke the camel's back," Zuri said flatly. "But don't worry, Jacky. We're going to wipe these upstarts off the face of the earth. I'm going to bathe in their blood come the full moon."

Shivers ran down my spine, but I kept my eyes on Hasan. Like me, his werecat form had gold eyes, which were on display. Ignoring Zuri's bloodthirst was easy when he had me locked in his gaze, studying me, trying to find some piece of a puzzle he was missing.

"Jacky, you don't have to represent the family. You know that, don't you?" he asked, looking over my face. I could only imagine what I looked like. I had dropped weight, lost blood, and fought more than a few times in the last week. I had been bitten, clawed at, and shot.

It seemed like every year, my life grew more dangerous as if it was making up for something.

"I want to," I replied, trying to put strength behind the words. "I wanted to do this, I wanted..." Closing my eyes, I considered my reasons when I accepted the responsibility. "I'm a member of this family, and you do great things for our kind. I just wanted to help you. I never wanted to rule, but I wanted to help and keep my own mistakes from coming back on you. It hasn't even been a year, and I've failed. Lani is out there with Mikkel, and she wants me dead. My only friend and I couldn't even keep her. Mikkel thinks I'm a disgrace with wolf magic and allies." I leaned over, ignoring how Zuri tried to hold me up. "This is all my fault."

"This is *our* fault," Hasan corrected. "But don't worry, I fully intend to remind them why I am the werecat who rules, and they are the ones who must learn to follow."

"Did you ever want to rule?" I asked, swallowing.

"No, but there were no other options. It was rule through the Tribunal or allow the werewolves to wipe our kind out." He stood and walked out of the room, leaving me surrounded by my siblings and the two humans who I had been hoping would never see me like this. They were the ones I had to keep safe in my territory. How would they ever trust me now?

"Dirk, take Oliver to the other room," Niko ordered. I heard the shuffling as the two humans left.

"Thanks," I mumbled. "I'm just tired. It's been a long week, but I'll be fine. I need some sleep."

"You mentioned Lani," Zuri pointed out, lifting my head again. "Tell us more while I bandage you up, please."

I dropped the blanket, exposing the newest of my injuries. While we could leave injuries alone as werecats, it was safer to treat them as needed. Zuri got to work, disinfecting them and cleaning out the dirt.

"She's helping them. Apparently Mikkel is her lover, though I'm certain he's fucking another of the females in their little group. None of them seem bothered by it."

"That's not relevant, and you know it," Jabari growled, coming around where I could see him again.

Niko and Davor moved to flank him, staring down at me as Zuri worked.

"She's pissed off at me. I think she hates me more than she really believes in Mikkel's cause. I lied to her through omission for years, caused a bunch of trouble that got her into hot water with other werecats with the Dallas incident, then proceeded to ignore the trouble I had made for months while she stewed on who I was. She stopped being my friend probably a year ago, and that's fine. I just never thought she would be my enemy." I laughed bitterly. "I called her. I called to check on her as things started to get weird around my territory because I was worried about her. Because that's my job, right? To keep an eye on the werecats of the area. She never breached my territory, so I had no idea...she was covering for them. She knew, and..." I sighed, trying to ignore how badly it stung.

"She'll be executed for this. You understand?" Jabari had no remorse. I nodded, knowing the fate of the werecats who had taken me, including Lani—especially Lani. "Now that we have you back, we can formulate a plan. I'll need to discuss it with Father this evening, and we're still waiting on Hisao and Mischa, but then we'll attack. They'll pay for this."

"Good," I said without remorse. I knew Jabari would kill everyone for the family. He would rather see us the last werecats left on Earth than see one of us hurt. He was a good older brother that way. I looked past him at Davor and Niko. "I'm sorry Dirk and Oliver happened to be around for this."

"You did everything right," Niko said patiently. "You put them where they would potentially be the safest before the trouble truly began. That's all that matters."

I was glad he agreed with my choices. I didn't think Dirk and Oliver were going to stick around and keep working at Kick Shot. There was no way in hell those two would ever go back to my territory.

Zuri finished up after Jabari left to find Hasan. I wrapped myself up in the blanket lying over the back of the couch just in time. Heath and his family walked in, and the moment Carey saw me again, she ran for me. Zuri backed away as my little human threw her arms around my waist and fell into me. I bit back a pained groan, trying my best not to show Carey or anyone else how badly I hurt. I clutched my blanket with one hand and tried to hug her with the other, pretending like nothing was wrong.

"You're not supposed to get hurt anymore," she whispered into my chest. I silently thanked myself for covering up when I had.

"I know," I mumbled into her hair.

"You can stay in my room with me," she offered. "Dad said you would be really tired. You fell asleep the moment you got away."

"I would love that." I wouldn't turn away such a generous offer. I pried her off me, which wasn't easy, and stood, feeling the ache of exhaustion and not having a proper bed for several days. "Let me use the restroom." I had been using a bucket for six days. A proper toilet would be nice too.

"Okay. I'll wait in my room." She scurried off, and I heard her thumping up the stairs.

Landon looked me over before nodding, then left the room. I had a feeling I had gotten his approval for some reason.

Heath, though, was still in wolf form and padded away without a single look at me, heading up the stairs as well.

"How was finally meeting them?" I asked softly, knowing the wolves could possibly still hear me.

"Landon is very protective of his sister," Zuri said thoughtfully. "A good thing for an older brother. I see Jabari hates him. They're very similar."

"Don't let him hear that," I muttered, shaking my head in dismay.

"Good wolves," Niko added. When I turned to him, he gave me a smile that was very wolfish. Knowing who he used to be and how he came to be a member of the family and a werecat, I could see why he was quiet, and his mannerisms were a little different from everyone else's. He probably understood Heath and Landon better than I ever would.

"That's it?"

"She loves you," Zuri whispered with respect and admiration. "Treasure that."

I swallowed the hard lump that quickly formed in my throat and nodded.

"I do," I promised. Carey was most of my world—her brightness, her quick wit, her strong but fragile heart, her courage, and her love. She brought me out of the dark more than anyone else ever could.

"Good. Go. Get some rest. We won't move on Mikkel until you're up and ready."

"Really?" I was a little surprised. Did I want a piece of those assholes? Definitely. But I had figured my family would go without me to get it done and avenge me while I healed.

"He owes you a pound of flesh," she reminded me with a sharp, dangerous smile. Bloodthirsty Zuri was terrifying.

I went upstairs, found a bathroom, used it, then proceeded to find Carey. She was already getting ready to lie down, staring at two stuffed animals. It wasn't even her bedtime, but I had a feeling it had nothing to do with being tired.

"You can have this one," she decided, holding out a wolf with blue eyes. I took it with a smile. "I'm too old for stuffed animals, but sometimes..."

"I get it. Thank you for sharing your room."

"Lie down and go to sleep," she ordered, patting her small bed.

I did as she demanded and knew a twelve-year-old was watching my back as I slept.

CHAPTER TWENTY

T he door opening woke me up, and I sat up quickly, staring.

"Yes, Hasan?" I asked, a little annoyed and still tired.

"I brought clothing for you," he said kindly, holding up the bundle in his arms. "If you could dress and meet me downstairs, I would be glad. There's much we need to talk about."

It felt like a flashback, but my initial reaction was much different. Over eleven years ago, I had woken up to a door opening, my hearing too sensitive, and saw a man I barely knew. A guy who had taught me and Shane how to ride horses while on our trip to a remote island. He'd terrified me then.

Eleven years later and the hardness in his eyes and posture betrayed the kind words he had said, and terrified me again.

"Is there a plan? Are Mischa and Hisao here?" I

asked, swinging my legs off the bed, ignoring the aching of the bruises. I didn't care about being naked in front of him. If there was one thing Hasan made very clear at the beginning of our complicated familial relationship, it was he didn't look at me in any way that should be considered uncomfortable. His eyes never wavered off mine, and he never had any sort of reaction. He was a father, first and foremost, before a man.

"There is, and they are," he answered, holding out the clothing. "Are you feeling better?"

"I think so. Sorry for being...fragile, earlier," I said, taking the bundle. Turning away, I tossed it on the bed to see what he had given me. One of them must have gone to my house and grabbed some of my clothing.

"We understand. Heath said you fought hard to get to him."

"You talked to him again?" I pulled on underwear and pants, then looked back at him as I picked up the sports bra.

"Of course I did. Does that really surprise you?"

No, but I'm not sure I'm comfortable with it, either.

Shrugging, I pulled my shirt on. I didn't really know how to answer. I'd never imagined the two sides of my life would cross to this effect. One of the family meeting my wolf was something entirely different than the *entire* family.

"Would you like a hand?" he asked, offering an arm.

"No, thank you." I didn't want to feel weak like I had after the rescue. I didn't want to feel fragile, not with how much power surrounded me. I wanted to live up to them, not be the one they needed to coddle. "Food would help more than walking assistance."

"I'm going to assume they starved you," he said quietly, holding the door for me. "Niko and Zuri have been fighting over the kitchen to make food for everyone since you laid down."

"So, everyone's noticed," I said with a snort.

"It's hard to miss. You've probably lost over ten pounds, and I know how hard it is for us to keep weight if we're not properly sustained."

I didn't look at him as I walked past, keeping my eyes down. I wasn't an invalid. I trotted down the stairs and went to the kitchen, following the scent of food, walking in to see several dishes on the counters, steam coming off them. Before I looked at my siblings, an errant thought ran through my mind.

Ah. Richard liked brown, just as much as his father.

Standing in the house, staring at the kitchen but able to see a peek of the dining room, I could see all the warm tones. Richard had balanced the brown with reds, which would've a warm effect if it didn't look so much like dirt. The counters were light tan, paired with dark cabinets. Even the dishes were brown with designs on them, peeking into view underneath the mountains of food my family was cooking.

Which brought me to the surreal scene happening in the kitchen.

Zuri was standing over a pot on the stove while Niko was pulling something out of the oven. They worked around each other like they had done it every day for centuries. It was nearly magical in its own right. Neither of them noticed I was there yet, so I continued to look around, peeking into the dining room, taking a better look at who was in there.

Heath sat at his dining room table, bemused, watching my siblings take over his kitchen. He noticed me after only a second, and I caught the bemused expression turn into a wider smile, then disappear. A hand touched my shoulder.

"Get something to eat," Jabari ordered.

I sighed as Niko and Zuri turned to me. Zuri's eyes narrowed.

"How long have you been there?"

"Only a moment," I answered, swallowing.

"Food. Eat. Now. No one else has been allowed to eat until you woke up because you..." She used a wooden spoon to point over my body. "Need it."

I didn't argue. Niko handed me a plate, which I allowed, but when Jabari started to help me spoon things onto my plate, I snarled, took the spoon away, and did it myself. My older brother was smart enough to take two steps back. When my plate was full, I went into the dining room and sat across from Heath at the dining table, realizing quickly there was a new awkwardness between us. I searched his face for any indication of what he was thinking, but he kept it blank and looked at his phone.

"What are you doing?"

"Checking my email," he answered truthfully.

"Ah."

I hated it already. I was used to talking to Heath about everything under the sun. Was he angry with me for what I said in the truck?

"Where are Carey and Landon?"

"Landon took her outside to play on the four-wheelers. She doesn't like this house."

"Because Richard used to own it?"

He looked up, his eyes narrowing.

"Who told you?"

"Landon, when we got here."

He nodded, then went back to his phone.

"Sister!" a woman yelled across the house. "Where is she? I smell her!"

"Over here!" I called out. Heath sighed heavily and got up, leaving the dining room as Mischa blew in like a winter storm. I smiled at her, trying to put Heath out of my mind. Something never quite lined up with Mischa for me. She looked and dressed like a model or movie star, her eyes were the color of snow at night, her natural platinum blonde hair cascaded in a long fall, straight and silky, and she dressed in high-end designer clothing.

Yet she lived on the road and never settled in one place. She acted like a rock star who couldn't put down roots and traveled to places most humans didn't dare live. She didn't have a speck of dirt on her, though, nor any other signs of the hardships from the life she lived.

She was a pretty drifter, Mischa. Prettier in person than she ever was on camera.

"You're alive," she breathed out. "They told me, but..."

I didn't get the chance to say anything as she smothered me in a hug, but this time, I didn't wince. I was seated, and she was standing, which made it uncomfortable, but it was a hug.

"Let her go, so she can eat," Zuri snapped.

"Shut up. You got to tend her. I'm going to shower her in affection now," Mischa growled back.

"Both of you stop," I tried to order, pushing Mischa off me. "I want to eat. I'll talk, but don't hover. Actually, Mischa, why weren't you here earlier today?"

"Hisao and I were chasing down some possible leads. We didn't find anything, but Father told us the wolves could be getting close to finding you, so we headed this way. Then we got here, and you'd already escaped. Good work, kid." She grinned, all teeth, and sat down next to me. I looked over her head and saw Hisao quietly coming into the archway between the living room and dining room, then leaning against the wall. He just nodded.

"Thanks. It was good timing and luck, mostly. What's our plan now?"

"Our plan is for everyone to eat, including the poor family we've intruded on, then discuss how we're going to crush Mikkel and his motherfucking friends," Mischa answered, still grinning. "Time to fight with the big cats."

"I fought with Jabari already," I reminded her. Mischa snorted.

"Against vampires. Not hard prey. Other werecats, though? That's a good fight."

Is that what you call it? Fuck, my entire family is insane.

They all filed into the dining room, even Hasan, and started eating. It was like a Thanksgiving from hell. I didn't say anything, just shoved food in my face. When Carey came in with her family behind her, I looked up, desperately hoping any of them would save me. Carey, however, wasn't feeling protective. Her eyes wide, she looked over my entire family together at one table and around the dining room. She was in awe.

"It's not polite to stare," Heath whispered down to her, purely for her benefit. A whisper like that was something every supernatural in the room knew to ignore for the young girl's pride.

"Dad..."

"Find a seat."

Mischa jumped up, smiling. "She can have mine. You must be Carey. I saw you out on the four-wheeler. Very cool."

Carey's face turned bright red as she sat down, her eyes never leaving the beautiful woman talking to her. I was completely forgotten in favor of my cool and interesting family. The same thing had happened when Jabari visited my territory, so I wasn't surprised. It was a cruel and funny reminder that kids had short attention spans.

Landon made no move to find a seat, but Heath was interesting. He went to Niko and looked down at the werecat, who glanced up to see the Alpha staring at him. Interestingly, I saw the visible effort Niko made to remain sitting before giving in and giving Heath a seat at his own table.

"Old habits die hard," Davor teased from across the room. "How did you figure it out, wolf?"

"Figure out what?" Heath asked, looking up from his plate. "He was sitting in my spot at my table."

Davor's eyes narrowed, but it was Niko who sighed.

"My parents were werewolves. Niko the Traitor," he explained. "I thought Jacky would have told you."

"Jacky doesn't tell me your family secrets," Heath said blandly. "But, really? How did you end up a werecat?" Heath seemed to lighten up in the span of a heartbeat as he and Niko started a lively conversation about the War and Niko's life. I could see Heath grow more comfortable by the second, probably because he finally had someone in my family who understood him just a little, other than me.

I turned to Carey, who was still enamored by Mischa, but now Zuri was joining the fold. Turning away from my two older sisters completely charming and spoiling her, I looked at Hasan, Jabari, and Hisao. They weren't saying anything, but the looks they were giving each other told me there was some kind of conversation going on there.

The entire scene seemed too surreal. I finished up my food faster than everyone else, took my dishes to the kitchen, and went out the back door. Sniffing the air and taking in the scenery, I was glad to see I was still in East Texas, though I didn't know exactly where. The door opened and closed behind me, and I caught Davor's distinct scent.

"You didn't enjoy dinner? Zuri and Niko worked hard on it just for you," he said with a small bite.

"I spent a week being held captive. The idea of kicking my feet up..." I shook my head. "It just felt weird."

"We're waiting on the little one to head off to bed," he explained. "Hard to plan killing a lot of people when young ears are around."

"Where did Oliver and Dirk go?"

"They ate upstairs. This is too much for Oliver. He's... proper. Doesn't know how to handle this much authority and power in the room without working. Dirk...you've met him." Davor snorted. "I don't know how Niko puts up with him."

"They're family," I said, side-eyeing him. "I mean, that's why we all put up with you."

He growled. "And here I was, trying to come out and see how you were doing."

"You started it by guilting me over the hard work our siblings put into dinner. You weren't off to a very good start," I snapped back.

He looked at me, measuring me. I allowed it, waiting for the judgment I knew was coming.

"I don't like you," he said finally.

"I don't like you, either. I'm amazed you're even here." Was it harsh to say? Yes, but I wasn't in a very good mood.

"You're family," he snarled at me, stepping closer. "Of course I'm fucking here. We can't tolerate another loss."

"I'm not going to get myself killed. If you haven't noticed, I've done everything in my power to not die," I said in frustration, not understanding the brother squaring off with me.

"You've done a bang-up job so far, haven't you? You just do as you please, and if you don't die, then you've done the right thing. Is that it?"

"Better than being a fucking asshole every time I open my mouth like someone I know," I snarled, pushing him away. "I don't fucking get you, Davor. Everyone says you hate me because Liza died, and you think I'm some fucking replacement, but I think you just want to hate me. I never hated you, but you..." I waved a hand at him. "You can't even treat me with a shred of respect."

He looked down at his chest, where I had touched him. He seemed a little confused that I would put my hands on him.

"You just shoved me," he said.

"Damn right, I did." I straightened, squaring my shoulders. "I've been through enough this week. I don't need you right now."

He didn't say anything more, walking inside and leaving me with no small amount of confusion. The next thing I knew, Hasan was walking out, an annoyed expression on his face.

"Did you shove your brother?"

"Yes."

He heaved a large sigh. I wanted to reach out and throttle the man.

"Jacqueline."

"He's a total asshole to me! I came out here to have a moment of peace, and he came out to be a prick!"

"I know."

"Then..." I inhaled, trying to control myself. "What am I supposed to do?"

"I'm not mad at you, just a little exasperated my children must always resort to physical violence to deal with each other."

"Why is he like this?"

Hasan's eyes were sad. "That is something I can't help you with any more than I have. You and Davor might never like each other, and he never has to give you a reason why. Could you live with that?"

"I could try. At least this time, he attempted to be nice by coming out to check on me," I muttered, shrugging.

"It's a start," Hasan agreed. "Alpha Everson is taking his daughter upstairs so we may use the living room for our meeting. Hisao wants to strike at midnight."

"Do you think they might have run by now? They know I escaped with Heath. They'll know we're going to come for them."

"They'll have already run," Hasan said, nodding. "But we can hunt them down. Don't worry."

I nodded, accepting that, and followed him in. He held the door again, and I walked in, going to the living room. I stopped at the back as Hasan moved into the middle. Davor slid up next to me.

"Sorry. I was an ass. You're my sister, and our enemies targeted you, fought you, and captured you. I...

don't think enough before I speak sometimes. I went out to make sure you were okay and then let my attitude get the better of me." He was deathly serious. I looked at his face and noticed it was a little pale. Looking past him, I saw Hisao watching us closely. The assassin's eyes narrowed as I stared.

"Apology accepted," I said quietly. "It's fine. We don't need to get along, but maybe we can turn the hostility down a little."

"I agree," he said, heaving out a sigh. "Thank you."

I was never going to ask if Hisao threatened him or not. I was just going to take the apology at face value and try to move on with my life.

And hopefully, not have any fucking nightmares about the look on the assassin's face across the room. It was distinctly too pleased.

"Let's get to work," Hasan said loudly, now that Davor and I were done.

CHAPTER TWENTY-ONE

"We're going to hunt in pairs," Hasan began. "Alpha Everson has already marked the location where we should begin on a map." He pulled it out of his blazer's inside pocket and dropped it on the coffee table. "Now, the wolves won't be joining us because this has stopped being their fight. While Heath is an ally, and he helped immensely in finding Jacky, he does have a family, and we're going to respect that. Are we all okay with that?"

"Yes, sir," half of us said loudly. I was more than all right with Heath sitting this one out. I was amazed he had even helped to find me. While they didn't get the big rescue they probably wanted, it had given me a chance to run. I was going to take it as a win.

"Should we officially consider him a friend to the werecats?" Zuri asked, reaching for the map. "I know he's the werewolf liaison to us now or whatever strange title the North American Council gave him, but maybe we should recognize his efforts."

"We will discuss it once we've put down this resistance. It could put him at risk, and I don't want to make those decisions without his input," Hasan answered. I raised an eyebrow, and it caught his eye. "Yes, Jacqueline?"

"Anyone who doesn't respect us already wants to kill him. Mikkel wanted to drop his and Landon's bodies at the feet of the Tribunal werewolves as a warning that any werewolf coming too close to our business wouldn't be tolerated. At this point, I think a public sign of our support and protection will help him, not hurt him. He might need it."

"He already has your public display of support," Niko pointed out.

"And look at what good that did him," I replied. "I'm a young werecat nobody really knows and has no reason to respect."

"Then you need to give them a reason," Hisao whispered. "Kill enough of them, and they'll fall in line."

"That's why Mikkel hates you," I said in annoyance. "Kill your enemies instead of listening to dissenters. If I start killing werecats to protect werewolves…"

"A nightmare waiting to happen, bigger than the one we're dealing with now," Zuri finished. "We'll figure this out after we take Mikkel down. He didn't attack the werewolves. He attacked you and this family. We're justified in killing him and everyone who allies with him.

Let's handle that first, then all of you should leave the politics to me or Father."

I was grateful there had been no large family gatherings when I lived with Hasan. If I had faced the different personalities and conflicting ideas while I was still young and new to this extent, I would have run away.

"Let's get back on topic," Jabari called out. "Leave other discussions for after the hunt."

"When was the last time we did a family hunt?" Mischa asked loudly.

"Does it matter?" Davor asked with a snort. "We're doing one tonight."

"We've done this before?" I was more confused than anything else.

"During the War when we realized the wolves were overwhelming us in numbers," my Russian sister said with a smile. "And we showed them."

"Moving. On," Jabari snarled. "Father..."

"This is why we don't do family hunts anymore," Hasan whispered to his oldest son. Everyone in the room heard, and most of my siblings began chuckling.

Werecats didn't have a natural inclination to respect leadership, to bend to the dominant or more powerful force. Even I was finding it hard to stay on topic, feeling the need to revolt ever so slightly against the idea of Hasan leading the conversation, wanting to join in with the others.

Hasan snapped his fingers twice. Even though Jabari had called us all back to attention, Hasan's comment had led Mischa and Davor into another conversation, and even Zuri joined in.

"Up here!" he growled. "We need to focus."

"How the hell did Mikkel get a bunch of werecats to work together well enough to invade my territory?" I asked myself out loud. "We can't even focus when we need to kill these people." Everyone looked at me. When no one said anything, I shrugged. "It's a valid question. When I worked with the wolves in Dallas, they were pack-oriented, willing to follow the orders of one person and work toward a common goal. We don't even like when someone tells us to set the table or sit quietly while someone else talks."

"He probably deals with this as well," Hasan said, nodding. "It doesn't change our plans. We'll go to the spot where Heath picked you up and begin our hunt. We're hunting in pairs, and Jacqueline, you'll be with me."

There was a collective gasp.

"Father..." Zuri said softly. "Are you sure?"

"I don't need a babysitter," I cut in as Hasan stared at me, ignoring whatever Zuri was about to say.

"It's not about babysitting. It's about a show of power. You'll fight by my side, watch my back, and you'll finally get to see me fight against another werecat."

"It's a great honor," Jabari added, looking down at me. "He'll expect you to keep up."

I nodded slowly. Weird.

"Father, are you sure? You'll be their main target. Even if they've scattered, the moment they catch your scent on the wind with Jacky, they'll come for you."

"Yes. Jacqueline has proven herself a capable predator I can rely on," Hasan answered. "And I want all the werecats to know I trust every single one of my children to live up to the legacy of this family, no matter their age. Just because she's young doesn't mean they can write her off as weak."

"Well, thanks," I said. "I'll do my best."

"You won't do your best. You'll do what is necessary, even if it asks for a great deal more than what you've ever given before," Hasan corrected.

I nodded once, his message loud and clear.

"The rest of you will pair as follows—Jabari and Zuri, Davor and Mischa, Niko and Hisao. Watch each other's backs and cover weak spots. Stay close to one another and don't leave your partner for prey without making it clear you've caught a scent, and they will follow." Hasan rubbed his hands together, looking at all of them. "Any questions?"

"How long do we hunt?" Hisao asked. "Is there a time you wish to have us back?"

"Until they've all fallen. I don't care if we must chase them all around the world. We'll see them dead before we go home. Because of that...Jabari, did you bring them?"

"Father, you know how much I hate—"

"Did you bring them?" our father asked again.

Jabari sighed and went outside. We all heard a car door open and slam, then he walked back in, holding fanny packs.

"One of each pair will have one of these to carry

cellphones and other technology. I've had Jabari developing them, against his will, after the Washington incident. They are fireproof and waterproof. If it's broken off, one of you will carry it. Don't let it get stolen, please." Hasan grabbed one and tossed it at me. "You'll be holding onto ours."

"Obviously, because you would have these made but never force yourself the embarrassment of wearing one," I muttered. "Though this would have come in handy when I was taken. I wouldn't have lost my bag so easily in the chase."

"Don't encourage him," Davor growled. "He'll have us wearing hiking packs by the end of the year."

"He already had us wear packs during the War," Niko added in a whisper. "After about a century, we convinced him to stop making us do it when we traveled."

"Well, neither of you were run out of your territory, trying to hold a duffel bag in your teeth," I answered, then realized we had once again gotten off topic. I looked up at Hasan, who was beginning to lose his patience with us. "Sorry."

"You're all lucky we aren't leaving until nightfall," he said with a growl. "Davor, help Niko load up our vehicles. Zuri and Jabari, let's go over the map and pick hunting zones to start with based on our best estimations of where they may have run. Jacqueline, eat more. Hisao, make sure she does that."

Everyone scattered, and I was left with the most terrifying of my siblings hovering over my shoulder.

"Let's go," he ordered, grabbing the shoulder of my shirt and lifting. I didn't fight it, standing as he wanted and following him into the kitchen. "Why did they starve you?" he asked as we left the family in the other room.

"They didn't starve me the entire time. They actually fed me drugged food to begin with, but I was too smart to fall for that. Eat slow enough and our bodies burn off the drug before it can take effect. Then they realized I was never going to talk, never going to give them answers, so they started keeping the food. Mikkel gave me some bread once, but that was when he'd decided to torture me if I didn't start talking within twenty-four hours."

"Did he? Torture you?" Hisao asked softly, leaning over me as I tried to make a plate of food.

"No. I escaped," I answered. "Please back off."

"I've trained people to handle torture before. I could do the same for you," he said gently. "It might prove useful."

"No, thanks," I said, quickly stepping away from him because he didn't move. "Don't be so fucking...intense, please. It's creeping me out."

"I've trained assassins as well. If you're worried about defending the wolves, I could teach you some of the techniques—"

"Drop it," I snapped with a snarl.

He leaned back, his hard eyes seeming distant. For a minute, I wondered if Hisao was missing something, some key piece of humanity that kept the rest of the family chained to at least some level of decency he couldn't be bothered with. Since I highly doubted Hasan would have raised him to be this way, it had to be something he grew into over the centuries he'd been a werecat.

"I just want you to be safe," he said finally. "And I know skills that can keep you safe because it seems you live a very dangerous life. I have a feeling it won't get safer for you any time soon."

"And you're a good judge of these things?" I found that hard to believe.

"I've trained a variety of supernaturals, many from young ages, to do what they can do now. Three of them are Tribunal Executioners. I met all of them at their worst, trying to live lives they were wholly unequipped to handle. They never wanted to admit to me they were in over their heads, but I knew. I've never raised and Changed a werecat. They are my legacy. So, yes, I do think I'm a good judge of these things. Especially since every single one of them would be dead now if not for me."

"Are you saying I'm going to die if I don't listen to you?"

"I'm saying it's a possibility, and I would hate for that to happen, little sister."

That bothered me. Not the very words he said but the way he said them. There was very little emotion from him about the possibility I was going to get myself killed. Very little emotion about training the killers of the supernatural world, the Tribunal Executioners. I hadn't met the ones who would have killed me after Dallas, something I was eternally grateful for. It was worse to find out he had trained a few of them.

"Did Hasan ask you to talk to me about this?" Even while it bothered me that he trained the ultimate killers of the supernatural world, I considered it. If Hasan wanted me to learn more, I would strongly consider taking Hisao up on the offer. My thoughts drifted to Lani, and a wave of blood red anger hit me. I imagined the ways I could kill her for her betrayal, and the things Hisao could teach me to make me dangerous enough to never be toyed with again would certainly help.

"No, and I'm certain he's going to be angry at me later, but I call things as I see them." He smiled, but there wasn't any humor in it.

That made me come back to reality. I didn't like the feelings I had just confronted.

"Well, I'm going to pass on your offer. I'm not interested in knowing any more about killing than I have already experienced." I nodded as if that ended the conversation, then walked around him. I hadn't passed on his offer because it made me uncomfortable to learn more ways of killing. If anything, the idea of learning more made me excited, and that was what made me turn the offer down. I wanted Mikkel's blood in any way I could get it. I wanted to hurt Lani. I wanted to kill anyone who wanted to kill me for just trying to do the right thing.

And that made me scared of myself.

When did that reaction become my default? What the fuck ever happened to just protecting the people I care about?

He didn't say any more as I sat down at the empty dining table and ate. When my plate was empty, he took it before I could stand and walked back with it into the kitchen. I didn't pay him any mind, still trying to think about how tempting his offer was. It would have been useful before Washington with the vampires or Dallas with the werewolves. I wouldn't be seen as a target anymore as the weakest, youngest member of the family.

I would be able to kill anyone who threatened me or those in my territory.

I would be known as a killer.

A small part of me was completely okay with that. The better part of me was not.

He brought the plate back out with more food and dropped it before me.

I didn't get a chance to tell him I wasn't hungry anymore because Hasan walked in.

"If you two are ready, we're going to head out."

"Yeah." I jumped up and left my incredibly strange assassin of a brother behind, staring at the plate of food. He met us outside a moment later and stopped me from getting into the SUV beside Zuri.

"You'll fight your hardest tonight," he said in a whisper. "And if you aren't up to the task, I'll be in your territory in the coming days to teach you better."

"Hisao," Hasan snapped. "She'll be fine. Go to Niko."

"Yes, sir," he said, walking away.

"Excuse him. He gets amped up when there's killing to be done, and he wants all of us to be at our best no matter the situation. He takes it as his personal responsibility," Zuri explained. "I'm certain you'll be fine."

"Let's hope so," I muttered, closing the door.

I looked back at the house as we started moving.

Heath never came down to say goodbye.

CHAPTER TWENTY-TWO

I t was a longer drive than I remembered, but I had slept through most of it last time. For the majority of the drive, I only thought about Heath. How he'd acted from the moment he helped me escape, then barely spoke to me at his home.

It hurt in hindsight.

I also thought about Mikkel, and what I was about to do with my werecat family, a family he wanted to see brought down a peg or several. I thought about Lani and how everything had turned sour between us.

It made me so angry.

I tried my best to make everything right, to clean up the messes I left behind. I only ever wanted to do the right thing, but apparently, that wasn't good enough. Not for her.

I knew I would never be good enough in her mind.

That still hurt. It also pissed me off. I wanted to tear

her limb from limb to ease the pain and anger in my chest.

I had one friend, and she betrayed me because I had kept my personal business a secret. Because I hadn't wanted to live like all the other werecats. Because I didn't see werewolves as the enemy, but saw some of them as friends.

I stewed on that until we stopped on the side of the road.

I got out without a word and began to strip, using the vehicle as cover like the rest of the family. Hasan grabbed the pack I would wear from the trunk and held it while I finished throwing my clothing into the back seat.

"Jacky, I hear you're fast. Race?" Davor grinned from the other SUV.

"You'll lose," I promised and began Changing, letting it tear through my body and accepting it, riding the pain instead of fighting it. I was beginning to understand that was what made my Change so fast. The natural inclination was to fight pain, to try to ignore and stop feeling it, but I let it happen, accepting it, and it ended quickly. When I had lived apart from the family, I had a very 'get on with it' attitude about being a werecat and needing to Change. I really wanted to think that was what helped me in the end.

I was done before Davor and moved to knock him over, making someone else growl.

"Jacqueline, that's unkind," Hasan snapped. "Get over here."

I moved back to him and angled, so he could strap the pack on me. It was literally a fucking fanny pack!

"This is the ugliest thing I have ever put on in my life, and that's low bar," I said, not considering the entirety of my company.

Hasan jumped a little, surprising me into jumping as well. Someone growled, and I turned to see everyone staring at me with wide eyes, including Davor and Niko who weren't even totally finished Changing.

"Ah. Yeah. This is the first time everyone has heard me do this except Jabari," I said, trying to keep all of my words in the open. That was a little thing about pack magic. I could focus on one head and talk to it, or I could throw the words out into a void, not considering who would hear them, only the feeling I wanted them to be heard.

"That is very strange," Hasan said softly. "How do the wolves live with voices in their minds?"

"I'm not sure where you're going with that." If I could have frowned, I would have.

"My mind is my space," he said, looking down at me. "It feels...like a violation for you to speak there. It's very uncomfortable."

"I can't read your mind if that's a concern."

"No...but maybe you should leave the speaking for when it's absolutely necessary. It could prove distracting to many of us." He ran a hand over my head, scratching behind my ears for a moment before turning away. I stepped away as he fell and began his Change. He was a little faster than me, maybe by a couple of seconds. I chalked it up to age and experience, which was what he always said.

Once we were all ready, Hasan took the lead and found my trail, and we followed it backward. It was less than twenty-four hours since I had escaped, so it still smelled fresh. That worried me, and I figured it worried my family as well. With the scents so fresh, there was no way of telling which one would be the right one to follow to hunt down the dissenters.

It felt like it took forever to find the cabin-like house in the woods with its wood walls and earthy tones. It felt so alone, so foreboding. Part of it was too normal, which made it more intimidating. This had been a normal home. People had once lived here, probably happily, and now there was a dungeon in the basement that could have been the place where I died.

Don't think about it, Jacky. You escaped, and now it's time to get back at them.

I lifted my head and sniffed the air as my siblings sniffed around me, moving more cautiously toward the house now that it was in view. I was hoping to smell one thing in particular and caught it—blood. I followed the trail, lowering my head to sniff closer to the ground, trying to find the source of the scent. It took me around the house, Hasan following me. He was probably curious about what I was looking for since none of us were going to waste time on something that didn't matter.

To me, at least, this mattered.

I found it near the dirt drive of the home. The kitchen door I had escaped from had to be at the back of the house, and this was the front. I saw a long mound of dirt and padded over to it, digging when I arrived, the scent of blood and decaying flesh becoming more prevalent.

There he was. Sam, the werecat who had been too excited to torture me.

Hasan bumped me with his shoulder, and I decided I had to explain.

"He was going to torture me. He's the one I shot. I was hoping to find him dead. There's only six left, then. Well, as far as I know."

He huffed, nodding his head. I took that as a good thing even as he minutely shook his head afterward as if he was trying to get my voice out of it.

We walked around the building and met with the rest of the family. Hisao, prominent with almost black coat with black stripes and gold eyes like mine and Hasan's, stood near the back door, sniffing around. He looked up at us, then turned to stare into the doorway. Hasan snorted and nodded his head when Hisao looked back at us.

I guess they don't need me to pass around messages. They've been in werecat form together often enough to have a good understanding of each other's body language.

I watched as Hisao and his partner, Niko, walked into the house. Jabari and Zuri moved to the back door, Zuri peering in after them. After a moment, Zuri and Jabari went in as well. When Hasan stepped forward, I growled softly.

"I'm not going back in that house," I said sharply. I

didn't care if he was in charge or my father. If he went inside, he was going alone.

He didn't move again, looking down at me. He was a little bigger than Jabari, but it was probably by a matter of ten pounds and an inch of difference. None of the family was nearly the same size as me, which should have intimidated me. I was tiny compared to all of them.

My feet didn't move, and I didn't relent under his gaze. There was no chance in hell I was ever going back in there. I never wanted to see that basement again, and I knew that's where my feet would take me. Hasan would want to see where they'd held me, and I would follow.

So, I didn't move.

Everything was quiet as Jabari walked out, then Zuri. Neither seemed bothered, but in werecat form, that was hard to determine. Jabari was only a few feet out of the door, and Zuri was right behind him when everything went wrong.

It was like a movie, only it was my worst nightmare because it was real. In a split second, everything went from still and silent to complete mayhem. The boom that came from the house and the power of the shockwave from the blast sent me off my feet even though I was around five hundred pounds of feline. Blood and smoke filled the air as the dark night was illuminated by the fireball erupting from the house. Windows blew out with the distinct sound of shattering glass. Wood creaked and collapsed with the earth-shattering sound of pure destruction as the building's materials exploded out and fell in on themselves.

Someone roared. A feline scream pierced the air.

Objects hit me—shards of glass, pieces of wood, splinters, rocks, pieces of the house—cutting into me, digging into my flesh. I was probably bleeding in two dozen places by the time it was done.

I was also off my feet. My vision was blurry, and my ears were ringing. A second roar seemed very distant. A third after that, but it seemed closer. Still too far away. My sensitive hearing was blown, and I could hazard my eardrums were ruptured by the initial explosion.

I tried to stand, growling at the pain. I had hit the ground hard. After a few staggering steps and several blinks, my vision began to clear, but it didn't reveal anything good.

In front of me, the house burned, large chunks of wood falling.

"NIKO! HISAO!" I screamed into the night. I turned to see where the rest of my family was and noticed none of them were ready to help me save our brothers. Jabari was standing over Zuri, but he was looking to the woods. Blood poured down his side, but I had no idea what the extent of his injuries were.

Snarls and growls forced me to look that way as well.

I turned just in time to see Mikkel's werecats running for us before one of them took a leap and attacked me.

I wasn't able to ready myself before the large female landed on top of me. I went to the ground, screaming as claws raked over my ribs. I brought my back legs up and kicked, but she dodged. It took a moment, but I recognized her scent—Fiora. I considered the numbers while she danced around me, trying to snap at my weak points while I got to my feet. Spinning, I swatted the air between us to drive her off while also trying to find my balance again. I staggered every few steps, still too disoriented to properly fight. She snarled and jumped on me when I stumbled a fourth time, and her large canines grazed my back. I roared in pain, but I was grateful she didn't get ahold of me.

I bumped into another werecat as I tried to create distance between us. I didn't know who it was, but by the snarls and growls going on around me, it wasn't an appreciated bump.

Fiora moved around me, snarling. She was playing with me, and I knew it. She was probably angry I had killed Sam and left her locked in that cage, and angry that Sam wasn't the first of their group I had killed. Two of them had fallen to me, and they had been winning. Now, she wanted to repay that in kind.

She jumped for me again, and this time, I dodged, but poorly. She shoulder checked me on her landing, knocking me to the ground again. The smoke was thick now. My eyes watered as I continued to try and dodge Fiora's attempts to attack me, realizing too late, she was efficiently driving me away from the rest of my family. My back to the trees, I could see my family fighting for their lives behind her and the house that had become smoldering wreckage, probably holding two of my brothers dead inside.

I wasn't expecting the claws that grabbed onto my hindquarters and pulled me down.

23

CHAPTER TWENTY-THREE

I rolled and kicked up with my back legs, able to shake the new attacker off. My nose was unable to smell who it was thanks to the overriding smoke, but I knew the werecat. I had seen Lani's feline form before.

With a roar, I swiped up with my front paw, rejuvenated. Fiora had brought me back to the woods for Lani to attack me. This was a special revenge just for me, and with the explosion, they could get away with it. Two of my family had been in the house when it exploded, and Zuri and Jabari were probably both severely injured.

They could get away with making sure I died because they had tipped the scales in their favor.

I tried to roll and screamed as claws ripped at my side. Fiora tried to lie on me, to hold me down so Lani could tear me open. I bit into the closest flesh I could, listening to Fiora scream over me and try to pull away. I let her momentum help me to my feet and shoved her down, keeping my fangs buried in her.

Lani rammed me, and I released Fiora before the force of the hit pulled my fangs out of my mouth. She swiped at my head, but I reared up to meet her in a classic feline move. We tried to hit each other, our large feet slamming whatever we could hit. I hit her once, claws out, and knew I raked open her cheek when Fiora rejoined the fight.

The air was knocked out of me as she pushed me down, her head going into my vulnerable gut. I brought my back legs up again and kicked, hitting her.

Now, the air smelled of blood and smoke—everyone's blood. There were so many scents that telling the difference- especially as I got on my feet and sized up my two opponents- was impossible.

I was limping now, unsure which injury caused that, but I was pleased to see Fiora was favoring her right front leg, and Lani had blood covering half of her face. They separated and prowled around me in opposite circles, keeping me close between them.

I tried to turn to keep an eye on either of them, but every time my back was exposed to one, she took a swipe. I hissed as the backs of my legs were torn up, and I couldn't protect them, not from both of the females. The limp grew more pronounced.

"Is this what werecats do now?" I asked, knowing they couldn't answer. *"We toy with our prey and fight unfairly? Do you think that your cause justifies this? How do you think other werecats will feel when they learn you*

took down Hasan and this family with cheap tricks and human technology?"

I needed to bait them into breaking their fucking torture circle. I needed one of them to present an opening I could exploit. When getting at them that way didn't get the reaction I wanted, I decided to get mean.

"You're both just Mikkel's whores, doing his fucking bidding, but let me tell you, girls, he's not all that if he has you doing this. Hasan would never ask anyone to do something so dishonorable because he was jealous of someone else's power. Mikkel is an impotent, disgraceful mess, and you both choose dick over honor and respect."

I didn't know which of them would be more offended, not really understanding who cared more about Mikkel. Lani roared and jumped for me.

She met me where I was, and we clashed again, fur and blood flying as our claws tore into each other. Fiora came up behind me and grabbed the scruff of my neck, her saber teeth puncturing through, and yanked me away, putting me in an awkward position. I pushed back, remembering how I knocked both wolves and vampires off my back and rolled onto her, knowing my weight would cause her problems. She let go, probably because my weight would have knocked the air out of her, but was able to get me with the same classic back-leg kick I had used.

I nailed a strong hit to Lani's face, batting her away before turning back to Fiora. I lifted up and dropped both of my front paws on her chest to hold her down, claws deep into her ribs, scratching her bones. Before Lani could recovered, I sank my fangs into Fiora's neck, puncturing her windpipe and jugular. Blood flooded my mouth, pouring out onto the soil.

Lani roared and attacked me again. This time, I didn't release Fiora. I tore out the precious body parts as I faced Lani. When Lani slammed into me, I was ready, feeling victorious already. With one dead, the other was much easier.

A roar echoed from the rest of the fighting. I heard bone crunching, and Lani jumped away, her head turning. I didn't get distracted, rushing her. She dodged, still much healthier. She looked at Fiora's body, then at me.

"We're finishing this," I snapped at her.

Another roar made me want to look, but I didn't take my eyes off her. A feline scream made my heart ache. I didn't know who was winning or losing out there.

But Lani had a view over my head and must not have liked what she saw.

She turned, without giving me another look, and ran.

I took two steps, then stopped again, listening to the fighting behind me. Lani was running for her life. That told me she was one, a coward, and two, losing, at least in her view of things.

I turned and ran back for my family. Jabari stood over a dead body, tearing it up. Zuri was on the ground, but I could see her chest rising and falling, a large piece of metal, like rebar, sticking out of her ribs.

Jabari didn't look up at me, lost in his rage as he yanked a back leg off the dead body underneath him.

I turned, trying to see what I could do. Davor, a blond-looking werecat, was being pressed hard by his opponent, and while I hated Lani and Fiora, their double team tactic worked, so I ran for my brother.

"Davor, fake him out," I ordered, running at full speed. My body screamed in protest, but adrenaline was able to keep the pain dull enough for me to focus.

Davor didn't miss a beat, pretending to limp and misstep. The other werecat took his chance, lunging for my brother. I leapt and hit the side of the enemy, sending both of us rolling in the dirt. It felt like two trucks in a head on collision, but I didn't let that bother me. I clawed at the other werecat as Davor ran for us. The enemy werecat kicked me off and snapped at me.

Davor rushed in and was able to get a holding bite onto the werecat's front leg and shook hard enough to break it. I grabbed one of his back legs and did the same, listening to the screeching scream of pain, more of a distressed yowl. It made my ringing ears worse, but I didn't care. I continued to pull the leg into an unnatural position, so I could dodge the working leg.

"Hold him. I'm about to yank this fucking thing off."

He pulled the front leg in the opposite direction, and together, we maimed the werecat between us. I wasn't able to completely remove the back leg, but it was fucked up. Davor was able to tear off the front, and bleeding out, the werecat died before Davor grabbed the back of his neck and shook it hard enough to break it.

As we finished, a satisfied roar filled the air, and I turned to see Mischa standing over a burned body, her silver and white coat covered in blood. She roared a second time, proud of her kill.

With her safe, that only left one fight—one duel that could decide everything.

I saw them from where I was, two massive werecats brutally beating on each other. Mikkel was a similar size to Hasan and Jabari, proving he was old and strong, living long enough to achieve such a great size. He was also an experienced fighter.

Unlike the messy way I had fought against Fiora and Lani, Mikkel was purposeful, and so was my father. They were obviously choosing their attacks carefully, refusing to leave openings to the other. I started walking toward them, but Davor blocked my way, shaking his big head. I growled.

"Move. We can end this now!"

He turned to the burning wreckage, and I understood.

He had faith that Hasan would win. We needed to try and get to Niko and Hisao. Hopefully, they were still alive.

Mischa must have seen us. When Davor and I reached the smoldering rubble, she was right there beside me. We dug furiously, trying to move big pieces and get into the shell of the structure. It didn't take long for Jabari to finally join in, helping me move a beam by crawling underneath it and lifting with his back. I got under him and moved further into the home. When I found no way further, I backed out.

A roar was heard, and we all turned together. Mikkel

and Hasan were both bleeding, and Jabari walked away from us, his head high. I knew what was happening. Jabari would inherit it all if Hasan fell, and his first act of leadership would be to kill Mikkel before the other werecat could celebrate.

I was too distracted by the fight for a minute as my werecat father and Mikkel clashed one more time. That werecat had beaten me. He'd had his friends beat me. He had turned Lani against me, so no matter how hard I worked to do better, it didn't matter.

Davor gently pushed me aside to keep working in my spot.

I had no words of encouragement for Hasan. He would win. I had to believe he would win.

One good hit to Mikkel's jaw broke it, and Hasan dove for the last bite, ripping out the male's throat. When he roared in victory, we joined him, not caring if it brought human attention. Not caring if it was a bad time. Victory was had.

For the most part. Turning back to the smoldering rubble, I knew we still had to find Hisao and Niko.

And in the back of my mind, I knew my fight wasn't over. Lani had run, and this wasn't going to be over until I felt her die between my teeth.

Hasan and Jabari joined us in the digging. We sniffed and hoped to find evidence that either of them had survived. It was hoping against the odds. The blast had been huge, and the fire afterward probably fatal, but I tried to believe.

There was nothing else anyone could do except

believe. Mischa stepped back and Changed back to her human form to begin directing us.

"Jabari! Is Zuri stable?" she asked first.

He looked back and nodded his head. I turned to see Zuri still slowly breathing, the metal still deep in her chest. By my best guess, it had punctured a lung, but if she didn't move and no one removed it, we had a chance to save her. It worried me that we couldn't do anything for her and try to find Niko and Hisao at the same time.

"I can help her," I said to everyone. *"Make sure she remains stable."*

"Do it," Mischa snapped. "Now."

I left the rubble and went to my oldest sister, Changing back. She lifted her head, which was a good sign.

"The explosion did this to you?" I asked, knowing it was probably a yes.

Her big head nodded, and I saw her body convulse from the pain of the movement.

Open pneumothorax caused by the rebar. Depth unknown. Bleeding slow. Patient, supernatural. Healing factor, moderate. If that rebar is moved at all, she'll suffer possible catastrophic damage. No sign of fluids in her lungs yet.

It had been a long time since I entered EMT mode, assessing my sister.

"Can you feel all your toes?" I needed to know if she had broken her spine. "Blink once for yes, twice for no. Don't move again."

She blinked once. I sighed in relief and began to feel

her side. Her breathing was a little shallow, but her pulse was still strong.

"Did you know not to move?"

She blinked once.

She was a damn good patient, especially since she'd had to lie here while everyone was fighting.

"We're going to have to call for a medevac," I called out. "There's no way we're moving her in this form with the bar in her, and we can't take it out."

"Keep her safe, then," Mischa answered. "We still have the packs. We can call for help. That's not a problem."

I nodded. Everyone else was still in the rubble of the house. I was losing hope for Niko and Hisao, but Zuri was my patient, and I had to stay with her. She was vulnerable, and who knew what could happen at this point. Lani was still out there, and Zuri was an easy target.

Someone roared in the house. Mischa looked over to me.

"Never mind. Get in there. They might need you."

I didn't pause to think about the debris, the smoldering pieces of the building, or my bare feet and bleeding injuries. Everything done to me was superficial in comparison to Zuri, and I could suffer through them. Suffering through things was something I was getting surprisingly good at.

I climbed down into a hole my family had made, Hasan waiting at the bottom, positioning himself so I landed on his back.

"Thanks," I said, coughing as the smoke in the basement filled my lungs. It was awful. Waving it out of my face, I tried to focus and see through it.

"Oh fuck," I gasped. "MISCHA! CALL FOR HELP! NOW!"

24

CHAPTER TWENTY-FOUR

I ran for the cell and tried to get through the bent, mangled door. Hisao's eyes opened, and he growled. That kept me from looking at Niko. Hisao would need to move before I could help Niko, anyway.

"It's me," I snapped. "Let me see."

He tried to stand but groaned, falling back down. His front leg was broken. From what, I couldn't tell, but I could reasonably guess Jabari and Hasan had already moved it.

"Blink once for yes, twice for no. Are you bleeding?"

He blinked twice.

"Can you feel your back legs and toes?"

He blinked once.

"Do you think you can try to stand and move away for me? Limp if you have to. I need to see Niko, Hisao." I needed to see if what I thought I saw was real, but I needed the massive, dark cat out of my way.

Jabari came forward and gently grabbed the back of

Hisao's neck without giving him a chance to answer. Ever so slowly, he helped Hisao up onto three legs and began to walk as far away as they could get.

I put a hand over my mouth, blood and smoke making me want to choke and gag.

Hasan growled behind me.

Niko was pinned down by a large beam. His back was broken. The only reason I knew he was somehow still alive was the very slow and low rise and fall of his chest.

Plus, death had a distinct smell.

"Niko..." I whispered. "We're going to get you out... Hasan...Can we fix this? Can we..." I fell apart. I should have been solid and steady, the one trained in these sorts of situations, but he was a brother I liked, and there was Dirk to think about.

I should have been grateful they were alive, but I was heartbroken by the sight. I walked closer carefully, wincing as I stepped on hot pieces of metal and wood. Splinters entered my feet, but I wanted to get next to him.

I gently touched his forehead. He was unconscious. Hisao might have somehow stayed awake even through the smoke, but Niko had no idea we were there.

Bones cracking behind me, along with a pained grunt, made me turn. Hisao was Changing back into his human form. When he was done, I stared at him incredulously.

"What the hell are you doing? You know that sped up the healing in your arm, right? It's definitely going to need rebreaking now!" I wanted to strangle him.

"It's fine," he said with another grunt of pain. "How's Niko?"

"You don't—"

"Answer me," he demanded. I looked around him.

"Get him out of here," I ordered. "Now. I don't need him breathing down my neck." When he tried to interrupt, I changed my tactic. "Plus, you can help Mischa watch Zuri."

"What happened to Zuri?"

"Rebar, punctured lung. It has to remain in, but someone should be monitoring her. Mischa needs to call for help if she hasn't already. Now. If she can't get anyone, have her call Heath."

"Why the wolf?"

"He might be able to use some of his contacts with the Dallas pack he used to be the Alpha of. We need helicopters or something, and they need to already be on their way. Now go! I'll stay with Niko. You've been down here long enough; I'm worried about lung damage."

He stepped back and nodded. Jabari moved toward him, and Hisao carefully climbed on, favoring his right arm, which was bent in the middle.

Fucking idiot just wanted to fucking talk, and now, his arm is going to be fucked up, goddamn it.

Hasan didn't leave, coming up close behind me to sniff his youngest son.

"He's alive," I whispered. "Hasan..."

A large chin touched my shoulder.

"His back is broken," I finished.

I had never heard Hasan whimper. He didn't for this,

even if I did as I finished the words. He stayed solid as we watched Niko breathe. With Jabari and Hisao gone and knowing there was nothing I could do for Niko yet, I looked around the basement. The cell bars were holding up a large portion of the wall, and though they had bent, they didn't collapse. That was probably what saved them in the end. They must have been in the basement already, looking at where I had been kept, starved, beaten, and nearly tortured. I saw other, small timbers that had come down from the building above. One must have hit Hisao and broken the leg, but he had been closer to the bars and more protected. Niko hadn't been so lucky. The beam wasn't crushing him, but it was holding him down and had probably hit his back, causing the break.

"We can fix that, right?" I asked softly.

Hasan nodded slowly.

That was good. It calmed me a little. I had no idea how we were going to get Niko out, but if we could fix him, make him better, it would be worth it, whatever we had to do.

"Medical teams are on their way!" Mischa yelled. "Zuri is still stable!"

"Thank you!" I kept my eyes on Niko, sad the yelling didn't wake him. I touched his cheek, feeling his coat and pulling bits of debris from it.

It felt like forever, but his breathing changed, and I knew he was going to wake up. There was fresher air in the basement as the smoke rose up and made it out. There was too much dust in the air, but that was okay.

"Hey, Niko," I said gently. "Don't move. You've been injured, and help is on the way."

His eyes opened slowly, and saw me, then saw Hasan behind me.

"We won," I told him. "We just need to get out of here now."

And once we were out, I was going to hunt down that bitch, Lani, and make her pay for all of this. She was the last, and I wasn't going to let her hide for long.

Both must have smelled my anger. Hasan stepped away and looked down, almost as if he was protecting Niko from me.

"Lani got away," I explained. "Once everyone here is safe and healing, I'm going after her. I won't let her get away with any of this. Maybe if it was just me, but not this."

He nodded and stepped out of my way again.

When help finally arrived, Niko was sleeping again. The damage done to him was too much for him to try to fight the pain to stay awake. It only took ten minutes of comforting him to get him to close his eyes again.

The help came in the form of a helicopter at first.

"Take Zuri!" I yelled up. "Take her!"

When the helicopter left, Mischa's face appeared in the giant hole above us.

"They took Zuri, Jabari, and Hisao," she called down. "An ambulance is on the way for Niko. The rest of us need to get back to our vehicles on our own. Hasan, they're going to take them to the airport in Dallas, then fly them to Minnesota."

I had no idea what was in Minnesota, but I was guessing a hospital. It seemed far, though. Too far to make me comfortable, but then, I had no idea who 'they' were and why we were trusting them with our family. Those were questions I intended asking later.

When the ambulance came, Mischa called down again to tell us we needed to get out of the way. I climbed onto Hasan's back and let him carry me up, instead of Changing.

When we were topside again, I didn't blush or try to hide my nudity from the humans. They looked at me and the rest of the group with wide eyes.

"He's in werecat form. Are you strong enough to carry him?"

"They aren't, but we are," a man said, coming out of a second car. I didn't catch a scent, but I knew a vampire when I saw one now. I snarled, and he lifted his hands. "We're employees of Isaiah, the male vampire of the Tribunal—"

I snarled louder, and Hasan stepped in my way. Mischa grabbed my shoulder and pulled me aside.

"They're here to help," she snapped. "Do not attack the help. They're strong enough to get Niko out and help the humans. We need them, and it was a big fucking favor to call in to get supernatural-sensitive help. Isaiah even offered his plane, so we can take ours to follow. Don't ruin this."

I fell silent and watched intently as the two vampires jumped down first, two humans following with a stretcher designed for the safety of obese patients.

Hasan Changed back to his human form next to me, and Davor walked to Mischa's other side. We were the last of the family left, waiting for Niko to come out and get to the hospital.

"What's in Minnesota?" I asked as I heard them talking in the basement about the beam and how best to free Niko.

"One of the best hospitals for supernaturals, Mygi Hospital. Most of their staff are briefed on our kind and heavily watched to make sure they don't leak anything. A lot of the staff are supernatural as well and experts in healing our kind. It's attached to a supernatural pharmaceutical company. The pharmaceutical company has had a lot of very troubling problems recently, but the hospital remains the best place for Niko."

"That's good. I didn't know we had a supernatural drug company." I was trying to distract myself as Niko's cry of pain made tears well up in my eyes.

"It's..." Hasan sighed. "Tribunal business. If you ever wonder what gives me more headaches than you, my children, it's the Tribunal and the other supernaturals I have to keep an eye on." He put a hand on my shoulder. "Aside from that, it's the hospital I would have sent you and Jabari to after the vampires in Washington. I trust it more than any other place on Earth when it comes to healing. Everyone there is very dedicated and has magics no other hospital has access to since they've pooled it all into one place."

"Will everyone be safe?" I couldn't bring myself to

trust anything. If I had learned anything over the last month, it was that paranoia was a close friend.

"Politics are left at the door," he said gently. "That's enforced by the Tribunal."

"Good."

Another cry of pain and I was forced to turn away. Mischa wrapped an arm around me.

"I thought you used to be an EMT," she teased gently.

"You didn't see him," I whispered. That made her wince.

I was able to collect myself and turn back to see them bring him above ground. We all huddled around the stretcher for a moment until one of the vampires held up a hand, indicating we needed to back off so they could load him.

"We should go," Hasan said as the ambulance began to move.

Together, we Changed and started the long run back to our vehicles. The next time we planned to see any of our family would be in Minnesota at the Mygi Hospital.

I already knew how I was going to spend the trip.

Plotting how to find and kill Lani.

CHAPTER TWENTY-FIVE

The trip to the airport was a blur. The flight to Minnesota was a weird mix of restless napping we all needed and eating to keep our energy up. I was the worst of the group who didn't get taken. The bruises from the beating were fading well, and my muscles didn't scream, but there was still the terrible toll my body had taken over the last eight days. Mischa sat next to me on the spacious plane, curling an arm around me, Davor on my other side. Strange, since he and I didn't like each other, but it helped me feel a little safer, and I figured that was the point.

When the plane landed, we practically ran to get into the cars waiting for us, and the trip to the hospital was at illegal speeds.

"How are we not getting pulled over?" I asked.

"You need more exposure to the supernatural world at large," Davor said, shaking his head. "Fae spelled vehicle. Called a Look Away spell or something. It keeps humans from looking too closely at something and makes them forget about what they might have seen. It keeps human cops from taking much interest in us. I take it you don't have any fae you know outside your territory to get it done on your vehicles?"

"Nope," I said. "Only the one who..." I tapped my head. "And that was enough fae for me for a lifetime."

"Well, thank the gods you're going to live longer than a lifetime," he said, giving me a look. "Meet some friends, get some better work done. You have enough money. If Hasan let you leave his home, you're probably incredibly wealthy, and you live like you aren't, so you probably still have most of it. Use some of it and get with the times."

I sighed. "Back to the asshole."

"Sorry," he muttered, looking away. "It's just...the supernatural world has a lot to offer, and you just ignore it all. You ignore a lot of things. I know Hasan probably taught you much of this, but you seem like you've forgotten it."

"I mean, probably," I said, admitting I didn't retain nearly enough of what he taught me. I kept a lot of the important stuff, like anything having to do with werecats, but I never wanted to dive into the deep end of the supernatural world, so there were a lot of little things I didn't keep. That had been proven in Washington when I forgot the all-important detail that vampires don't have scents and are hard to feel in a werecat territory. I should have started brushing up on my knowledge after that.

"Do you practice the runes?" he asked.

"Sometimes." *Not enough.*

"At least there's that," he said, shaking his head again.

"Can you stop? I'm worried about Niko, and I don't need this from you. This might all be over for you, but it's not for me."

He looked back at me, frowning.

"What?"

"Lani got away," I snapped. "That...bitch ran off when Jabari killed another one of them, after I killed Fiora. She realized they were losing and ran like a fucking coward. Once I know Niko is okay, I'm going after her and fucking ending this. I don't need you..."

He reached out and grabbed the hand I was waving at him.

"I'm sorry," he said more genuinely. "If you need it, I'll go. Or any one of us. We'll do it. I know she used to be your friend, and that's not going to be easy."

The unexpectedness of the offer caught me off guard. I gently pulled my hand away.

"I'll handle it," I promised. "But, thanks."

"You'll need to pick one of us to go with you, anyway. Hasan will probably make sure of it. You're younger than her, so having backup in case you fall is mandatory."

"Thanks for the heads up. I'll decide who to take after we see everyone together again."

"Okay. And Jacky, we don't like each other, but I am your older brother. I'm going to give you a hard time because it's how I'm built, but that doesn't mean you can't rely on me for help with these kinds of situations. This is our family, and if one of us falls, we all fall. I was alongside everyone else, prepared to reveal werecats to the world to save you from a Tribunal Execution."

"That means a lot," I said, trying to smile. I had never really thought of him waiting to do that on Hasan's order. Most of the rest, sure, but it really had been all of them.

"You shoving me made me realize I might not have ever made that clear to you," he said, rubbing his hands together like he was getting antsy.

We pulled up in front of the hospital, killing the conversation. We jumped out, seeing Hasan and Mischa in the car in front of us, then walked in together. A human saw us and waved us to follow.

"Good morning, Hasan. We've secured a private room for all of your children once they're done with their procedures." She smiled at all of us, her face getting slightly confused at the sight of me. Before she had the chance to say anything to me, Hasan gestured for her to walk.

"Lead the way," he ordered. "How is everyone? They got here before us if I was told the correct information."

"Madam Zuri's injuries were easy to address once we could secure her and remove the rebar. We simply patched her once it was removed and laid her down to rest. She's already on the mend and in the private suite. Mister Hisao is still undergoing his procedure. We're trying to figure out the right dosage to put him under to rebreak the arm, but it shouldn't be much longer before we wheel him into the room as well."

"And Niko?" I asked. "He..."

"He's currently under heavy sedation, and our best

experts are working on him to realign his spine," she answered kindly. "We've also got our best witch healers and fae healers there to encourage the regrowth of his spinal cord. His doctors and healers will have more information once the procedure is complete."

A hand grabbed my shoulder and squeezed. I looked up as we walked to see Hasan holding me.

"He won't walk out of this hospital," he explained to me. "But he will walk again and much faster than any human would. Dirk has been working for you, and I would like that to continue, because I want Niko to stay with me at home when they discharge him. Dirk can't go home to Germany."

"He can stay with me." I wasn't going to ship the young man around the world. He knew me, and that would be easier than giving him to another one of the strange members of the family.

"We also need to talk before you hunt Lani down. I made you a promise."

I stumbled and looked up at him as he grabbed my elbow.

"I'd forgotten our deal," I said, swallowing. "Where...When..."

"The rooms here are soundproof, and I feel comfortable using them to talk," he said gently. I nodded slowly in response.

We followed the nurse, Mischa and Davor quiet behind us.

She opened the door for us, then handed a key card to Hasan.

"We can have more made, sir, but we prefer to have fewer keys for high priority rooms, so if you must have other copies, please try for only maybe one or two more and send people out with them in pairs."

"Of course. One should be enough for now," he said, smiling at the nurse.

I could smell Zuri as I walked into the large private suite. It was more than big enough to fit everyone in the family, with three couches, space for the three hospital beds that would eventually dominate the space, and a large TV on the wall. There was even a door to a private bathroom. I opened it and looked inside to make sure.

"This is all soundproof?" I was too paranoid. Werecats had betrayed us, and Lani was still out there.

"Relax," Hasan said, grabbing my elbow again to pull me along. "Come see your sister."

I swallowed, not wanting to see her. She was hurt because I wasn't strong enough, wasn't fast enough. If I had gotten away that full moon, none of this would have happened the way it did. But Hasan pulled me to her anyway, and we stood quietly, watching her breathing. She was tucked under sheets that exposed her outline, but she was in human form now.

"I'll need to ask them when she Changed," my father said, leaning down to brush his fingers against her cheek. "Mischa, go find Jabari and ask him why he isn't with his twin."

"Yes, sir." She left the room as quickly as we had entered.

"Davor, watch the door to help Jacqueline feel at

ease. We might as well get this conversation out of the way."

Davor gave one jerky nod and left as well.

I stepped back from him as he moved to sit down on one of the luxurious couches. Alone with him, with answers right in front of me, I found myself put on the spot and unable to speak. I wanted to get Lani. This could wait.

Right?

"Ask your questions, Jacqueline."

"You let Shane die," I said, swallowing. "Why?"

"Because I knew he would never survive the Change, and he was too far gone to save in his human life, just like you. You could survive, so I made the choice."

I could smell the truth, no hint of a lie, but the problem with that statement was he believed he was telling the truth. There was no possible way he actually knew. He just decided not to risk it.

"How? How could you have possibly known Shane wouldn't live through it?"

"I'm Talented," he said softly. "Sit down. While the walls are soundproof, I don't want to test that by turning this into a screaming match."

I understood his reasoning, so I sat. He had sat in the middle, making it impossible to get any distance from him, but sitting on a different couch wouldn't have fixed the problem.

"Some werecats, mostly very old ones, have what we call Talents, small abilities that are unique. Our family, as old and as powerful as we are, only has two, mine and Zuri's. Well, Zuri inherited hers from my mate."

"I heard Jabari talking to you about this before. You think Heath's self-control, his ability to cover his emotional scents might be a Talent."

"Having now lived in his house for a few days, I'm certain of it, but since wolves have short life spans, they probably lost the knowledge of it. It doesn't really matter. He has a useful skill. Most Talents are very useful. Mine is...more dangerous, however, and I've grown used to hiding it. Only my mate and my children know of it, with the exception of you."

"Why?"

"You'll understand once I tell you what it is," he explained. "Jacqueline, I can...smell out how likely someone is to survive. Before you jump in and say anything, understand that modern technology is catching up to what I can do, and my need for secrecy might become obsolete, but I'm an old werecat and can be stuck in my ways."

My hands started to shake.

He can what?

"Keep...keep going," I ordered.

"Take you and Shane. When I met you, you were a bright couple looking to learn how to ride horses. You were trying to have children. You were fighting against the way things were done by having your honeymoon two weeks before your wedding. You wanted it to be a small wedding, didn't you?"

"Yes," I answered softly.

"I remember you talking about it. I thought it was charming." He sighed. "You always had this look about you, though, that you were meant for other things. Like that life was the one you were settling for, and you would be happy, but you craved something else."

"Don't presume to know—"

"Don't lie to me," he said softly. "When I Changed you into a werecat, you had four glorious years where you were thinking of reaching for those goals."

"At the cost of Shane," I snapped. "And you know it. Now tell me...*everything.*"

"I can smell what science is trying to tell humanity now. The likelihood of someone surviving the Change. Sometimes, the answer is a clear yes, sometimes, it's a clear no. Sometimes, you can flip a coin. If I taste their blood, the answer becomes clearer. Sometimes, very rarely, I can be wrong. It's not perfect. No is always no, but yes...is not always right."

"What..."

"I have raised more children than I have werecat children. I love children. It's one of the things you and I have in common. We bond well with the youth. We like being parental."

"Yeah..." I never really considered that. I loved having Carey in my life. I loved...the idea of her, the friendship, and those precious moments where I could almost be the mom I always wanted to be, and I loved how she loved me. I never really thought Hasan looked at the world the same way. That he cherished being a father, guiding someone and being there for them. Seeing the world from a new perspective and listening to charming stories about homework and playing with friends.

"I had two sons, both human, who did not survive the Change. One of them should have been a clear yes. One of them was a coin toss." He looked away from me. "And yet...they didn't survive. I believe I can smell the genetic markers that make someone more or less likely to live through it, but each person must also have something unidentifiable, something...*more* to survive. Over the centuries, I have tried to find what that something more was. A will. A need. A purpose. Maybe even a touch of magic."

"Me?"

"You...you felt right. Your scent made it very clear to me the likelihood you would survive was strong. Probably the highest likelihood I smell in people. You also had... something. I saw it when we met. I saw it every time I saw you staring at the ocean, your eyes filled with wonder and exploration, and a need to see it all. You had something. I wanted you as a daughter. I thought 'yes, she would do well with Zuri and Mischa' and 'Jabari would get a kick out of her.' You seemed to fit like a puzzle piece, and I couldn't deny that."

"And Shane?"

"He had nothing," Hasan said with a gentleness I knew well. It was the same gentleness he'd used to explain to me the car accident and that Shane was dead. "And if I had tried, I knew for certain I was going to doom him to an excruciatingly painful death."

"Why didn't you tell me sooner? About why you...left him to die..." Hasan truly believed he saved Shane from more suffering, truly believed he'd made the right decision, even if it broke my heart in half. "I might have...understood..."

"Imagine what a Talent like mine could do in this world, Jacqueline. Imagine what would happen if... Mikkel knew I could do it. That they could bring their human children to me, and I could tell them if their child would live or not."

"That's not a bad thing," I growled softly.

"Imagine if the werewolves found out, then," he said, his voice growing hard. "Silver is just as effective on me as it is on you or any werecat or werewolf. Imagine the danger I put myself in, letting the world know before science started to figure this out for them, that I could save their humans...or make them an army."

I sucked in a breath, my eyes going wide. I understood.

He was protecting himself. For hundreds of years, thousands of years, he protected his Talent, kept it from the public, to keep anyone from capturing him and using him.

But something else bugged me.

"Hasan...you said you could see me in the family before the car accident...did you..."

"No. No..." He groaned and leaned over, rubbing his face. When he sat back up, he turned to me and grabbed my shoulders. "I didn't cause the accident. I followed you and him around my territory because I was interested in your lives, making sure everything about your vacation was perfect. But that storm was a big one, and I can't control the weather. I wish someone had told you two to stay off the road, but I made it a point to never interfere in the lives of humans on my island, especially ones who didn't work for me. You were not the first, and you won't be the last adult human I meet who I wished I had met sooner. I have met many, many people in my years. You were only the first I had a chance to save and bring in, though."

As the realization settled, as his truths were told, I began to think in other directions. My mind turned with the implications of his ability. Science was still a long way off from being perfect. They were trying desperately to identify every gene that might make someone more or less likely to Change, but they were still failing at an alarming rate. Hasan didn't fail nearly so often.

"And this is why I waited over a decade to tell you," he whispered. "Never ask me because I don't want to hurt you by refusing to answer."

"What?"

"My children must decide on their own with their children if they wish to attempt the Change. I will not interfere. I will not tell you if your human family would survive. I will not tell you if Carey could or not. I will never tell you any of it."

My eyes went wide. How had he known? Had my siblings tried before and failed to get that information?

"You don't want..."

"I made that rule because not everyone is meant to be

a werecat. There's a violence in our world that needs someone with a strong spirit, or it will eat them alive."

"Liza..."

He sighed. I could almost hear his thoughts, but I certainly wasn't going to ask him to voice them, and if he chose not to, that was okay.

"So...the car accident happened, and you knew I would live, and Shane wouldn't. Even if you had Changed him, he wouldn't have survived."

"I kept trying to tell you it was because he was too far gone, but..."

"But if he could survive the Change, he would have lived through his injuries. Our curse would have healed him if he could accept it, but he couldn't, so he had to live human or not at all," I finished for him, understanding why he felt terrible. He'd kept his Talent a secret from me, the key piece of information I was missing.

"You're very smart," he said softly. "And now, you know the entire truth."

"You could make an army," I whispered.

"Daughter," he murmured, running a hand over my head. "I already have."

Jabari, Zuri, Mischa, Hisao, Davor, Niko...and me.

That sent shivers down my spine.

26

CHAPTER TWENTY-SIX

Davor and Mischa still weren't back twenty minutes later, and Zuri wasn't awake. We had no word on Niko or Hisao, either.

"You can ask me anything," he finally said. "We're going to be here for a while."

"I need to get to Lani..."

"You'll wait for word on your siblings," he said sternly.

"Who Changed you?" I asked, purely curious, and since I was stuck, he was right, I had the chance to know everything.

"The first werecat," he answered. "But that's all I'm saying about it and said werecat."

I moved away from him, eyes wide again.

What a troubling thought. He was made by the first werecat, and he'd made an army of loyal children. Terrifying.

"Three wars," I whispered.

"I'm not talking about the early days," he said stiffly. "They were a very long time ago."

"Okay."

"Anything else?"

"Where's your mate?"

"Your mother lives in Africa, though I couldn't tell you exactly where. She left that information with Jabari and Zuri."

"She's not my mother," I said, narrowing my eyes. "Right?"

"If you meet her and say that to her, know that I loved you, and you will be missed," he said softly.

"You're not joking, are you?"

"No," he said, a small smile forming. "It was a promise she and I made centuries ago. My children are her children. Always and forever, even if she never wants to come out and meet any of you. She vowed to never Change anyone."

"And she's just...hanging out somewhere in Africa?"

"Yes. The modern world never appealed to her, and she thought Rome was too modern for her," he said, that small smile never leaving.

"Do you ever see her?" Felt pretty weird to know Hasan had a mate who was alive but never left her bubble.

"She visits me," he said softly. "You heard all about Gaia and Titan. Mating and love are strange things for a species who only wants to be alone. We come to compromises and understand that forever doesn't mean right next to each other."

"Yeah..." I could accept that. "How would you tell her about Zuri?"

"I actually think that's where Jabari has wandered off to. To send her word one of her twins was hurt. She'll come give me an earful about it. It might take a decade, but it'll come back to haunt me." He sighed, seemingly resigned and a little happy about it. It was clear in his eyes. He still loved her with every piece of his soul, and he would take his lumps for getting the children he shared with his mate hurt. He would take them gladly.

Perversely, I decided to ask more about this strange relationship. Anything to keep my mind off being stuck in the hospital when I wanted to hunt down my prey.

"When was the last time she gave you an earful?"

"Liza." That wiped away the joy. "You're feeling nosy," he commented.

"You said ask anything, and I know nothing about her. Shit, you haven't even told me her name. Isn't the remaining seat on the Tribunal hers?"

"Her name is Subira, and yes, it is, but she can never claim it. That's a story for another time."

"Subira," I whispered to myself, a pretty name.

"Be careful. If you say it three times, she'll appear."

"Don't try to be funny," I said, leaning back on the couch to get more comfortable as he chuckled.

It was another thirty minutes before Jabari and Mischa walked back in, Davor following them.

"How was the talk?" Jabari asked. "Mischa told me."

"Good. Learned new, interesting things," I said blandly. I didn't want to make a big deal of it. It settled something between Hasan and me, and that was enough. "Any word on Niko or Hisao while you were out there?"

"Hisao is almost done; he just needs to wake up. They don't want to move him because they know who and what he is. Niko might take a few more hours," Mischa answered, sitting on Hasan's other side. "Jabari called Mother."

"I figured," Hasan said with a sigh.

"She's going to yell at you. Between everything Jacky has been through, my injuries in Washington, Zuri, Niko, and Hisao here, she's not happy." Jabari looked at our father with a raised eyebrow. "She thinks you're willfully putting us in danger."

"Did you tell her Jacky is much more of a handful than the rest of you?" Hasan asked with a yawn. I gasped as Mischa snorted in laughter.

"No."

"Then you are mean, and you don't love me," Hasan declared. "What have I done to you, my oldest son?"

"Nothing, I'm just mean, and I don't love you," Jabari replied with a small smile of his own.

They were joking, and I was boiling with anger.

Mischa fell asleep, leaning on Hasan. I got up for Jabari to sit down and began to pace, and continued to pace as they all fell asleep, waiting on news. All except Hasan.

It was interesting to see him with my siblings like this. It felt like they were all children again. Maybe because I had never been his child, never raised by him like the others were, it struck me as strange.

Finally, someone knocked on the door.

I pulled it open before anyone else could even stand and saw a nurse who didn't smell human.

"Hisao is awake again, and we're allowing him to walk here. He needs to wear his cast for one week."

"Yeah, we'll make sure he does that," I promised. I looked over her shoulder to see my terrifying brother coming down the hall, a cast wrapped in black adorning his broken arm. When he was inside, I grabbed the nurse before she could leave.

"What about Niko?"

"Another couple of hours," she said, looking down at my arm. "Watch yourself, cat." Her eyes flashed a vivid green, a warning. I let go of her, backing up into the suite and closing the door before anything else could happen.

"Get this thing off me," Hisao snarled at someone behind me.

"I heard the nurse. One week," Hasan snapped. "Sit down, and don't wake Zuri."

"Too late," my eldest sister said airily. Her head rolled, and she smiled at the majority of the family sitting on the couch. Then she sniffed the air and rolled her head to see me, seeming surprised. "I thought you wouldn't be here?"

"Why?"

"Lani is still out there. I heard you talking about it before the helicopter came. I thought you would go after her once we were all safe."

"I made her come," Hasan said. "The moment all of you are in this room, and things are looking up, I'll let her pick one of you as backup, then the hunt for Lani can continue."

"Good," Zuri said, pushing herself to sit up. When Jabari growled, rushing to her, Zuri snarled viciously. I raised an eyebrow as Jabari halted a foot from the bed and out of his twin's reach. "We need to crush all of them. If one escapes, they might as well have won."

"I'll handle it," I said stiffly. "She's mine." *Because I should have seen it coming. I shouldn't have been so naïve to think she was my friend.*

Zuri nodded slowly. "It's personal. Let me go with you."

"Sister," Jabari groaned. "You..."

"Lani could never defeat me, and I'll continue healing. They pumped a lot of magic in me. The wound is closed. Other than a little stiffness, I'm fine. But I think I'm the best choice to go with Jacky."

"Agreed," Hasan said, nodding.

"Cool. So, when Niko gets in here, we're going," I said sharply. Zuri arched an eyebrow at me, and all of her regality, her presence filled the room with that look. "Sorry. We'll leave when you're ready."

"Better," she said softly. She patted the bed next to her legs, keeping her stare on me. I walked over and sat. "Stay with me," she said softly, rubbing my back. "We'll finish this together."

Why do I have the distinct feeling she understands what I'm feeling?

As Niko was wheeled into the room, two long hours later, a phone began to go off.

"Damn it," Mischa snapped angrily, the ringing continuing as she searched through a large bag. My attention stayed on Niko, though, as the doctor began talking to Hasan. Mischa missed the calling, cursing silently at seeing a blocked number.

"He'll need physical therapy for a few months and no trauma to his back, so the fragile healing will become stronger. As you know, even the best of magics have a hard time with these sorts of injuries, but he got here as fast as you could bring him, which was a good thing. We gave him the best possible care, sir."

"I know," Hasan said, patting the doctor's shoulder. I looked down at Niko but didn't want to touch him. He was still in his werecat form, which was probably for the best. If he had Changed, who knew what healing his back would have been like.

We huddled around him, hoping he would wake soon. Zuri went back to sitting on her bed, staring intently at Niko just like me, with Jabari next to her.

We didn't get much of a moment, though, as a phone started going off across the room again. Mischa started cursing wildly, rummaging through the same bag to find the damn thing. I was barely listening when she answered, and the other person began talking. She said something loud for the room, but I didn't hear her.

"Jacky," Hasan snapped.

I shook myself out of whatever I was in and looked back at her.

"It's for me?"

Mischa looked at me with worry and anger, though hopefully, the latter wasn't my fault.

"There's a fire in your territory. Heath is there now."

"Where..." I needed more.

"Kick Shot. It extends behind your bar into the woods, but no one knows where it originated. Heath and his family are safe. They still have Oliver and Dirk with them. They were driving past when they saw the emergency crews there."

"I do," I said softly. Back to the task at hand, then. Lani was making a play. "That bitch set my bar on fire, and it might spread to my fucking house if it isn't already on fire," I growled. Lani knew how important Kick Shot was to me. More importantly, that meant Lani was in my territory. And so was Heath, probably taking everyone to his home. My chest tightened. My territory wasn't safe for him, Carey, or any of them. I had to get back.

"Hasan, I'm leaving."

"Zuri, are you ready to go? Do you think you can manage this? I know you got the best of care—"

"I'll be fine," Zuri hissed.

I started for the door as I put the pieces together.

"Lani didn't join the fight until Fiora backed me into the woods," I said, turning back to them. "Who wants to bet, she's the one who set off the explosive at that house that trapped Niko and Hisao and nearly killed Zuri?"

"She needed time to Change," Hisao said, nodding. "Kill her for us, would you?"

"On it," I growled. Zuri grabbed a bag from Mischa

and went into the bathroom. When she came out, she looked ready to go. "Do we have a ride?"

"Take our plane back to Dallas," Hasan ordered. "We'll wait here until this is settled."

Zuri grabbed the door and pulled it open.

"Let's go. It's time for you to learn how to serve and fulfill an execution in the name of Hasan." She walked past me and left the hospital to the surprised glances of the people around. I followed her out, focused on my goal. Before getting on the elevator, though, I heard something curious.

"She looks exactly like you. Really. You have to see her, it's crazy."

I turned, frowning. Something about it bothered me. Zuri stopped ahead of me.

"Jacky, let's go," she said. I turned away and started walking again when I couldn't find who was talking.

"There she is," that same voice whispered, now trying to be hushed.

They were definitely talking about me, but when I got onto the elevator, I put it in the back of my mind. Zuri and I wasted no time jumping into one of the loaned cars and getting back to the airport.

"This is an execution?" I asked as we parked by the plane.

"Yes. It would have been for Mikkel and the others as well, but they wanted all-out war, and they got it. Lani is taking her revenge. She knows she can't win this." She turned on me at the bottom of the stairs into the plane. "Where do you plan to begin the hunt?"

"Her territory," I answered. "But first, I want to make sure she isn't hanging around mine and a threat to Heath and his family. Or Oliver and Dirk."

"Good. She'll go home and try to hide. It gives her the best chance of winning the fight. If she runs, she knows we'll hunt her down."

"Zuri?"

"Yes?"

"Have you done this before?"

Zuri sighed, turning away.

"Yes."

She walked up the steps, and I had to hurry to keep up with her. There was a story there, but it was, like many other things, for another time.

The only thing I wanted to consider was my plan to hunt down and kill the only friend I'd had for six long, lonely years.

CHAPTER TWENTY-SEVEN

When we landed in Dallas, Tywin was waiting for us at the airport. I hadn't seen the werewolf Alpha in a long time, since before he was made Alpha of the Dallas pack. He stood with four other werewolves, his arms crossed, giving me a confused and worried look.

"We heard of a private plane jumping in and out of our airport. Then we heard Heath wasn't home, and when we sent wolves into your territory, it stank of other cats. Now, there's a fire at your bar. Would you like to explain why there seems to be a small war going on right outside my door, and why I was never informed of it?"

"Wow, what a way to greet someone who saved your fucking life," I said, snarling at the end. "Didn't tell you because it's not your business."

"Plus, the war is already over. We just need to clean up a loose end," Zuri added, shrugging nonchalantly. "Take it to the Tribunal. I'm sure our father will answer any questions your Tribunal Alphas will feel are necessary, wolf."

"Now you both wait a minute—"

Zuri and I started walking. I had a one-track mind and didn't have time to play politics with a wolf pack. Lani was running around destroying things, and Heath was still looking out for his daughter and two humans who belonged to my family. I was certain Landon would help him in a fight, but if Lani targeted them, there was a slim chance they would survive.

Tywin tried to grab my arm, and before anyone could react, I spun and wrapped a hand around his throat.

"I have been captured by my enemies, starved, beaten, and had to escape. I watched a building blow up and nearly kill not one but three of my siblings. I like you and your wolves, Tywin. Do not push me right now." I was normally easygoing and had no reason to dislike anyone there, even if Tywin's general Alpha attitude annoyed me. But he wasn't Heath. He didn't get to demand answers and expect anything from me.

And if I don't hurry, Heath could die. He could already be dead. I can't waste time on this.

The wolves around us had pulled weapons in that split second. Zuri stood at my back, ready to fight with me, even though not even twelve hours ago, she had been speared by rebar.

Tywin lifted his hands.

"I'll go through proper channels," he conceded. "Is everyone okay?"

"That's none of your business," I whispered. Not yet.

I was certain Zuri or Hasan would make some sort of public statement after this was all over, saying the family was attacked, and all of the resistance was quelled or something archaic like that. But not yet. Not while Niko was still in the hospital, and Lani was running around.

"Heath is a friend of mine," he said, not bothering to hide the growl.

"Sure," I hissed. "If he's your friend, why don't you fucking try calling him every now and then?"

I released him with a shove, wondering why I was suddenly offended for Heath and his lack of friends. He'd explained to me it was normal. I didn't understand why I was so angry.

"Jacky," Zuri said softly. "We need to go."

"I know." I turned on my heel and left with my sister, the wolves not bothering to follow us to the cars we had left at the airport earlier. Airports were semi-neutral territory, no matter who claimed ownership over the city and what species they were. Not everyone could skip them, especially if they needed to land and refuel. Unless you were an obvious enemy of whoever was in the city, passing through wasn't generally considered important. It was nice to give a nest or pack a heads up, but not required.

"You didn't have Heath let Tywin know you were traveling through Dallas?" I asked as we got into the car.

"We don't answer to a local wolf pack," she reminded me. "As you said to the vampires, we're the children of Hasan, a member of the Tribunal. We outrank them."

I shrugged one shoulder, accepting that answer.

Being part of the family, an active member, was changing me. I was beginning to truly understand what it meant. I wasn't sure I completely liked it, but I hoped at the end of it all, I would still just be Jacky.

Jacky Leon, living by myself, and away from all the problems until another one landed on my doorstep, requiring me to become Jacqueline, daughter of Hasan. I wasn't sure I liked her very much.

"I just wanted to be a bartender," I whispered as we drove toward my territory.

"And you will be again," Zuri said in a serene, patient tone. "I want to be a fashion designer. I want to run restaurants. I want to do many things with my time. This is temporary. Is that what's bothering you? This?"

"How I behave when things like this are going on," I answered, swallowing. "How I feel."

"It's not a bad thing to be ferocious and dangerous or to be bloodthirsty when those you love and care for are in danger. Or when you've been betrayed. And when it's all over, you will know peace again, and you can put away the beast that we are. Just as you did after you were called to Duty. Just as you did when you came back from Washington after helping Jabari with the vampires."

"I'm scared I won't be able to turn it off after this," I admitted. "How am I ever going to...trust anyone after this?"

"You make it clear that you'll kill anyone you can't. They'll find ways to make sure you know you can trust them after that. That's a hard reality, I know, but you'll turn it off, eventually, go back to your normal life, and everything will be okay."

"First, I need to kill Lani." There would be no peace until that happened. The need to tear something apart wouldn't go away until I finished this.

Zuri didn't respond for a moment, but when she did, I was surprised.

"I killed one of my own sons."

I had to keep myself from jerking the steering wheel. "What?"

"Niko and Father both told you their stories, parts of them, secrets this family keeps. That's mine. My son was trying to build himself an army of werecats to conquer humans and install himself as a king. It was my fault. I raised him as a prince. I told him he was special, and he believed that entitled him to things none of us were willing to give him. He tried to kill us because we wanted him to stop. It was all my fault. Jabari offered to finish it, a brother looking out for his sister. Hasan offered. Mischa offered. Before you ask, none of our other siblings were born yet. But I did it. I killed him and the dozen werecats he had Changed within a decade. He killed many more humans in the effort. Too many." She turned to me. "Betrayal cuts deep, and being the one who stops the infection is hard."

"He was your...Zuri, I'm sorry."

"I understand some of your pain, Jacky. I do. That's why I'm telling you this. When this is over, just remember you are making the best choice you can, and no one is going to say you did the wrong thing. Killing Lani will not be easy on you, no matter what she's done."

Yes, it will be. It's going to be the easiest thing I've ever done.

Entering my territory, the first thing I noticed was that it was still my territory. The second thing I noticed was that Lani wasn't in it. The last thing I noticed was that Heath was. He was in his home.

I didn't turn toward Kick Shot. I jerked the wheel hard to make the turn I needed and hit the gas to fly down the road.

"Where are we going?" Zuri asked.

"Heath is here. I want to see him, make sure he's okay."

Zuri nodded, accepting it.

I was still speeding when I made it to his street, hitting the brakes hard to make the turn into his driveway. He came running out of his house, naked relief on his face when he saw me get out of the car.

"Jacky...Oliver and Dirk told me about the explosion and the fight. I was worried."

"What are you doing here? Why aren't you at the safehouse?"

"I'm a big wolf and can take care of myself," he said with a small growl.

"He is," Zuri agreed, stepping up beside me. "Good to see you, Alpha Everson."

"I wish everyone would stop saying that."

"It's who you are," Zuri said nonchalantly. "Once an Alpha, always an Alpha with you wolves."

"True," he conceded.

"Why are you here?" I asked again, glaring at him. He could have been killed. She could have gone after him. Was he insane?

"Because this is my home, and I wanted to make sure it was still standing. Plus, Carey and Landon were getting tired of me, and Carey hates the safehouse. I decided to come here for the day and tonight to make sure it would be safe, then bring them back tomorrow morning if nothing happened. We'll house Dirk and Oliver until you're done and...find them a place, I guess."

"Lani's going to die tonight," I promised. It was already after dark again—a full twenty-four hours of fighting, running, cars, flights, waiting...hoping. "She's not going to make it to sunrise."

"Then I have no reason to worry," he said softly.

"I saw Tywin," I said before an awkward silence could set in.

"Yeah...he's been blowing up my phone for a couple of hours. I was wondering why. Do I want to ask?"

"Probably not," I said, able to break into a small smile. I decided to explain anyway. "I gave him a good thumping for trying to stop us when we landed."

"He'll take it."

"Will he?"

"Yes. He's a good Alpha, but..." Heath smirked. "He's not on the North American Werewolf Council. Not like I was. He's going to take his thumping from you because you're Jacqueline, daughter of Hasan. He'll take it to the Council, they'll take it to the Tribunal, who will talk to

Hasan, and they'll argue about it, but in the end, he'll just have to take it."

I wished Zuri wasn't there. Heath wasn't acting normal. Hadn't been acting normal with me since he left the truck when we arrived at the safehouse. I wanted to ask him why, but I knew I couldn't with her hovering.

"We should go," she said, breaking me out of my thoughts.

"Of course," I agreed, nodding. "Stay safe, Heath."

"Good luck," he whispered, heading back into his home.

We got back into the car.

"What was that?" my sister asked, almost a little too wise.

"None of your business," I answered. She chuckled.

"You're his friend. You can admit it, little sister. You're allowed to be his friend, no matter what you think. We're all okay with it, even if it's unconventional."

"Thanks. So...to Lani's territory."

"Yes. She'll have gone to ground. If she didn't come after Heath, then burning down everything you cared about was her priority. She probably didn't even think one of the wolves would come back."

We hadn't started moving, which was a good thing because Heath jogged back outside. I rolled my window down to hear what he had to say.

"I forgot. Your house? It's fine. They caught and stopped the fire in time. It's a lovely place, by the way."

"Oh, you saw it?"

"Yes. I just figured you should know, then you never

asked. When you're done with everything, your home is still standing, waiting for you."

"Thanks."

He patted the top of the car and backed off. This time, I didn't let conversation keep me from driving away. I pulled out and started down the dark road.

"How far to Lani's territory?"

"A few hours."

She closed her eyes, took a deep breath, and fell asleep as if someone had snapped their fingers and cast a spell on her.

And I drove, staring at the dark road ahead of me.

I'm coming for you, Lani.

CHAPTER TWENTY-EIGHT

I stopped only feet from the territory line.

"Zuri, we're here," I said softly. She snapped awake, alert and ready to fight. "Do you think she'll be here?"

"I think it's the highest probability, but no one has been acting normal since this started," Zuri said with a sigh. I cut the engine and got out with Zuri following me. We both stripped down and tossed our clothing in the backseat. Before Changing, I knew there was a conversation she and I needed to have. I had let her sleep the entire drive, but that meant I hadn't been able to ask her a few more questions.

"How does this work?"

"We're going into her territory together. If she's still here, she'll know why we've come. If not, we go to the center and try to find the freshest trail, then begin a proper hunt. I'll Change back into my human form to declare the execution, and your duty is to keep her from attacking me. Once you and she begin the fight, I'll Change back in case I'm needed, so don't worry about me being helpless for long."

"If I lose?"

"I kill her, and don't worry, I'll be able to."

"If I win?"

"Depending on your injuries, I'll drive you home or back to the plane to go back up north to the hospital with the family. That will also be your call when this is over. I'll prepare a statement about it once Niko is on the mend and no longer so vulnerable. We go back to our lives, Jacky."

"Okay. I just wanted to make sure that was somewhere in the plan. Going back to normal."

If I even could at this point. So much killing, so much fighting—it was changing me. Everyone had to notice because it was scaring me.

I started my Change, and Zuri was done at the same time. We walked together, crossing into Lani's territory, which reeked of fear and anger. I felt the pull to the center of the territory, knowing Zuri felt it as well. It was the best place to find her, and if she wasn't here, the best place to start the hunt.

This was my first time in another werecat's territory since Washington, where Gaia's rage was strong even after her death. Lani's feelings weren't as powerful. They didn't scare me off, but they were there, reminding me of that trip to the woods of Washington and the monsters that had tried to claim those mountains.

Thinking about that made me want to visit Hasan's

when this was all said and done, to go to a territory that wasn't hostile to me but welcoming and warm. He also had beaches, water, and a big house I could hide in.

Maybe that would ease my soul a little. Maybe that would help wash away the paranoia and pain of the last month.

We found her ranch, and I stopped at the fence line, sniffing the air. There were no lights on in the home on the hill, surrounded by empty fields. I thought Lani had an active ranch with herds, but there didn't seem to be any now. The smell was certainly around but no cattle.

"I wonder where her herds went," I said to Zuri, who only snorted in return. I wished for a second it was Heath and not her. Heath could talk to me in werecat form.

We jumped the fence and started walking across the field. As we drew closer to the home, the porch light came on, and Lani walked outside. She stood on her front porch as we stopped only ten feet from her.

Zuri began to Change back into her human form and stood regally next to me when it was done.

"Lani, daughter of Arobi, son of Lesna, I have come as a representative of Hasan, ruler of the werecats and member of the Tribunal of Supernatural Law. You have been sentenced to death by combat execution. If you don't wish to fight, submit now and let us be done with this. If you defeat your executioner, another shall finish the duty. If you run, we will chase. There is no escaping justice."

Zuri's words were impressive and professional. They lacked emotion, purely there to convey a message of death without making it personal. I couldn't have pulled it off. This was personal, and I would make sure Lani understood that by the end. Her last sight would be me over her. Her last breath would be the one I claimed to remove her from this life.

This was very, very personal.

Lani lifted a hand and waved something around.

"You'll come inside and talk to me, or I'll blow up everything within a hundred feet of this house. Me, both of you. Everything."

"Well, Zuri, this might be a problem," I said, taking a deep breath.

"Why?" Zuri asked Lani, her chin held high with all the regal energy I loved her for.

"Because I refuse to die to her when I was fighting for what was right."

"You were a coward who ran the moment you realized your side was losing," I snarled.

Lani's thumb caressed something.

"Don't be so mean, Jacky. Come inside, and we'll talk this out," she said. "I'm not dying tonight unless I take one or both of you with me."

"Let's go, sister," Zuri said softly, running her hand over my head. She started walking toward the house. I only took one step before Lani had something to say.

"Wait." Lani held up her free hand. "Jacky, get to your human form. I'm not letting you come into my house like that."

I grumbled but complied when Zuri looked back at me. I caught her fear in the wind. My sister was scared of this as well, even though it didn't show on her face. Lani was smart. She had played us, knowing how the family tried to do everything honorably, by the books, the same for everyone.

In human form, I didn't have pack magic. I didn't know why that was since werecat land magic worked in both forms, but I was going to have to talk now. It ruined any chance of me trying to plan something with Zuri in secret.

We walked up to the porch, and Lani pulled a gun from the back of her pants, pointing it at me, of course, then pointing it to the door. Zuri went in without a fight, and I followed close behind, trying to hide the shake in my hands.

This woman had blown up a house on top of our brothers. There was no telling what she would do to Zuri and me alone, with no backup, just to escape the justice she deserved.

"Why can't you just admit defeat? And why did you set Kick Shot on fire?" I asked softly as the gun touched my back. Lani walked around me, keeping the gun pointed at me, but she also looked at Zuri, making sure my sister wasn't about to make any sudden moves. We moved into her large living room. I didn't need to look down when I kicked something.

I distinctly knew what chains sounded like.

"Because I'm not losing," she said simply. "Because I didn't risk everything to throw it away in some fight we couldn't guarantee. I loved him, you know. If you're here, I take it he's dead. That's how your family handles everything. I set Kick Shot on fire so you would come after me faster. I wasn't going to wait forever, and I knew I would have the upper hand here."

"You tried to handle it the same way," I snarled.

She lifted the barrel and wiggled it a little.

"No, we didn't. We captured you and asked Hasan to step down. We asked, and he never replied. He said he would kill us. We needed to escalate because he went straight to killing like he and that entire family you're a part of always does. You kill everyone who gets in your way, anyone who dares challenge your power. That's what you do." She sighed. "I just can't believe I was so blind for so long about the lot of you."

"Lani, we can discuss this," Zuri said calmly. "I can rescind the execution order. I have that power."

"Of course you do," Lani growled. "Jacky would never let you. Right, Jacky? Even if she rescinded it, you would still come after me."

I didn't say anything because denying it would be a lie, and she would know. Saying she was right made me feel like a murderer.

"Come on, Jacky. Say something. Tell me how much you've changed since you've taken on the wolves and Daddy saved you from the Tribunal and his own fucking Laws."

"You were my friend," I said softly. "And you betrayed me."

"You betrayed the werecats, so I think we're even," she snapped. "Wolves. She took in fucking wolves, the very kind who continuously try to kill us for whatever reason, and none of you thought to deal with it." She directed the accusation at Zuri. "You're all hypocrites. Every single one of you. If it had been at the Tribunal, we all know Hasan wouldn't have stepped in."

"You also would have never gotten into that position," I snapped. "You would have probably been fine with letting Carey Everson, a little human girl, die if it kept you out of any drama or trouble. So stuck in your fucking ways, you can't even think about what the right thing to do is."

"No, I actually agreed with you, Jacky. I just didn't think it would get past you. I figured you would get executed, and..."

"And what?" Zuri asked softly.

"Mikkel was saying if Jacky had died, we could have risen up against the Tribunal and Hasan for not seeing she was a good werecat. We could have done this years ago."

"I'm not sure I'm following," I said, frowning. "Am I a good werecat or a bad werecat?"

"You were a good one. You were great with performing your Duty and helping the human. It was perfect. Then you made a public showing with that Alpha, letting him live in your territory. Being his friend. His ally. It's one thing to protect a little girl, it's a completely different one to cross a line."

"We've been down this road," I said tiredly. "Next, you'll tell Zuri how you tried hard to forgive me after I helped in Washington, but then I was declared Hasan's representative of the continent. Mikkel convinced you it was nepotism, and that I was weak. I don't need to hear it all over again."

"Then you don't have to," she said. "Behind you, there are chains on the ground by the wall. Zuri, you'll wrap Jacky's legs and arms together when she sits down."

"Of course," Zuri said softly.

I sat down next to the chains, breathing hard, remembering what it was like to be chained in that cell while Lani's real friends beat the hell out of me. Zuri knelt beside me, starting her work. She looped them around my ankles, and I moved so that she could then loop the chains around my wrists.

"With two more of you dead, I just need to rally the werecats still on the fence, and we can finish off your family," Lani said.

"More?" I said. "Everyone is still alive. The plan with the house blowing up didn't even kill one of us. Lani...all of your friends...they died for nothing." I pitied her for that. I pitied the idea of fighting so hard for something, and walking away a total failure. I pitied her for picking the side that lost os handily. They shouldn't have. I fought hard because I wasn't willing to die, but the likelihood my family only walked away with injuries had to have been small. They were bad injuries, but we still walked away.

None of her friends did.

Fury. The room was filled with the scent of her fury.

But I pressed on.

"Maybe if you had stayed, you could have defeated

me before I went to help Davor," I said softly. "Maybe you could have turned the tide of the fight."

"I should have let him torture you sooner," she snarled. "I tried to bring you to our side, and I should have let him rip your fingernails out. I should have let him direct Sam to break every bone in your fucking body." Lani bent over, getting close, the barrel of the gun to my head.

It put her in the terrible position of being right next to Zuri, who worked very slowly as if she were scared of spooking Lani into blowing up the building. Lani couldn't see Zuri's face, but I could. I could see the small smile form even though her head was ducked to stay out of Lani's way. A very demure way to behave for such a regal woman.

It was an amazing act.

Lani was breathing hard in her anger, too focused on threatening me. I ducked right when I saw Zuri's hand begin to move, going not to the gun, but the explosive trigger.

The gun went off above my head. I fought with the chains while Zuri fought to take the trigger from Lani, the two females snarling at each other as they struggled. I waited for the building to go up any moment, but another gunshot made me cry out as the bullet went into my shoulder.

Lani was firing blind.

Finally, Zuri got the trigger. With the chains on my legs, it was difficult, but I kicked the gun from Lani's hand.

Lani stumbled away, realizing she had lost both her bargaining chips. I fought to get the chains off while Zuri went for the gun.

Neither of us was ready to pursue Lani as she darted out the back door of her house, pulling something out of her pocket.

"Jacky, we need to go," Zuri snapped.

"Why?"

"JUST MOVE!"

I stumbled, standing with the chains on. Zuri had done them too tight, and I was struggling. Zuri picked me up, realizing I couldn't move fast enough and started running with me toward the closest door to the outside, back out the front door onto the porch. She didn't stop.

But she'd only made it a couple of steps when everything behind us turned into a thousand tiny little pieces, and a big fireball rose up, sending out a shockwave that blew us off the porch.

CHAPTER TWENTY-NINE

I struggled to move, reaching out to find Zuri. A hand grabbed mine, and I tried to open my eyes. I didn't know how much time had passed since the blast, assuming it probably knocked me unconscious there for a moment. It could have been an hour or a second.

"Were you hit by anything?" I asked, grunting in pain.

"No," she moaned. "But I think I'm done with this for a good long while."

"Me too," I said, trying to push myself up. "How?"

"Her phone, most likely," Zuri said, moving closer to me. I could hear her shuffling in the grass even though my tender, barely healed eardrums were ruptured again, and my ears rang. "A back-up plan in case we got the trigger. She's too smart to not have one."

"Fuck..." I finally made it up onto all fours, staring at

the ground. "How far do you think she's going to make it?"

"She wouldn't have set it off if she was close enough to feel any damaging effects. We're in for a chase," Zuri answered. "Are you up for it?"

"Me? Zuri, you were magically healed after being spiked on a bit of rebar. Are you?"

"I've been through worse," my sister said. I saw her outline stand and a hand come out. "How do you think I knew not to move once I realized something was in my lung?"

"How are you so...regal and put together and deal with shit like this on a regular basis?" I grabbed the hand, and she helped me onto my feet.

"Experience." She touched my face, frowning at something by my ears. "Ears drums?"

"They ruptured last night. Probably were nearly healed, then this..."

"Of course. Change, and let's go hunting."

I nodded and curled over, letting it take me into my werecat form. The Change healed us a little bit each time we did it. It couldn't be done excessively, but it sped up the natural process. It was how Hisao had mended the bones in his arm, even though I got pissed at him for doing it.

I was nearly done when something crashed into me. My right side was clawed up, opening up all the scabbed injuries from the previous night before Zuri yanked whatever was attacking off me. I didn't put it together, that it was Lani until it was too late.

Attacking a werecat in the middle of the Change slowed everything down. My body didn't know which way to go, traumatized by the pain. Screaming, snarling, and growls could be heard.

It took me a minute longer than normal to finish shifting into my werecat form. I struggled to my feet, knowing I was bleeding badly. I saw Lani get Zuri into the dirt, and I started moving, ramming into her with a roar. I reared up and swiped fast with both of my front paws. On a good day, Zuri and I could have taken her, but we were both rattled and injured. We weren't fresh in any way. I was still pretty starved, weaker than normal, and not close to recovering from the last week of abuse. Zuri was fighting against injuries sustained from two blasts. Magically healed or not, she wasn't at her best either.

Lani hit my chest, giving me four bloody red lines. I hit her across the face, knocking her down. Zuri came up beside me and tried for a killing bite to Lani's soft underbelly, only to be met with Lani's back legs kicking out. Zuri roared in pain as one cut her face. I was dizzy as I landed on my front paws and tried to focus, going for Lani's neck but moving too slow. Lani batted my face away with ease and was back on her feet before Zuri and I could do any more.

Zuri and I went side by side, stalking toward her as she backed off and tried to circle us. I lunged, striking out at her back leg, but not able to grab hold. Zuri turned fast to stop Lani from getting at mine, snarling as she raked her claws over Lani's face. Lani screamed, and I went for her back leg again, this time grabbing hold and using it to yank her off her feet.

"Back off, Zuri. She's mine. I need to do this."

My sister stepped back, leaving the fight and moving to a good position to watch. Lani hissed at me, realizing I must have wanted her to myself. I directed what I said next to her.

"I don't know if you're right or wrong about Hasan and my family, but this wasn't the way to do it, Lani. Trying to kill everyone I care about was the wrong move if you wanted me to sympathize with you."

Lani snarled again, and I let her stand. We started circling, finally getting to a point where it was an even fight. This was it.

"You resorted to cheap tactics. I can't see how you think you're better than them. My family might have made some tough decisions and mistakes while ruling the werecats, but they're honorable. At least they have been when I could see them. Zuri and I didn't come here to blow your home up while you slept. We weren't going to stab you in the back. You could have had a fair fight, and it would have been over. You did this."

I didn't know what she was thinking, I just felt the need to talk to her as we circled, knowing the next attack was the last.

"And I might have made mistakes, but I'm trying to do good, Lani. I just want to do good. I'm sorry my definition of good isn't the same as yours. Obviously, my definition of loyalty isn't the same as yours. You must think you're loyal

to the werecats of our world, but all I see is someone who forgot the meaning of it."

She roared and charged me. We met, rearing up and clashing, claws ripping out fur. She dropped onto her front paws first, and I dragged my claws down her side as I fell, making her stagger enough for me to knock her over and take a fast bite at her throat.

It was over, my saber teeth sliding through her jugular and windpipe. I didn't tear out her throat. I felt her blood pump into my mouth as her life faded.

When it was over, I released her and started walking away, overwhelmed.

I'd done it. I'd killed Lani, once my only friend.

Even dead, her betrayal still cut deep.

Zuri followed me in silence.

I was limping by the time we made it back to the car, exhausted. I could have let any of my healthier siblings do this. I could have let any of them go after Lani and end this.

I thought I could carry the burden, but it hurt. Deep in my soul and through every muscle of my body, it hurt.

Changing back into my human form took time. Zuri handed me a first aid kit from origins unknown. I was almost annoyed that she was in so much better shape for all the shit that had happened in the last two days.

"Let me wrap some of those," she said softly.

"I've got it," I mumbled, grabbing a bandage to handle the worst of it on my right side. I was weak from blood loss but not down and out yet. I didn't want to be coddled.

I had just killed my once only friend. Comfort was the last thing I wanted from my sister.

It took thirty minutes for us to get into the car, and I let Zuri drive.

"Let's get you to the hospital—"

"Take me home," I ordered in a whisper. "I'll survive. You know I will. Just take me home."

"Jacky..."

"Please. I just want to go home."

She nodded in the dark car. I closed my eyes and drifted into a light sleep.

30

CHAPTER THIRTY

"Jacky."

I opened my eyes, groaning as the car slowed down and parked. I looked out the window to see a burned husk of a building and wondered where Zuri had taken me.

"We're here. Do you want me to walk you home? I don't feel comfortable just letting you go without looking over you, and..." She sighed. "It doesn't get easier when it's this close to home. Being alone isn't a good idea."

"She wasn't even a good friend," I said softly. "I was so angry with her. I wanted to kill her from the moment I saw her with Mikkel. And then..."

"And then you killed her. I know."

"She was my only friend," I whispered, the emotions threatening to choke me. "There was a time she was my only one."

"I know."

"When I wasn't talking to any of you, and none of

you wanted to talk to me, I had Lani. When I was called to Duty, I had her to talk to. And..."

I killed her.

"She tried to kill you first," Zuri reminded me. I hadn't realized I'd spoken that last part out loud. "In time, the hurt will ease. You'll get up one day and remember you did the right thing. And she was no true friend."

"She said as much." She had pitied me, being all alone. And in the end, I was just nothing more than a scheme her lover could exploit.

"Are you sure you're going to be okay alone?"

"I need to be alone." I opened the door and got out, stumbling a little. I held up a hand before Zuri could get out. "I'm fine. I can treat everything and get some sleep. I'll be okay."

"Hasan is going to kill me."

"He can come here and fight with me about it," I growled weakly.

I didn't want Zuri taking care of me. I didn't want anyone. I pushed the door closed and waved at her, then started the slow walk around Kick Shot into the woods behind my home.

It felt longer than usual, and everything seemed different. Maybe it was the evidence of the fire Lani left behind, an obvious mark on my property, like the one she left on my soul—a dark streak of destruction.

The metaphor fit, and I hated it.

I staggered into view of my home and sighed. Going inside seemed like a bad idea, but I knew I needed to get in and clean up so I could get some sleep. I needed to sleep, so I could wake up tomorrow, a new day, and make a meal.

And try to pretend like my home hadn't been violated. Like my trust in my own kind hadn't been destroyed. Like my faith in the loyalty Hasan commanded hadn't been broken.

I made it through my front door, almost freaked out by how nothing was out of place. They hadn't ransacked my house. Everything was just as I left it, with a little bit more dust. It felt wrong. It felt lifeless and sterile.

I realized with a sudden need, I didn't want to be alone, and Zuri was gone.

There was one person in my territory, though. One person I trusted to treat my injuries like he had now a few times.

I found my spare car keys and staggered back out of my lifeless house, heading for my car.

Heading for Heath Everson.

I RANG HIS DOORBELL, even when the sound was obnoxious and hurt my ears. I didn't have the strength to knock hard enough to get his attention.

I heard him walking around, coming toward the door. It opened immediately, and I stared at grey-blue eyes, eyes I hadn't realized I wanted so badly to see. The moment they were there, framed in dark curls, I wanted to cry.

He took one look at my body, his nostrils flaring as he scented me and cursed.

"Jacky," he gasped, grabbing my elbow.

"She's dead. I killed her." Helping me cross the threshold of his home, I leaned into him for strength. "And Zuri brought me home."

"And she left you alone like this?" he growled. His arm snaked around my waist, and his body heat felt good.

"I asked her to. I thought I wanted to be alone, then I was alone, and it wasn't what I wanted, and..."

"You came here," he finished for me. "I've got you. Let's get you cleaned up, cat."

He helped me walk to his living room, and I sat down without a fight on his ottoman, not his couch. I didn't want to get blood on his couch. I would have preferred not to be on his carpet at all, tracking everything on me around.

He stepped back and frowned.

"No...you need a full shower. What did you do? Run into a burning building?"

"She tried to blow up her house with us in it," I answered hoarsely. "Apparently, the first time worked so well, she wanted another go. She didn't want to die without taking one or both of us with her. In the end, she ran out of the house, trying to catch us still inside." I coughed at the end of that, holding my ribs.

He picked me up, cradling me as he carried me up the stairs into the back bedroom. We passed through into what must have been the master bathroom.

"We've been naked around each other before," he

stated plainly. "So, please don't fight me. You need to get all of this off, so I can treat everything properly. I'm worried I can't get everything cleaned out."

"Okay." I didn't have much fight left. I lifted my arms, and the shirt came off. He growled softly as I undid my pants, and he started unwrapping the terrible job I had done with the bandages.

His warm, calloused hands were familiar to me now, totally professional as they worked. I appreciated them. They reminded me of bad times, sure, but there were good moments during bad times. Maybe they could help me get through this.

Once I was naked in his bathroom, I noticed a slight shake to those hands as he surveyed the damage.

"You should have gone to a hospital," he murmured, his fingers barely grazing the long, terrible lines of my fight with Lani and the bite marks and cuts from my fight with Fiora and my escape. I looked down to see in his bathroom light, some of the bruises from my beating had never really faded, still the light, sickly yellow.

"I know," I said, swallowing. "I didn't want people around."

"Well, I'm here for you. I've got you now," he reassured me. He reached into his shower and turned it on. "Tell me when the water feels good."

I got in without bothering to check, wincing as it started out frigid. Then it heated up to near blistering, and that made me happy. He helped me clean off; soot, dirt, and blood went down the drain. I couldn't believe I'd walked through a hospital with a lot of this on me. I couldn't believe Tywin tried me at all when I was in Dallas. I was glad I never looked in a mirror.

When Heath grabbed his shampoo, I frowned. I tried to step away, and he got into the shower, letting the water soak his clothing.

"We're not done until I say we are," he growled at me.

I let him lather my hair with the shampoo and rinse it as well.

Finally, the water turned off, and a large, soft towel was given to me.

"I'm burning these clothes," he said, kicking them out of my reach. "You can borrow something of mine."

I didn't fight. I had none left in me. If he wanted to put me in clean clothes, that was okay. That was one of the reasons I think I came here. He wouldn't bend like Zuri. He wouldn't accept my independence, not when I genuinely needed him. He would force his care on me, and that was okay.

He didn't pick me up this time, guiding me back into the bedroom and making me sit on the edge of his bed. He ran out and brought back a first aid kit, getting to work, making sure everything was clean, stitched if needed, and bandaged.

I needed him. At that moment, I had desperately needed him, and he hadn't turned me away. He hadn't considered a werewolf shouldn't help a werecat, or a werecat shouldn't need his help. He didn't make anything awkward, even though the attraction had been impossible to deny before everything happened.

He just helped me.

"You never said goodbye," I reminded him as he worked. Something to make the feelings in my chest remember he wasn't perfect. No one was perfect.

"When?" He frowned, looking up.

"When I was leaving with my family. You went upstairs with Carey, and you never came down and said goodbye to me." I didn't know why I held this expectation he would or even should, but I held it against him that he didn't. "Actually, you barely looked at me once we made it back to the safehouse."

"I was trying to be careful. With your family there, I thought maybe I shouldn't be right next to you. I didn't want to slip. I'm so careless around you now, Jacky. I didn't want them to know how I..." He ran a hand over one of my bare hips, and there was nothing professional about the touch. It brought goosebumps as he added just a small amount of pressure and growled softly. The scent of his arousal filled the room and dissipated.

"Oh." He didn't want them to notice the barely contained, small flame between us.

"Yeah..." He leaned over. "Let me finish this so you can get dressed, please. I can't do much more of this and continue to be a good friend."

Friend. That word. It changed my mood in a split second.

When he was done, I got dressed in his clothes, a pair of sweats and a hoodie much too big for me, and we sat on the edge of his bed together.

I noticed everything now. How our shoulders were

touching. How our thighs met. We sank together, thanks to the mattress.

But my mind hovered on the word friend like it was a curse.

"I killed my only friend tonight," I whispered.

"She wasn't your only friend," he said, seeming hurt. "I'm your friend."

There was a small lie to the words, just a tiny one, hidden in the feelings swirling around.

"No, you aren't," I said, swallowing.

"Really? What am I? Because I really thought we were friends."

"Liar. We both know what you are."

"Tell me. I'm a stupid man. Please tell me what I am," he said, something teasing to the words.

"Off-limits," I murmured. I leaned over and decided I wanted to see. I wanted to see if his lips were as soft as they looked. I wanted to see if maybe that bit of physical interaction would make me feel better.

He didn't move as my lips found his. When I tried to pull away, my mind trying to rationalize what I was doing, he leaned in, keeping our mouths together. I caught my breath as he wrapped one of those warm hands around my back and pulled me a little closer.

Whatever coldness and pain was in me disappeared for a minute as my body came alive during that kiss. It was like a spark accidentally hit tinder left too close to a can of gasoline. What should have been a small attraction became overwhelming. Whatever we had tried to ignore was now consuming.

When he finally stopped, his eyes were wide. I was certain mine were too.

"I should go," I said quickly. I struggled to stand up, my body sore. Everything was bandaged tightly, reducing my mobility.

"Jacky, wait, please..."

"I'm leaving. We..." I shook my head.

What did I just do?

"You shouldn't drive," he said, trying to stop me, but I was glad he didn't put his hands on me. I didn't know if I had the strength to resist melting back into him. "Jacky..."

"I'm going home," I said, trying to put weight behind it. "Don't send Carey to me next Monday. I need...I need time. Okay? I'll let you know when I'm ready for her. Please? I'll figure out where to put Dirk and Oliver as fast as I can. I just need some space."

He looked despondent. Slowly, he began to nod.

I took my chance to run.

CHAPTER THIRTY-ONE
MARCH 23RD, 2020

I woke up, sighing heavily as I stared at my ceiling. Last night, a statement went out from Zuri, well, from the family. Niko was now secured on Hasan's island, deep in his territory and away from the world. Hisao was healed. I was healed.

And the world of werecats knew not to fuck with us. Not any time soon. Any threats would be met with deadly force by all of the able members of the family. There would be no bargaining, no games. We would destroy them.

With that out there, I knew what today meant.

Today was the day I needed to get back to my life.

The first thing I did was text Heath. I'd had my time to rest. I wanted Carey back. If I was going to face a Monday like it was any Monday, I wanted to do it with my favorite person—a charming, nearly thirteen-year-old with a strong, big heart.

Today, when I looked in the mirror, I considered

what had happened as I did every day. It still hurt. It all still hurt too much, but I hoped every day it would hurt a little less. Zuri was right. Eventually, things calmed down, and life came back. The hurt would fade too. The hurt from Shane had faded, and it helped, knowing Hasan truly couldn't have saved him and hadn't just put him through more pain by trying.

I was in the shower when my phone rang the first time. When I got out, I frowned when I saw the call was from an unknown number. It started ringing again before I had the chance to put it down. I answered, standing in my bathroom, dripping wet.

"Jacky Leon speaking. May I ask who's calling?"

"I'm Coyotl, son of Tenoch, and I'm a werecat living in Mexico. I just wanted to make it clear to you, Jacky Leon, I am sad to hear of your recent troubles. Please, also send my good wishes to your father. I respect him very much and would like that known."

I pulled my phone away from my ear and looked at it in confusion. When I put it back, he was still on the line.

"Why?" I asked.

"Ah..." He was obviously at a loss for words, thanks to my confusion. "I'm the first to call, aren't I?"

"Yes?"

"Oh, okay. You'll be receiving, hopefully, several of these for the next few days. Hasan will explain it to you, I'm sure. We should have all made the call long ago, but you were a new face, and I was wary. I didn't know what to think of you. I'm certain many others felt the same way. But have no doubt of my loyalty, please. I had nothing to do with Mikkel and his schemes. If there is anything I believe needs the attention of Hasan or yourself, I will let you know. That is my duty as a werecat to the leading family of our kind."

I understood now. He didn't want any repercussions from what happened with Mikkel and Lani. He was calling to make sure I knew he wanted to be in my good graces, and therefore, he would be in Hasan's good graces.

"Well, thank you for the kind words about the unfortunate incident," I said casually. "I'll let Hasan know you called."

"Thank you...Is Jacky Leon what you wish to be called?"

"When discussing official items, it's Jacqueline, daughter of Hasan, but if you just want to make a social call to check in or even talk about nothing, Jacky is fine."

"Ah. Okay. I'll remember that."

He understood that was an important distinction. I wanted him to remember I was a daughter of Hasan and would act like one when it was needed. That, I learned, was no idle reminder. Not after I saw the power of my siblings and their willingness to do whatever was necessary to keep our father in his position.

"Have a nice day, Coyotl." I didn't want to make a passing remark about how a werecat was named Coyote, so I decided it was time to get off the phone.

"You as well, Jacqueline, daughter of Hasan. I'll pass along my email to you. It is the best way to get ahold of me."

"Thank you."

I hung up first and put the phone down, staring at it.

This is because of the statement we put out yesterday. I really hope he's wrong. I don't want to answer more phone calls. That's going to get annoying.

I texted Hasan, deciding it was easy to avoid making calls. He sent me back a quick confirmation and a picture of Niko looking angry in bed.

I couldn't help but laugh. I forwarded the photo to Dirk, who sent back several laughing faces. Everyone knew Niko was going to be okay at this point unless he did something stupid, so we were all trying to have a bit of fun with him.

I fiddled around my house, waiting on Heath to text me back. Was this it? Was he not going to bring Carey?

Before I could text him again, my phone rang, and I dealt with the same thing as Coyotl, this time from a werecat named Audrey. I texted Hasan with her name as well.

It was nearly four when Heath got back to me.

Heath: We're on our way over. I'll walk her to your place. Also, I have something for you.

My heart pounded. He had something for me? Hopefully it wasn't a restraining order.

I'd tried my best over the last weeks to not think of how I ran out on him. The hot and heavy kiss during a weak moment. I hoped time and distance would kill whatever was between us.

And I prayed the coming meeting wasn't awkward.

I felt him moving through my territory and knew

when he was at Kick Shot's ruined remains. I felt him walk through the woods and went onto my front porch to see him and Carey come through the trees.

Carey saw me and started running. I grabbed her and swung her around the moment she wrapped her arms around my waist.

"Dad said you needed some time alone. It's okay. I'm not mad," she said, her face pressed against my chest. I ran a hand over her head.

"I did. Thank you for not being angry." I hadn't been in a good place when I walked out on Heath that night. I hadn't been in a good place for two weeks after that. I had really needed the time to myself.

"Carey, can you go inside and wait for Jacky?" Heath asked, walking up the steps. I tried to get the door for her, but she was in the house faster than I could move, which was startling and impressive. When I looked back at her father, he gave me a wry smile. "She's missed you."

"I'm sorry."

"There's nothing to be sorry for."

There's a lot to be sorry for.

I looked down at his hands and saw he was carrying a folder.

"What's that?"

"For you, if you're interested." He held it out, and I took it slowly, flipping it open to see designs, blueprints. I looked up at him in confusion. "Rebuilding Kick Shot," he explained quickly. "I figured these could give you a place to start."

"Can I hire you?" I asked softly. I searched his gray-blue eyes, hoping for some sign he didn't hate me now. I didn't want Heath Everson to hate me.

"Yes."

An awkward silence settled between us. There was so much I wanted to say, but I couldn't find a way to put it out there. I tried to start easy, tried to get something going.

"Heath—"

He didn't let me finish. His warm, calloused hands caught me, and his lips met mine with a demanding force. It was a proclamation, a statement of want and need, freeing. My body melted into his, the folder in my hand forgotten.

Fire burned in my gut. My heart raced. My only thought was about how wonderful it felt.

He wanted me.

And damn everything, I wanted him.

Then it was over. He didn't go far, his lips brushing against mine as we stared into each other's eyes.

"I've been waiting weeks to do that," he murmured against my lips. "Too fucking long, Jacky. I've been waiting too long."

"We're technically immortal," I reminded him and earned a growl for it.

"I want to have secrets with you."

"No one can know," I said, knowing it would be hard...so hard. "Carey can't know. My family can't know."

"Landon will figure it out." He sighed, then kissed me again. "He'll keep it to himself."

"Oliver and Dirk—"

"We won't tell them."

"We...Heath, we might never get more than this. Stolen kisses when no one is looking. Anything more and people could start asking questions." I dropped the folder and ran my hands up his chest, the only thing between us a thin black shirt.

"I'm okay with that," he whispered. "For now. We can play it by ear."

I nodded and kissed him this time. I was hungry for him. I hadn't been truly hungry for a man in over a decade, but now, I was hungry for a man I should have never considered.

It was asking for trouble.

But I was Jacky Leon. I was Jacqueline, daughter of Hasan.

And I was the family troublemaker, it seemed.

We broke apart right as Carey yelled out.

"Come on, Jacky! You and Dad can work later!"

"I should get inside," I whispered.

"I should go," he said at the same time. He grabbed my wrist, keeping me from going inside just yet. "Jacky, if there's anything you ever need from me, just ask. Anything. I'm here for you."

"Thank you."

"For?"

"Reminding me I have some loyal people in my life who aren't required to be."

I went inside, smiling as I found Carey breaking into my kitchen cabinets to start cooking dinner with me. It was like the last two months never happened.

And that was the last bit of healing I needed.

Keep reading for more information about the next release, special news, and more.

DEAR READER,

Thank you for reading!

Jacky, Jacky, Jacky. Always getting into some trouble, and now she's kissing a werewolf. I warned everyone the romance was coming and now she's kissing the werewolf. We'll see how this plays out in the future.

I also left a very tiny hint about book four somewhere in this book. You can try to go find it. That's all from me this time around.

I'm very excited about Jacky kissing that werewolf. Very excited indeed.

If I still have you, head over to my website to get the latest updates on the next book in the series. Head over to my website and sign up for my mailing list! There are exclusive teasers for those who are signed up: Knbanet. com/newsletter

Also, I have a Patreon, where I write a monthly short story or novella. You can check that out here: Patreon. com/knbanet

And remember,

Reviews are always welcome, whether you loved or hated the book. Please consider taking a few moments to leave one and know I appreciate every second of your time and I'm thankful.

THE TRIBUNAL ARCHIVES

The Jacky Leon series is set in the world of The Tribunal. Every series and standalone novel is written so it can be read alone.

For more information about The Tribunal Archives and the different series in it, you can go here:

tribunalarchives.com

ACKNOWLEDGMENTS

I'm very bad at giving really public praise. I shower people in praise in private. But that's not everyone's love language and that's okay.

So this little page shall now be dedicated to everyone who helps me get these books from the concept to the release and beyond. From my PA, to my editor and my proofreader, to my wonderful friends helping me through the hardest moments. To my husband, who doesn't read my books, but loves that I write them and is willing to listen to me talk about them for hours.

And to you, the reader, for without you, I wouldn't have anyone to share these stories with. I'm a storyteller at heart and you have given me the greatest gift of listening.

I love all of you. Thank you for continuing to go on this journey with me.

ABOUT THE AUTHOR

KNBanet.com

Living in Arizona with her husband and 5 pets (2 dogs and 3 cats), K.N. Banet is a voracious... video game player. Actually, she spends most of her time writing, and when she's not writing she's either gaming or reading.

She enjoys writing about the complexities of relationships, no matter the type. Familial, romantic, or even political. The connections between characters is what draws her into writing all of her work. The ideas of responsibility, passion, and forging one's own path all make appearances.

 facebook.com/KNBanet

 instagram.com/Knbanetauthor

 bookbub.com/authors/k-n-banet

 amazon.com/K.N.-Banet/e/B08412L9VV

 patreon.com/knbanet

ALSO BY K.N. BANET

The Jacky Leon Series

Oath Sworn

Family and Honor

Broken Loyalty

Echoed Defiance

Shades of Hate

Royal Pawn

Rogue Alpha

Bitter Discord

Volume One: Books 1-3

The Kaliya Sahni Series

Bounty

Snared

Monsters

Reborn

Legends

Destiny

Volume One: Books 1-3

The Everly Abbott Series

Servant of the Blood

Blood of the Wicked

Tribunal Archives Stories

Ancient and Immortal (Call of Magic Anthology)

Hearts at War

Full Moon Magic (Rituals and Runes Anthology)